诗经·国风
英文白话新译
"Airs of the States" from the *Shi Jing*
A New Trilingual Translation of the World's
Oldest Collection of Lyric Poetry

贾福相　译著
Translated by Fu-shiang Chia
with a Foreword by Stephen H. Arnold

北京大学出版社
PEKING UNIVERSITY PRESS

著作权合同登记　图字:01-2009-5015号
图书在版编目(CIP)数据

诗经·国风——英文白话新译/贾福相译著.—北京：北京大学出版社,2010.7
ISBN 978-7-301-17205-6

I.诗… II.贾… III.古体诗—中国—春秋时代—英文 IV.I222.2

中国版本图书馆CIP数据核字(2010)第096070号
ⓒ台湾书林出版有限公司
本书经台湾书林出版有限公司授权在中国内地出版发行

书　　　　名：	诗经·国风——英文白话新译
著作责任者：	贾福相　译著
责 任 编 辑：	刘　爽
标 准 书 号：	ISBN 978-7-301-17205-6/H·2504
出 版 发 行：	北京大学出版社
地　　　　址：	北京市海淀区成府路205号　100871
网　　　　址：	http://www.pup.cn
电　　　　话：	邮购部 62752015　发行部 62750672
	编辑部 62767315　出版部 62754962
电 子 邮 箱：	zpup@pup.pku.edu.cn
印 　刷 　者：	北京大学印刷厂
经 　销 　者：	新华书店
	850毫米×1168毫米　A5　13.75印张　300千字
	2010年7月第1版　2010年7月第1次印刷
定　　　　价：	28.00元

未经许可,不得以任何方式复制或抄袭本书之部分或全部内容。
版权所有,侵权必究　举报电话：010-62752024
　　　　　　　　　　电子邮箱：fd@pup.pku.edu.cn

献给我的祖父,贾安之。
当我七岁的时候,
他领我走进了诗的花园。

For my grandfather, An-Chi Chia,
who led me to the garden of poetry
when I was seven years old.

目 录
CONTENTS

译者小传 ·················· 08
Translator's Biography

致谢 ·················· 010
Acknowledgements

桥 ·················· 012
"Bridge"

史蒂芬·亚诺尔教授序 /
郑惠雯译 ·················· 014
Foreword, by Stephen H. Arnold
Translated by Heather Cheng

自序:"多识鸟兽草木之名"
是诗经余绪吗? ·········· 040
Preface: Is "To Learn the Names
of Birds, Beasts, Grasses and
Trees..." Unimportant?

导言 ·················· 047
Introduction

后记 ·················· 062
Postscript

周南 / Airs of Zhou-nan

1 关雎(鱼鹫) ·················· 2
　Kingfisher

2 葛覃(葛麻) ·················· 4
　Cloth-Vine

3 卷耳(卷耳) ·················· 6
　Cocklebur

4 樛木(弯曲的树) ·············· 8
　Crooked Tree

5 螽斯(纺织娘) ················ 10
　Grasshopper

6 桃夭(桃树) ·················· 12
　Quince Tree

7 兔罝(兔网) ·················· 14
　Rabbit Nets

8 芣苢(车前草) ················ 16
　Plantain

9 汉广(汉水宽广) ·············· 18
　Broad Han River

10 汝坟(汝水岸) ··············· 20
　Ru River Banks

11 麟之趾(麒麟之趾) ········· 22
　Chi-lin's Foot

召南 / Airs of Zhao-nan

12 鹊巢（喜鹊巢） ………… 26
Magpie Nest

13 采蘩（采蒿菜） ………… 28
Collecting Mugwort

14 草虫（蟋蟀） ………… 30
Crickets

15 采蘋（采野菜） ………… 32
Harvesting Ceremonial Vegetables

16 甘棠（杜梨树） ………… 34
Pear Tree

17 行露（露水） ………… 36
Evening Dew

18 羔羊（羔羊皮袍） ………… 38
Lamb Skin Coat

19 殷其靁（雷声轰轰） ………… 40
Thunder Rumbles

20 摽有梅（梅子熟了） ………… 42
Falling Mei Plums

21 小星（小星） ………… 44
Small Stars

22 江有汜（江有潟湖） ………… 46
River Lagoon

23 野有死麕（野地死獐） ………… 48
Dead Deer

24 何彼襛矣（多么艳丽哟） ………… 50
So Beautiful

25 驺虞（驺虞） ………… 52
Zou-yu

邶风 / Airs of Bei

26 柏舟（柏木小舟） ………… 56
Cedar Boat

27 绿衣（绿衣） ………… 58
Green Coat

28 燕燕（小燕子） ………… 60
Swallow

29 日月（太阳与月亮） ………… 62
Sun and Moon

30 终风（风暴） ………… 64
Storm

31 击鼓（鸣击战鼓） ………… 66
War Drums

32 凯风（暖风） ………… 68
Warm Wind

33 雄雉（雄野鸡） ………… 70
Cock Pheasant

34 匏有苦叶（葫芦叶黄了） … 72
Gourd with Yellow Leaves

35 谷风（谷风） ………… 74
Valley Wind

36 式微（晚了） ………… 78
It's Late

37 旄丘（旄丘） ………… 80
Mao Hill

38 简兮（壮丽） ………… 82
So Glorious

39 泉水（泉水） ………… 84
Spring Water

40 北门（北门） ………… 86
North Gate

41 北风（北风）·············· 88
   North Wind
42 静女（静美的姑娘）······ 90
   A Fair Maiden
43 新台（新楼台）············ 92
   New Tower
44 二子乘舟（两人乘小舟）··· 94
   Two Men in a Small Boat

鄘风 / Airs of Yong
45 柏舟（柏木小舟）········· 98
   Cedar Boat
46 墙有茨（墙头有蒺藜）····· 100
   Burdock on the Wall
47 君子偕老（白头偕老）····· 102
   Married for Life
48 桑中（桑林中）············ 104
   In the Mulberry Field
49 鹑之奔奔（鹌鹑奔走）····· 106
   Quail Walk
50 定之方中（定星在空）····· 108
   Ding Star in the Evening Sky
51 蝃蝀（彩虹）·············· 110
   Rainbow
52 相鼠（看那老鼠）········· 112
   Look at the Rat!
53 干旄（牛尾旗）············ 114
   Ox-Tail Banner
54 载驰（马车疾驰）········· 116
   My Wagon Flies

卫风 / Airs of Wei
55 淇奥（淇水之湄）········· 120
   The Bank of the River Qi
56 考槃（铜盘）·············· 122
   Brass Gong
57 硕人（美人庄姜）········· 124
   Madam Zhuang-jiang
58 氓（布贩子）·············· 126
   Cloth Peddler
59 竹竿（竹竿）·············· 130
   Bamboo Pole
60 芄兰（萝藤）·············· 132
   Pea Vine
61 河广（黄河宽阔）········· 134
   Wide River
62 伯兮（丈夫）·············· 136
   My Husband
63 有狐（狐狸）·············· 138
   Fox
64 木瓜（木瓜）·············· 140
   Papaya

王风 / Airs of Wang
65 黍离（黍穗）·············· 144
   Millet
66 君子于役（丈夫远征）····· 146
   My Husband Fights in the War
67 君子阳阳（君子喜洋洋）··· 148
   An Elated Gentleman

68 扬之水(河水激扬)········· 150
　　Swift Water
69 中谷有蓷············· 152
　　(谷地里的益母草)
　　Motherwort in the Valley
70 兔爰(兔儿轻轻跳)········ 154
　　A Rabbit Hops Gently
71 葛藟(野葡萄)··········· 156
　　Wild Grapes
72 采葛(采蒿藤)··········· 158
　　Gathering Ge
73 大车(大车)············ 160
　　Large Wagon
74 丘中有麻············· 162
　　(丘陵地有麻田)
　　Hemp Grows in the Hills

郑风 / Airs of Zheng

75 缁衣(黑色制服)·········· 166
　　Black Uniform
76 将仲子(二先生)········· 168
　　Qiang Zhong-zi (Second Son)
77 叔于田············· 170
　　(我的阿哥打猎去了)
　　My Man is Out Hunting
78 大叔于田············ 172
　　(阿叔出外打猎)
　　Shu is Out Hunting
79 清人(清城的壮丁)········ 174
　　Men from Qing

80 羔裘(羔羊皮袍)·········· 176
　　Lamb Skin Coat
81 遵大路(走在路上)········ 178
　　Walking on the Street
82 女曰鸡鸣(鸡已啼叫)····· 180
　　Cocks Are Crowing
83 有女同车(同车女子)····· 182
　　A Girl in Our Carriage
84 山有扶苏(山地有桑树)··· 184
　　Highland Mulberries
85 萚兮(黄叶)············ 186
　　Autumn Leaves
86 狡童(滑头男子)········· 188
　　Silly Man
87 褰裳(提起长衫)········· 190
　　Lift Your Gown
88 丰(体面)············· 192
　　Handsome
89 东门之墠············ 194
　　(东门外的土山)
　　A Hill Outside the Eastern Gate
90 风雨(风雨)············ 196
　　Wind and Rain
91 子衿(你的衣领)········· 198
　　Your Blue Collar
92 扬之水(山溪奔流)········ 200
　　Turbulent Water
93 出其东门(走出东门)····· 202
　　Walking Out the Eastern Gate

94 野有蔓草（青草蔓蔓）··· 204
　　Green Grass
95 溱洧（溱河与洧河）········ 206
　　The Zhen and Wei Rivers

齐风 / Airs of Qi
96 鸡鸣（鸡鸣）············ 210
　　Cocks are Crowing
97 还（敏捷）············· 212
　　You are So Agile
98 著（大门）············· 214
　　Front Gate
99 东方之日（东方之日）··· 216
　　Sun in the East
100 东方未明············· 218
　　（东方天未亮）
　　The Eastern Sky is Not Yet
　　Light
101 南山（南山）··········· 220
　　South Hills
102 甫田（大块地）········· 222
　　A Large Field
103 卢令（猎犬颈铃响）····· 224
　　Dog Bells Ringing
104 敝笱（破鱼篓）········· 226
　　Broken Fish Trap
105 载驱（轿车疾奔）······· 228
　　Carriage Running Rapidly
106 猗嗟（噢，啊）········· 230
　　Oh, Ah

魏风 / Airs of Wei
107 葛屦（草鞋）··········· 234
　　Straw Slippers
108 汾沮洳（汾水岸上）····· 236
　　By the River Fen
109 园有桃（园地有桃树）··· 238
　　Peach Trees in the Garden
110 陟岵（爬山）··········· 240
　　Climbing a Hill
111 十亩之闲（十亩悠闲）··· 242
　　Ten Acres of Leisure
112 伐檀（伐青檀）········· 244
　　Chopping Down
　　Sandalwood Trees
113 硕鼠（大老鼠）········· 246
　　Big Rat

唐风 / Airs of Tang
114 蟋蟀（蟋蟀）··········· 250
　　Cricket
115 山有枢··············· 252
　　（山地上有刺榆）
　　Mountain Elms
116 扬之水（清清流水）····· 254
　　Stream Water Runs Clearly
117 椒聊（花椒树种子）····· 256
　　Pepper Tree Seeds
118 绸缪（洞房之夜）······· 258
　　Wedding Night
119 杕杜（棠梨树）········· 260
　　Pear Tree

120 羔裘(羊皮袍子) ………… 262
　　Lamb Skin Coat
121 鸨羽(秃鹫羽毛) ………… 264
　　Vulture's Feather
122 无衣(无衣) …………… 266
　　No Clothes
123 有杕之杜(棠梨树) …… 268
　　A Lone Pear Tree
124 葛生(葛藤) …………… 270
　　Climbing Vines
125 采苓(采甘草) ………… 272
　　Gathering Licorice

秦风 / Airs of Qin

126 车邻(马车邻邻) ……… 276
　　Rushing Carriage
127 驷驖(四匹青马) ……… 278
　　Four Black Horses
128 小戎(轻兵车) ………… 280
　　Small War-Chariot
129 蒹葭(芦苇) …………… 282
　　Reeds
130 终南(终南山) ………… 284
　　Zhong-nan Mountain
131 黄鸟(黄鸟) …………… 286
　　Yellow Finches
132 晨风(鹞子) …………… 288
　　Falcon
133 无衣(无衣) …………… 290
　　No Clothes

134 渭阳(渭水之北) ……… 292
　　North Side of River Wei
135 权舆(思旧) …………… 294
　　Good Old Time

陈风 / Airs of Chen

136 宛丘(宛丘) …………… 298
　　Wan Mound
137 东门之枌 ……………… 300
　　(东门外的榆树)
　　Elm Trees Outside the East
　　Gate
138 衡门(陋室) …………… 302
　　Humble Shack
139 东门之池 ……………… 304
　　(东门护城河)
　　The Moat Outside the
　　Eastern Gate
140 东门之杨 ……………… 306
　　(东门外的杨树)
　　Poplar Trees at the East
　　Gate
141 墓门(墓门) …………… 308
　　Tomb's Gate
142 防有鹊巢(防备谣言) … 310
　　Avoid Gossip
143 月出(月出) …………… 312
　　Moonrise
144 株林(株林) …………… 314
　　Zhu-lin

145 泽陂（池塘岸上）……… 316
　　The Pond's Edge

桧风 / Airs of Kuai
146 羔裘（羊皮袍子）……… 320
　　Lamb Skin Coat
147 素冠（白冠）…………… 322
　　White Cap
148 隰有苌楚 ……………… 324
　　（隰地里有狝桃藤）
　　Kiwi Vine in the Wetland
149 匪风（大风）…………… 326
　　Strong Wind

曹风 / Airs of Cao
150 蜉蝣（蜉蝣）…………… 330
　　Mayfly
151 候人（小军官）………… 332
　　Man of Arms
152 鸤鸠（布谷鸟）………… 334
　　Cuckoo
153 下泉（下泉）…………… 336
　　Deep Spring

豳风 / Airs of Bin
154 七月（七月）…………… 340
　　The Seventh Month
155 鸱鸮（夜猫子）………… 346
　　Owl
156 东山（东山）…………… 348
　　Eastern Hills
157 破斧（破斧）…………… 352
　　Broken Axe
158 伐柯（作斧柄）………… 354
　　Making an Axe Handle
159 九罭（鱼网）…………… 356
　　Fish Net
160 狼跋（狼走路）………… 358
　　Wolf Walking

【附录】………………………… 360
夜读蒹葭 ………………………
Evening Reading of "Reeds"

关于封面的艺术 …………… 368
A Note About The
　Book Cover Art

译者小传

贾福相,1931年生于山东省寿光县贾家庄。六岁时遭逢二次大战,1949年5月参军,随舅父到了台湾,先进大甲中学,后在台中装甲兵子弟中学毕业,1951年考取师范学院(现师范大学)生物系。服役期间担任两年少尉翻译官,役毕在东海大学担任助教一年。1958年获西雅图华盛顿大学动物研究所奖学金赴美,1962年完成硕士学位,1964获得动物学博士学位。

从此,他开始了教书、研究和行政工作,在6个国家教过7所大学,编辑参考书4本,发表论文203篇,担任6家国际期刊编辑委员,指导硕博士生40余人,到他实验室工作的访问学者和博士后研究员计有23人。1997年于香港科技大学退休,退休后任台北海洋馆馆长3年。

他在加拿大阿尔伯塔大学任教24年,担任动物系系主任5年,研究生院院长10年,多次参与国内外大学行政会议,五种世界名人录榜上有名,2002年与友人合创Bioneutra生物科技公司,并被选为该公司首任董事长,2007年获选入北美企业总经理俱乐部会员。

1986年开始写散文,以笔名"庄稼",在台湾几家杂志和副刊发表文章,出版诗集散文集《独饮也风流》、《吹在风里》、《看海的人》、《星移几度》、《生态之外》五本。

Translator's Biography

Fu-Shiang Chia was born in Shandong, China in 1931 and moved to Taiwan in 1949 where he completed high school and got his BS in Biology in Taiwan Normal University. After two years of military service and one year as a T.A. in Tunghai University, he went to Seattle to attend graduate school at the University of Washington, receiving his MSc in 1962 and PhD in Zoology in 1964.

During his academic career he taught in seven universities in six countries, edited four reference books, published over 200 research papers, served on the editorial board of six international journals, supervised the completion of more than forty MSc and PhD degrees, and worked with over twenty visiting scientists and post-doctoral fellows. He retired from the Hong Kong University of Science and Technology in 1997 and after that, he worked for three years as the director of Taipei Sea World.

He taught in the University of Alberta for twenty-four years, during five of which he was the chairman of Zoology and ten of which he was the Dean of the Faculty of Graduate Studies & Research. He served on numerous university national and international committees and was listed in five editions of world *Who's Who*. Most recently he was one of the founders and Chairman of the Board of Bioneutra, Inc, a biotechnology company in Edmonton. He was selected as a member of the North America President & CEO Club in 2007.

He has published six books of prose and poetry in Chinese.

致谢

　　我很感谢加拿大爱德门顿市《光华报》林惠琪社长和迟文荣主编的鼓励和帮忙。也感谢台湾交通大学英文系主任兼语言研究所所长刘美君教授的邀请，得以在2005年于交大客座教授六周，讲"诗经翻译"获益良多。另外，过去三年我曾获邀去台湾师范大学，中山大学，爱德门顿市台湾同乡会、温哥华漂木艺术家协会、画家协会、读书协会、绿色俱乐部及中国文化研究院等多处讲演诗经，得到诸多听众指教。

　　译稿在美国华盛顿大学星期五港海洋研究所完成，郑惠雯、亚诺尔和我日以继夜工作八天（2006年3月4日至12日）。最难忘的是几次在炉火旁的讨论。我感谢星期五港海洋研究所的同仁们，特别是 Bob Schwartzberg 先生。最后，我要特别感谢妻子 Sharon 在我翻译诗经过程中始终耐心陪伴提供协助。

Acknowledgements

I am most grateful to Ms. Vicki Lim and Miss Grace Chi, respectively the Publisher and the Chief Editor of the weekly *Chinese Journal* in Edmonton, Canada for their encouragement and advice on this project. I wish also to thank Professor Mei-Chun Liu, who invited me to offer a course on translating the *Shi Jing* as a Visiting Professor for six weeks at National Chiao Tung University in 2005. During the past three years I have been invited to give lectures at the National Normal University and Sun Yat-sen University in Taiwan, and to many associations in Canada, from which this work benefited a great deal.

Miss Heather Cheng and Professor Stephen H. Arnold and I worked continuously for eight days (March 4 — 12, 2006) at Friday Harbor Laboratories of the University of Washington, USA to complete the first draft of the manuscript. I shall never forget this occasion and our discussions at the fireplace. I am also grateful to many colleagues at the Friday Harbor Labs, particularly Mr. Bob Schwartzberg. Lastly, but hardly least, I acknowledge the patience and assistance of my dear wife Sharon at all stages of this project.

In preparation for this Peking University Press edition, Dr. Arnold and I have corrected several typos and have changed/improved several lines in Chinese and in English. Being so few, and editorial in nature, these changes are not really sufficient to qualify this printing as a " Revised Edition". –F-S Chia, May, 2010.

桥

窄窄的桥
无边的海

古人走过来
今人走过去

东方人走出去
西方人走进来

听一听"喓喓草虫"
看一看"灼灼其华"
且唱：
"蒹葭苍苍"；"明星煌煌"
"月出皎兮"；"伫立以泣"
"七月流火"；"麻衣如雪"

生命流出了爱
爱是诗
诗的多样哟：
"有女如玉"；"巧笑倩兮"
"青青子衿"；"巷无居人"
"投我以木桃"；"与子偕老"
"如何如何,忘我实多"

过来过去,一段路
走进走出,生之旅

窄窄的桥
无边的海

注：引号中的句子都是引自国风诗篇。

Bridge

Narrow bridge.
Oceans wide.

People of the West cross to this side;
People of the East cross to that side.

People of yesteryear return;
People of today remember.

Together we look at "the bright cherry blossoms."
Together we listen to "the autumn songs of the cricket."
Together we sing:
"The reed plumes are infinitely white,"
"The evening stars are infinitely bright."

From life flows love,
From love, poetry
In myriad forms:
"Sweet dimples frame her teasing smile";
"The man in the blue collar has stolen my heart";
"Give me a peach"; "We shall grow old together";
"Why, why have you completely forgotten me?"

Remember, remember...

This side, that side...
Crossing,
We journey to each other

Across a narrow bridge,
Across oceans wide.

Note: Lines in quotation marks are phrases from "Airs of the States."

序

史蒂芬·亚诺尔
加拿大埃布尔达大学荣誉教授
比较文学暨电影研究系前系主任
郑惠雯中译

  贾福相翻译《诗经》国风160首，可谓半个多世纪以来中国内地以外地区首见全新的完整英译[1]。在此《诗经》国风全译本问世之前的近60年间，中国已成为世界强国，英语亦成为实质上的世界通语，这两件划时代的大事，适逢21世纪的来临及数波全球化发展，皆呼唤着一本如贾译这般贴近时代脉动的三语译本。然《诗经·国风》亟需新译最重要的原因，乃是因为它是现存世界文学中最早的诗歌文本，其中有些诗作已有3000多年之久。此一汇集人类遗产中最古老的诗歌文字，可谓已知人类文学文化的泉源与发轫[2]。虽然论古老没有比它更远古的了，而且只是口耳相传由当时的人记录下来，却毫不原始粗糙。如《诗经》这般精巧繁复的作品者应让各国人民共同欣赏和研究。

  贾福相翻译《诗经》国风的种子植于65年以前，他祖父是山东某地的公正人暨风水师。祖父教授他中国古典文学，福相自6岁起就站在黑板前，对着慈爱却又严厉的祖父背诵唐诗，一边背一边担心背错会被祖父鞭策。青少年时期他开始南北流离的生活，走过战乱的国土，食不果腹，无法兼顾生存与诗心的发展。1949年他18岁，舅父安排他随着军队到了台湾。

  过了4个月的军旅生活，他得以重入中学，而后进入师范大学生物系。中学时曾被怀疑是共产党间谍，入狱一周。大学毕业后做了两年少尉编译官，然后到美国华盛顿大学专攻海洋生物。他早期的学术游历，从美国一路到英国，最后终于在加拿大安顿下来，他在加国的研究工作非常出色，若以研究奖助金来衡量，排名加国自然科学家前十名。他不仅在研究和教学成绩卓著，在行政工作也同样杰出。曾担任埃布尔达大学动物系系主任五年，接着又担任研究生及研究院院长（Dean of Graduate Studies& Research）十年，该校博士生人数排名全加拿大第二，且于2006年获加拿大Maclean's杂志评为加国顶尖大学，这都是因为贾教授于该校多年耕耘的缘故（后来他于香港科技大学正式退休）。

我担任贾院长的第一副院长近十年之久，他休假或外出讲演时我就代理院务。我们每天一起工作，两年后他才向我吐露他私下也写诗。身为文学教授的我常遇到天真而欠缺才华的大学生、研究生甚至同事，拿着自己的"诗"请我评论。这种情境往往有些尴尬，被迫读了几页后，他们会期待评论家与非诗人的我给予专业建议。我有几句不伤大雅但又带有鼓励的评语，像是"这几个字不错"，或是"你抒发了颇为强烈的情感，谢谢你把诗给我看，可惜我现在没空多读，请继续创作"等等。这种时候无法完全诚实，尤其面对如此私人的感情，直言不讳并非上策。某日福相拿了一迭散文诗请我看，我突然有些不知所措，因为我俩的互动一向都是直来直往。当他缓缓以英文读出一首描写章鱼的中文诗，我竟听得津津有味，非常入迷。没想到我这位朋友贾福相，我们常常开玩笑介绍他是"潮间带动物性生活专家"，竟是个不折不扣的诗人哩。自此之后，我们开始一起研究诗作，后来也有数次合力完成作品的经验。特别是他退休以后，福相的诗作及饶富哲思的散文，几乎超越他在海洋生物及生态学的声名。

民歌"上市"的时间久远，其最"新鲜"的时候是刚诞生之时，当时作者的用意明显易懂。《诗经》里可能引用许多更古老的诗歌，只是我们已无从考据，因为找不到比诗经更早的书面纪录。当民歌逐渐老去，其根源逐渐为人遗忘，意义更为晦涩，许多特色便随之莫讳如深。举一首古老的英语童谣为例："绕着玫瑰转圈儿／口袋装满鲜花儿／灰啊，灰啊／我们全都倒下啦。"这首童谣至今仍广为流传，通常是一群孩童手牵手，一边唱一边转圈，唱到最后一句时大家一起倒地咯咯大笑。民间文学研究者近来才发现这首童谣蕴含的意义，原来是描写几世纪前鼠疫重创欧洲的情形。其中"绕着玫瑰转圈儿"一句，是形容鼠疫患者皮肤出现一圈红色脓疱；

"口袋装满鲜花儿"指的是当时人们相信,在口袋里塞满花朵可免于感染;最后一句"灰啊,灰啊/我们全都倒下啦。"是死者遗体通常会覆盖泥灰,以掩饰死因,当然"我们全都倒下啦"指的就是死亡。

我们虽然无法断定《诗经》中有多少诗篇有相类似的深度,但可以想见必然为数不少。以此类推,假设"绕着玫瑰转圈儿"是古英文,先翻译成现代英文后,再译为现代中文,如果在翻译时不求正确精准,那么最后得到的中译会是"围着雏菊……在草地上翻滚",如此一来根本无法追溯原意了(也以此告诫研究古文的学者)。我们要记得,好的翻译是一种发现与创新的努力,表层下隐藏或佚失的意义如同纸张的水印,只在某种光线下才会昭然若现。为了让诗歌长存,数世纪以来中国的诗经评论家,无论是个人还是学派,无不揣测着诗歌所隐含的历史或神话意义,可是他们却忘了,不管怎么说,这些文本其实就是诗而已。

将《诗经》介绍到英语世界的译者,获益于多如牛毛的中文批注,同时身为学者的他们,也或多或少会加入自己的见解。亚瑟·韦利(Arthur Waley)是公认的《诗经》翻译大家,实非浪得虚名。韦利学识广博,但稍嫌拘泥细节,其译作偶而失之于晦涩,清通不足,然而我们必须公允的说,《诗经》有些诗篇原文的确是暧昧模糊,令人无法完全了解其意。艾兹拉·庞德(Ezra Pound),第二位最常被称为英译《诗经》的"译者",由于坚持音韵优先于意义,往往使字面意思及引申含意都更为晦涩,她的文字游戏为《诗经》笼罩了一层不必要的迷雾。庞德的译写当中不时出现希腊文、拉丁文、德文、意大利文、普罗旺斯语、20世纪初美国黑人与白人俚语,以及其他语言,使原诗不时淹没于难懂的英文词藻之中。

那么多诗人学者翻译过的经典作品,为何还需要新译本呢?20世纪中叶美国诗人史蒂文斯(Wallace Stevens)所言甚是,尤其把"诗作"替换成"翻译":

〔……翻译……是〕一种寻找之举
找寻能够满足之物。它不一定总得
找到不可:场景已定;重复述说

剧本的字句。然后未来变成
其他东西。它的过去是纪念品。
它必须活着,要学习当地话语。
它必须面对时下之男人,会见
时下之女人。它必须思想……
且必须找到能够满足之物。
它必须搭建新舞台。

贾福相的译文正好满足史蒂文斯诗中隐含的标准,即有效地与时俱进,清通畅达、真实素朴的呈现。此外,《诗经》这类典籍译作的优劣良窳,由于原作语境久远而难以判断,英国诗人艾略特(T. S. Eliot)的《评论集》(*Critical Essays*)中有段话或许可以用以说明贾译之长处:

写诗时我一直追求的,
并非关乎诗意之事,而是诗作赤裸裸地
光溜溜地站立着,如此*透明*之诗作〔斜体为笔者所加〕,
甚至使人看不见诗作,相反地
我们的视线本当穿透诗作,
如是透明之诗,阅读它时,我们的意图
顺应着*诗所指之处*而去〔斜体为艾略特原文所有〕,而非
诗本身,这似乎才是值得尝试之事。

贾译的成就之一便是这种透明,以优美的英语再现中文之美的同时,他避免自己创造出一首首替代原诗的新诗作,因为那反而会遮蔽原诗,使之无法散发光芒。

我自己不懂中文,贾福相的《诗经》白话中译有待中文学者评断,然其英译的质量清楚可见。除了这点,贾福相的英译也不故弄玄虚。要描述其英译的方法和结果,稍早提到水印譬喻在此较不适用,另一个譬喻可能更适合:如果我们将原诗视为一潭深水,由当下的天空所映照,我们看到的是自己的历史文化脉络,看不见水

面下是什么或有什么,而这名译者将我们从表面给拯救出来,他像一名优秀的摄影师,有系统地将各种滤镜,置于他心中的镜片和目标物之间,我们因而得以看见镜面下的深度和细节,同时又充分保留表面的讯息,让时人能够体会诗的意义。

那么贾福相运用的是哪些"滤镜"呢? 首先,他是一名博物学家。对他而言,生物学名不只是一种儒家传统,而是必须力求正确的任务,代表着音韵的地位有时需略次于意义。《诗经》中俯拾皆是的动植物意象,是否挟带科学、社会学,甚至是人类学的重要意义,这点贾福相或许无法提供解答。然而他坚持从原典译为现代白话中文与英文时,需务求精准正确,最周全的阅读当包含如是之自然元素,甚至如潜藏的寓言——不论是已知或仍有疑义者——而且严格忠于原作的字面意思加以阐释。

贾福相运用的另一种滤镜,是其他译者未用的,即摘除镜片,将尺度从眼前移开。如前所述,许多英译者穷其气力翻阅数世纪以来译成欧语的《诗经》批注,结果反而落得莫衷一是。许多文化译介活动,似乎将那一层层包覆在外的训诂和注释看得比诗作本身还重要(这让我想起以前一位来自印度的同事 J.S. Das Gupta,他对德国学者研究印度文学的评语是:"德国学者钻研得比别人深,身上沾的泥巴也比别人多。")虽然贾福相几十年前就从祖父那里打下中国古典文学基础,但他有意将这些无边无际的注释题解搁置一旁,坚持阅读这些诗歌时,不在文化包袱里翻箱倒柜。他以个人深刻的中国诗学视角出发,看见其他人所看不见的事物,例如他发掘出许多首诗潜在的情欲元素,数世纪以来精英文化和学术研究将其禁锢于诗歌底层,不过这些诗歌其实是初民在较为自由的氛围下创作的。

性的议题一直让传统训诂学者头疼不已,今日之华文学术界也仍对其十分敏感。贾福相阅读诗经时完全将这些偏见抛除,他认为国风中至少有部分诗歌是在较为开放的社会环境中所作。然而在接下来的年代,直至今日,情欲的成分在中国文化中仍被压抑,轻则含糊隐晦一言以蔽之,重则于编纂成册时予以删除,藉由文学以外的道德教化观念加以消毒一番。中国文学界的编纂策略和操控,在读者和诗歌之间筑起一道隔阂,相较之下外国文学英译的历史较为多样,幸未受制于这种划一的标准。有一点值得提出,现代中国出版的唯一一本国风译本,只选译160首中的40首(Yea, Dai and Yang),而其中又只收录一首所谓的"淫诗"(第23首《野有死麕》),收录后又将它阉割了。贾福相的翻译也未刻意强化扩大原诗的性暗示,只是他忠于事实的信念,让他藉由忠实的呈现,使原诗可能的暗示重见光明。

对诗歌做跨越时间的新诠释(历时性),也可以是同一时间不同空间的诠释(共时性),译者在他所写的其他文章,尤其是散文中,不断强调跨文化的比较,更能让我们从封闭的传统中,挖掘出艺术潜在的能量,超越训诂传统所设下之限制。他以中文写了许多文章,讨论与性有关的议题,在中文脉络中显得大胆露骨,但英译之后西方人读来却顺耳温驯,同时他忠实呈现性暗示的策略,揭开中国文学的神秘面纱,重新赋予原已虚弱疲软者以活力朝气。

诗经国风的英译相较于中国从古至今的经学传统,保守的作风较不似后者那般统一,也不像后者那么势力庞大,然而二者不分中西却同样暧昧模糊、闪烁其词。一首诗或一篇译文要跨越历史长流持续产生影响,当须与时俱进,方能使当代读者亦感受到原作者为读者唤起的情感。如果原作唤起读者的七情六欲,其力道可能因时间之故慢慢淡去,除非翻译也能与时俱进,跟着时代条件与情境更新,才能再度唤起读者相同感觉。我们先举个与诗作无关的例子说明,就服装时尚的演进而言,在某个时代女性从头到脚包得密不透风,单是露出脚踝便能燃起观者的欲望。在今日多数国家,同样的效果需要大胆的暴露才能达成。诗也一样,在保守拘谨的年代里,情欲的元素潜藏隐晦,《诗经》和多年来的各种译本皆是如此。今日若要在性意象泛滥的世界里唤醒潜伏的情欲,今人的露骨远超过前朝的尺度,译者必须使古诗隐含潜藏的内容外显出来,而原本裸露脚踝所唤起的情欲,可能得袒胸露背才能在当代达到相等的效果。[3]

此处我以重新发现国风诸诗的情欲元素作为新译的根据,事实上还有其他各种理由可以支持《诗经》新译之必要,也值得在此稍加说明。首先,语言与文化演进的同时,译本也一点一滴地丧失其效力,到某一程度时,译文失去时效,读来不仅陈旧,甚至难以理解。此外,当诗中纳入俚语(寿命极短)、口语表达、谚语格言(通常指涉消失中的习俗),同时包含对其他短暂之艺术或改变之潮流等等所作的文化指涉,译本读来更易似走调般越发不对劲,需要重新调音,提供新的批注。

"翻译"根据古老的通则"系为诠释",因为英汉语言特质的差异,该原则说明了为什么今日有这么多不同的国风译本。中文并无字尾词形变化,非常洗练简洁,依赖语境来决定主词、数量、性别、时态等等,也比英语更为隐约、暧昧、间接、简练且含蓄。像国风这类的中文诗给了读者许多想象空间,因此很自然地同一首中文诗英译时,有些译本的诠释是一名女子在过去某时拒绝或想念一名男子,但有些则诠释为一名男子在此时此刻拒绝或想念一名女子。藉由如此不同译本的积累,原文的多样可能才得以显现。

在这诸多可能当中,处处皆是译者所必须面对的难题,英文无法直接对应古汉语(其于中国文化所处的地位,通常可比拟为中世纪的拉丁文,较其他欧洲语言优越,因为后者为口语方言,而用于书写及"高等"文化的是拉丁文)。中国古诗自民间搜集而来,经过朝廷文官乐师润色后,美化了原本较为俚俗的语汇。贾福相的国风英译,译文风格揉合雅正、古朴之词汇形式,未见土话或白话的粗鄙之语。因此,他撮合两种传统,呈现混血诗风,却不牺牲意义的清晰。他的翻译自然不矫作,不掉书袋卖弄学问,散发优雅气息。而生为庄稼子弟的他,少年历经流亡学生的岁月,中年成为鼓吹进步的教育行政者,这些曲折的生命经验,跨越社会阶层,跑遍世界各地,从乡巴佬到大教授,从科学家到诗人,这些都是暖身、都是准备,让他得以翻译《诗经》这般风格多元的作品。

性别意识抬头的今日,我们不得不对《诗经》里的性别议题多加注意。在多数传世的作品中,文学创作似乎是男性特有的权力,但《诗经》并非如此。国风160首中,只有一首诗的作者确定,诗人正是一名女性穆姬,《载驰》一诗出自她的手笔,约于2600年前写成。此外,当中有46首诗以女性为第一人称"发声",几乎等同于以男性发声的篇数(48首);另外57首可解读为男性或女性,其余9首是男女对话。而且十五国风当中的十四国,其男女作第一人称的篇数相当。数世纪以来,各地文学均有性别平等的发轫,我们须视此为中国文学本源的回溯,而非像西方那样缓慢、踌躇的线性"进程",以此含括更多女性作家。在此无庸置疑的,性别平等早已存在于这年代最早、以俗民为诉求的诗歌文学当中。

李雅各(Lee)、理雅各(Legge)和高本汉(Karlgren)将中国文化重要经典引进英语世界,译本各有千秋,皆有其重要性,韦利译作的经典地位依然崇高,只不过其语汇日渐褪色发黄;庞德的诠释特立独行,对一般读者而言从来就不易理解。贾福相将这些诗篇带入当代的同时,又能保存古味,他无意与其他时代的其他译者争高下,相反地其译作可视为一种补足。他在用字遣词上力求精准,朴实又不失丰富与诗味。甚至他也尝试使用音步与其他修辞技巧来提醒读者,虽然乐谱早已佚失,但国风的诗篇在很久很久以前都是可唱的歌曲,当中许多甚至可以伴舞。但是,他不在译作中刻意套用英诗的固定格式(英诗有无数种格律)来模仿中文古诗的体裁,其译作是为21世纪读者量身打造,亲切自然之余,又保存原诗异文化之特质与个性。

诚然,正如译者作为开场的小诗《桥》所言(请见前文),古老东方与现代西方二者在此译作中相遇,携手并进。诗人康明斯(e. e. cummings)曾写道:"诗:是不可翻译的。"再引用另一位诚实的诗人论诗之评语:"诗(翻译)没有结束,只有遗弃。"贾福相跟其他许多译者,都证明了康明斯所言只对了一半。我们应该庆幸,或许他的译作也不是"结束",但他四年多的坚持使我们受惠良多。译者并非都像斗牛士或悲剧主人公般,注定要失败丧命;他们当然不是傻子,但他们企及不可能之任务,因此情操更显高贵。

笔者也还不能"遗弃"自己的序言,须再对译者特出之处提供个人意见:第23首《野有死麇》(野地死獐)几乎无异于原创的现代英诗,情感细腻直接;第71首《葛藟》(野葡萄)深刻表达许多妇女的苦境,为不幸婚姻所困;第87首《褰裳》(提起长衫)语气暧昧,饶富意趣,尤其是与其他英译版本比较时,贾译更能凸显此特色;第99

首《东方之日》(东方之日)简单真挚;第113首《硕鼠》(大老鼠)抨击依赖他人的寄生虫,今昔皆然;第118首《绸缪》(洞房之夜)委婉描绘新婚夫妻如胶似漆之情景,口吻带有喜剧意味。第129首《蒹葭》(芦苇)给人一种他方世界的感觉,如梦地刻画本质而非实体,或许因其现代感及永恒感之故,《蒹葭》是其中我最喜爱的一首诗,可作为诗经导读之范本。

以上及本书其他许多诗歌,皆适于编入英语(或华语)学习教材以及世界文学选集。(译者便是顾及此类教学用途,计画于日后邀请专业朗读者,朗诵原诗与译文,制作朗读CD附于书后。)随着中国于本世纪的崛起,中华文化成为全球教育的一部分,未来英语仍是认识中华文化的中介语言,因此即使为求文化间的了解及多元文化的凝聚,对新兴全球文化有重大意义的文学作品,必须定期进行新译,贾福相的作品必能禁得起时间的淘洗。

---

[1] 显然相继出版的许多白话中译,其翻译与贾之白话及英译原则并不相同,贾之翻译原则详见于导言。

Jacob Lee 的 *The Chinese Classics* 是已知的第一本诗经英译,1861-1871于香港出版。我参考的最早译本为 **James Legge** 于1871年出版的 *The She King or the Book of Poetry*. The Chinese Classics, vol. 4(1898年再版)(出版年、地点不详),香港大学出版社于 1960年再版,文史哲出版社也于后几年再版(台湾,1971)。此处参考 **Legge** 之译文为维吉尼亚大学 Xuepen Sun 和 Xiaoqiuan Zeng 所制作之电子版本 URL:http://etext.lib.virginia.edu/chinese(1998)。

Ezra Pound 1936 (?) 全译本 *The Shih-ching: The Classic Anthology Defined by Confucius* 自1954年出版后,哈佛大学出版社已数次再刷。

Arthur Waley 的 *The Book of Songs: The Ancient Chinese Classic of Poetry* 于1937年问世(其中部分译诗早在1919年已出版),由纽约 Grove Press 再版数次,最近一次是1996年,Waley 之参考书目由 Joseph R. Allen 于 Grove 版本中更新如下:

Bernhard Karlgren 的 *The Book of Odes: Chinese Text, Transcription, and Translation* 1950 年于斯德哥尔摩由 Museum of Far Eastern Antiquities 出版，初版年月不详；然 Ezra Pound 于 1936 年的译本中引用其"发音指导"。最近的译本 *The Book of Songs: A Chinese Selection of Ancient Poems (Chinese-English)*, **Yea, Mong** 编，**Dai, Nai-Xien** 与 **Yang, Xian** 合译，北京 Foreign Language Publishing Company 于 2001 出版，虽然该译本仅选译 160 首国风的 40 首，仍非常有助于比较翻译学。

[2] 同样享此殊荣的是希伯来文旧约中的《雅歌》("Song of Solomon")，为宗教诗歌，另外则是梵文宗教诗作《梨俱吠陀》(*Rig Veda*)，不过《诗经》仍是现存最早之非宗教文集。

[3] 此处列举几位英译者对国风中情欲元素的翻译策略以兹证明。

国风第 29 首《日月》诗题与诱惑及变节有关……

Legge 晚期维多利亚时代文风过于拘谨，避重就轻地带过："...the man, / With virtuous words, but not really good./ ...Would he then allow me to be forgotten?" **Waley** 的策略也几乎同样间接婉转，他使用有些古味的动词 "requited"："Better if he had not requited me. /... /How should he be true?/ He requited me, but did not follow up." **Pound** 在此不同以往地显得非常保守："... his like of evil reputation?/ ... forgetting love?" 贾译 细腻但更为直接："How can such a person exist? He has no moral sense. / ...he has forgotten me completely./ ...He is not true to me."

国风第 45 首《柏舟》主题同上，各译者也都做出相似处理。**Legge**："He was my only one;/ And I swear that till death I will not do the evil thing." **Waley**："He swore that truly he was my mate, / And till death would not fail me./ ... That a man could be so false!" **Pound** 用了 "bull" 一字（性的暗示极为明显）让人如坠雾中，为了押韵之故又用 "traist" 一字，多数现代英语使用者都不知道该字的意思："My bull till death he were, /... / Shall no one be traist?!" **Yea, Dai** 与 **Yang** 的 2001 年译本，几乎不触及诗中明显的逾矩之举："Too much indignity I've been treated with./ ... / My heart stained with sorrow, / Cannot be washed clean like dirty clothes." 贾译 一如其翻译原则所示，暗示人性和道德的复杂："The ... man ... is my dearest./ I swear I will never change my mind./ Heavens, mother! Why don't you understand?"

国风第 23 首《野有死麕》，**Legge** 已经来到维多利亚时代大胆的界线："There is a young lady with thoughts natural to the spring, / And a fine gentleman would lead her astray." **Waley** 难得地直接点出主题："There was a lady longing for the spring; / A fair knight seduced her." **Pound** 也直言不讳："A melancholy maid in spring is luck for lovers./ ... / dead as doe is maidenhood." **Yea, Dai** 和 **Yang** 至少点出少女心中的热情："A girl is longing for love, / A fine fellow tempts her." 贾译 并未等到最后一段才讲明诱惑的诗题，而是在一开始便带出该诗题："A sensual young maiden, / ... / An oak tree deep in soft woods" — a clearly coital image.

Foreword

Stephen H. Arnold, Professor Emeritus
Former Chair, Department of
Comparative Literature and Film Studies
The University of Alberta

Outside of China, this translation by Fu-Shiang Chia of the 160 "Airs of the States" from the *Shi Jing* represents the first new, complete version to appear in English in well over half a century.[1] In the nearly six decades since a fresh, full translation last appeared, China has emerged as a world superpower, and English has become the *de facto* global *lingua franca*. This epochal pair of events, which have coincided with the beginning of a new millennium, marked by waves of "globalization," clearly cries out for an up-to-date trilingual text such as Chia's. The most compelling justification for new translations of the "Airs of the States," however, is the collection's distinction as the oldest extant book of lyric poetry in world literature — parts dating back 3,000 years. This gathering of the most ancient written lyric poems in the entire human patrimony[2] stands among the headwaters, the fountainheads of all known literary culture, which — in spite of such unparalleled antiquity and of its status as orature written down by contemporaries — has no taint of the primitive. A work of great sophistication, the *Shi Jing* should be available to all the world's peoples for appreciation and study.

For more than 65 years, this translation of the "Airs of the States" from the *Shi Jing* has been percolating in the mind of Fu-Shiang Chia, the grandson of a Shandong area circuit judge and *feng shui* master who taught him the classics of the Chinese literary tradition. From the age of six, Fu-Shiang stood between a blackboard and his loving but severe grandfather, having to recite his lessons while fearing a whack from a bamboo pointer if he made an error. A few years later, he became a teenage nomad, crisscrossing his chaotic homeland, barely finding enough food to keep body and poetic soul together. At age eighteen, in 1949, safe passage to Formosa/Taiwan as a soldier was arranged for him by an uncle.

After four months in the Nationalist army, Chia was allowed to go to high school, then on to the Taiwan Normal University as a biology student. When in high school he was imprisoned briefly, being suspected as a communist spy. Following his undergraduate degree, and after another stint in the army with the rank of lieutenant, he went on to graduate school in marine biology at the University of Washington in the United States. After a peripatetic early academic career in the USA and Britain, he eventually settled with his family in Canada, where he rose to distinction in his field — he was, for a time, ranked among the top ten natural scientists in Canada (measured by research grants) — combining his eminence in research and teaching with a distinguished administrative career, first as Chair of Zoology and then as Dean of the Faculty of Graduate Studies and Research at the University of Alberta, Canada's second largest producer of PhDs, and named by a national poll commissioned in 2006 by *Maclean's* magazine as Canada's leading university, a distinction owing not a little to Chia's long leadership there. (He ended his formal career at the Hong Kong University of Science and Technology.)

For nearly a decade, I was Dean Chia's Senior Associate Dean, and Acting Dean during his absences from the Faculty for sabbatical, and research and speaking stints. In spite of working closely with him on a daily basis, at least two years passed before he confided to me his secret double life as a poet. Professors of literature — my academic home — often have "poems" urged upon them by na — e, innocent and usually talentless undergraduates, and at times even by a graduate student or a colleague. Such occasions frequently result in awkward moments. After reluctantly reading whatever was offered for the professional opinion of a critic and non-poet, I was usually armed with a comment or two that were diplomatically neutral, yet possibly complimentary. "There are some beautiful words here," or "You've expressed some powerful emotions. Thanks for showing this to me; I don't have time for more now, but keep writing," etc. It is difficult to be sincere, and with such personal things, bluntness is rarely justified. But when Fu-Shiang brought out a sheaf of poems one day, I felt cornered, for our relationship had always been based on unmitigated honesty and truth. Yet when he began haltingly translating a poem about an octopus from Chinese into uncertain English, I found myself enthralled. My dear friend, whom we often introduced in a jocular way as "the world's foremost expert on sex in the tidal seas," was clearly a genuine poet. Thus began our study of poetry together, leading eventually to collaboration on a number of literary projects. Since that time, and especially since his retirement, Fu- Shiang's stature as poet and philosophical essayist has grown beyond his reputation as a marine biologist and general ecologist.

Folk poetry has a very long shelf life, but when it is most fresh, i.e. newly composed, the author's intentions are most discernible. Allusions in the *Shi Jing* to earlier songs in the popular canon surely exist, but are lost to us, since nothing prior to the *Shi Jing* has been found in writing. As folk poetry gathers antiquity, its roots become less evident and its meanings more obscure. Many of its features sink beneath the surface. An example from English language tradition is the ancient children's rhyme, "Ring around the rosie,/ A pocket full of posies,/ Ashes, ashes,/ We all fall down." This nursery rhyme maintains a lively place in our culture today as a dance song sung by groups of children holding hands, turning in a circle while they sing, ending with them all falling to the ground to giggle as they chant the final line. Scholars of folk literature have only recently rediscovered this rhyme's original significance as a song about the bubonic plague that decimated Europe centuries ago. The line "Ring around the rosie" described a round pustule forming on the skin, itself enclosed in a red circle, as the disease announced itself to a victim. "A pocket full of posies" refers to a popular belief at the time, which prescribed pockets full of flowers as a shield against the plague. Finally, "Ashes, ashes," expressed the practice of covering victims with ashes to render their illness less communicable at the time of their deaths — "We all fall down."

There is no way to determine how many songs in the *Shi Jing* might have such depths, but likely there are many. Imagine if, by analogy, "Ring around the rosie" were Old English, translated into modern English and then into modern Chinese. If care were not taken to achieve the greatest philological accuracy possible, we might end with something in modern Chinese like "Circling in daisies…we tumble in the field," and there would be no hope of retracing the meaning of the original. (Such admonitions are, of course, best directed at scholars of the original, classical language.) We must always keep in mind that translation is — when done well — also a labour of discovery and renewal. Undersurfaces and hidden or lost meanings lie like watermarks in the depths of paper, visible only under certain types of light. In keeping the songs alive, the long line of Chinese commentators on the *Shi Jing* have, as individuals and schools, speculated for centuries about historical and mythic meanings in them. In doing so, they have often forgotten that the texts are actually first and foremost, poetry.

Translators making the *Shi Jing* available to the English world have, of course, benefited from the mountains of Chinese glosses and, in their own rights as scholars, have added insights. Arthur Waley has been universally and most deservedly recognized as the dean of their ranks. But Waley's vast, meticulous erudition occasionally rendered songs more murky than clear, though it must be admitted that with some of the poems, clarity may never have been a quality, and with others, textual corruption has placed them forever beyond our understanding. Ezra Pound, the second most cited "translator" of the songs into English, constantly obscured both surfaces and depths by insisting on the precedence of music over meaning, thus enshrouding the *Shi Jing* in an unnecessary fog of multilingual word play, littering his adaptations with Greek, Latin, German, Italian, Provencal, early 20th century Black and White American slang and other languages, in many cases drowning the Chinese songs entirely in a stew of arcane English.

As further justification for a new translation of a venerable work of art which has already been translated by poets and by scholars with poetic gifts, an excerpt from "Of Modern Poetry" by the mid-twentieth century American poet Wallace Stevens seems apposite, especially if "translation" is substituted for "poems(s)/poetry":

> [...translation ... is] the act of finding
> What will suffice. It has not always had
> To find: the scene was set; it repeated what
> Was in the script. Then the future was changed
> To something else. Its past was a souvenir.
> It has to be living, to learn the speech of the place.
> It has to face the men of the time and to meet
> The women of the time. It has to think...
> And it has to find what will suffice.
> It has to construct a new stage.

Fu-Shiang Chia's translation skilfully meets Stevens' implicit criteria for effective modernization and limpid, unadorned presentation. Additionally, when assessing the quality of a new translation of an artistic monument such as the *Shi Jing*, whose poetic context is so remote from ours, a patch from one of T.S. Eliot's *Critical Essays* signals other strengths of Chia's work:

That at which I have long aimed in writing poetry, with nothing poetic about it, poetry standing naked in its bare bones, or poetry so *transparent* [italics mine — SHA] that we should not see the poetry, but that which we are meant to see through the poetry, poetry as transparent that in reading it we are intent on *what the poem points* at [italics Eliot's], and not the poetry, this seems the thing to try for.

It is such transparency that is among the most significant achievements of Chia's translation. While transferring grace from Chinese into graceful English, he restrains himself from creating a new, substitute poem which would be too opaque to allow the Chinese to shine through.

By force of ignorance I leave it entirely to others to assess Fu-Shiang Chia's skill in rendering the archaic, classical Chinese *Shi Jing* into contemporary Mandarin. In addition to those cited above, however, other qualities of Chia's English translations are less mysterious. To describe his method and results in English, our watermark analogy is perhaps less apt than if we were to view the poems as deep water, illuminated by our contemporary skies. The light of our own historical, cultural context is reflected back at us, leaving us almost clueless about what may lie beneath. Fortunately, we are rescued from superficiality by this translator who, like a good photographer, systematically places various filters between the lens of his mind and the poetic object it registers, thus allowing us to see considerable depth and details beneath the mirror surface, all the while leaving enough above-the-water information to keep the poem meaningful to his contemporaries.

What are some of the "filters" Chia uses? First, he is a naturalist. To him, proper biological nomenclature is not just a Confucian obligation. It is an imperative requiring accuracy, a fact which means that music must occasionally be subordinate to meaning. Whether the ubiquitous imagery of flora and fauna that informs so many of the songs of the *Shi Jing* carries scientific, sociological or even anthropological significance, Chia may not be able to tell us. But his insistence that accuracy be carried from ancient into modern Chinese, and further into contemporary English, ensures that the best possible readings involving these natural elements are guaranteed. Even lurking allegory — known or suspected — can be elucidated by strict, literal fidelity to originals.

Another filter applied by Chia, and by no other translator whose work I have assayed, is actually a filter removed, a scale lifted from the eye. As previously noted, many translators targeting English have driven themselves to bewilderment by consulting as much as possible of the accumulation of centuries of Chinese exegesis on the *Shi Jing* that is available in European languages. Encrusted, sclerotic commentaries seem more important to many of these cultural intermediaries than do the poems themselves. (Their efforts remind me of a comment made by J. S. Das Gupta, an esteemed colleague from India who — when evaluating German scholarship on Indian literatures — opined: "The Germans dive deeper and come up muddier than any other group.") Though schooled in them by his grandfather decades ago, Chia has deliberately ignored these endless annotations, instead insisting on reading the songs without rummaging through their cultural baggage. This reliance on his own personal and deeply Chinese poetic filters has allowed him to see what others have often been blind to. The best examples of this show his sensitivity to the latent eroticism of many songs, an element which centuries of high-cultural, scholarly prudery has driven far beneath the surface of songs composed by less politically correct poets of humbler origins.

Sexuality has provoked anxiety among traditional exegetes, and remains as an irritant today in Chinese academia. Chia irreverently banishes such prejudices from his reading. It is obvious to him that at least some of the "Airs of the States" were composed during less conservative times. In subsequent eras, right down to the present, the erotic elements have been pushed underground in Chinese culture, moving them — at best — from manifest clarity to obscure latency, and — at worst — some songs have actually been removed by mandarins from the canonical gathering of poems — purged for specious moral rather than literary reasons. Chinese readers have thus had barriers put between these poems and themselves through editing and manipulation by members of the literary establishment. It is worth noting, for example, that the only published version of the "Airs" to come from China in recent years contains only 40 of the 160 songs (Yea, Dai and Yang: see endnote one, below), and the only one of the "lascivious" songs that has been included (#23, "Dead Deer"), has been emasculated. Chia's translations do little if anything to amplify sexual suggestiveness of the originals. His allegiance to truth has him merely bring it back out of the closets and shadows through honest presentation.

Such updating of poetic material across time can also be required across space, within the same time frame; thus Chia has in other publications, especially essays, shown how cross-cultural comparisons allow us to see what is covert in art of a more cloistered tradition than its own exegetical tradition has allowed. His own articles on sexuality, rather daringly explicit for the Chinese context in which they are anchored, will seem tame to westerners once they are translated, but meanwhile their unapologetically honest treatment of erotic suggestions will help raise the scholarly, institutional veil on sexual content in much Chinese art, thus making what might be flaccid, regain its turgidity.

With respect to prudery, the history of *Shi Jing* "Airs" translations into English has been less homogeneous and less monolithic than the long line of translations from ancient to modern

Chinese, but vagueness and evasiveness have nevertheless crossed the cultural divide. For a poem or a translation to remain effective along an historical continuum, it must be frequently freshened up in order to continue to provoke in modern readers, emotions similar to those the poet wished to elicit in his or her contemporaries. If the original evoked erotic sentiments in its audience, such sensations may die over time unless translations are updated into new registers required by new historical conditions and contexts. To illustrate this first from outside the domain of poetry, we can refer to fashion in garments. In one age, women might be covered from head to toe, with the mere exposure of an ankle piquing ardent desire in an observer. Certainly today, in most parts of our globe, considerably more exposure is necessary to attain the same result; likewise in poetry. In an age of prudery and restriction, eroticism appears only as vague suggestion, as it often is in the *Shi Jing*, and even more so in its translations over the ages. Today, in order to render erotic undertones available to our more jaded world that is bathed in sexual imagery that far exceeds the bounds of some earlier eroticism, a translator has to make the suggestive content of old poetry far more overt. An ankle needs almost be made a bare breast in order to register on the contemporary eroticism scale at all. [3]

I have dwelt here on the need to recover eroticism in the "Airs" as a primary justification for an entire retranslation of its fifteen books. There are, in addition, more mundane, yet still compelling reasons for such an undertaking, and they are worthy of cursory review. As languages and cultures evolve, the potency of any translation inevitably begins to wane, until the points are reached when it becomes stale, outmoded and ultimately incomprehensible. Furthermore, when their poetic diction involves slang (which rapidly becomes obsolete), colloquialisms and proverbial speech (which often refer to vanishing customs), and also includes cultural references to other ephemeral art or to changing mores, translations begin to sound off-key and require replacements, plus new annotations.

"Translation" — according to an old axiom — "is interpretation." The qualities of the Chinese language in comparison to English, make this rule supremely pertinent to our inheritance of various versions of the "Airs." Uninflected, Chinese is utterly terse, requiring context for clarification of subject, number, gender, tense, etc., and is far more allusive, ambiguous, oblique, elliptical and reserved than English. Chinese poems like the "Airs" leave much of the imaginative work to their readers. It should also come as no surprise, therefore, that the same Chinese poem when translated into English can be about a woman rejecting or missing a man in the past in one translation, and about a man rejecting or missing a woman in the present in another. Only the accumulating totality of translations gradually reveals some of the multiplicity of potentials in the original.

From among these potentials arises the conundrum of styles the translator must wrestle with. Classical Chinese has no English equivalent. (Its position in Chinese culture is often compared to Latin's position in relation to other European languages during the Middle Ages, *i.e.*, they were spoken, vernacular languages, whereas the language of writing and "high" culture was Latin.) Having been gathered from commoners, the old Chinese poems were passed through the writing brushes of court mandarins, whose style most probably elevated humble diction to a more refined idiom. In his English translation of the "Airs," Chia has largely crafted a middle style between courtly, archaic diction and form without descending into peasant patois or *pai hua*, with their colloquial vulgarities. Thus he has melded two traditions, creating a hybrid poetic style while maintaining denotational clarity. His renderings are unpretentious, anything but pedantic, yet still graceful. This comes as no surprise from a man born a peasant, who was forced to be an itinerant beggar in his teens, and who lived his mature life as a progressive mandarin.

His meandering life through all social classes and many lands, from bumpkin to sage, from scientist to poet, prepared him well for translating such an eclectic collection of styles as those found in the *Shi Jing*.

Our contemporary preoccupation with gender bids us to dwell a moment on that issue in the *Shi Jing*. In most of the literature descending to us from antiquity, literary activity seems to have been almost exclusively a male prerogative. Not so in the *Shi Jing*. Only one of the 160 poems/songs has a known author, and that is a woman, Muji, who composed "My Wagon Flies" (#54) about 2,600 years ago. More significant is the fact that 46 poems "speak" with the voice of a female persona, almost exactly the number (48) that employ a male persona. Fifty-seven of the poems could be sung by either a male or a female, and nine present males and females in dialogue. As well, the balance between the sexes of personae is almost equal in 14 of the 15 States from which the "Airs" were collected. The long march toward gender parity which has taken place elsewhere in world literature over many centuries must be admitted to be a recovery of our Chinese origins rather than a slow, stumbling march of linear "progress" — as it has been in the West — to include more women writers, for here in humanity's earliest, secular, poetic literature, gender parity already existed, without a doubt.

Lee, Legge and Karlgren will always enjoy the distinction of having introduced the Anglophone world to these Chinese cultural monuments. Arthur Waley's magnificent work will doubtless always be canonical, but his vocabulary has begun to yellow. Ezra Pound's renditions, rife with idiosyncrasy, have never been comprehensible to common readers. Fu-Shiang Chia makes these poems once again contemporary, while preserving hints of their antiquity. In doing so, he has not competed with his peers from other eras. Rather, his work complements theirs. His language is as lexically accurate as possible, and plain without being spare or un-poetic. When possible, he has used meter and other devices to remind us that these "Airs" were all, once upon a time, sung — and many danced — though their scores have disappeared into the fog of antiquity. What his translations do not attempt is to find rigid forms in English (of which there are many) in which to mimic the strictly formulaic templates of the ancient Chinese sources. The poems have been made companionable for a 21st century audience, without sacrificing either their exotic foreignness or their careful specificity.

Truly, as Chia's own introductory poem "Bridge" implies (it follows the "Table of Contents," above), the twain of ancient East and modern West have met and joined hands in this volume. e.e. cummings wrote, "Poem: that which cannot be translated." To paraphrase another honest poet whose topic was poetry, not translation, "a [translation] is never finished, it is abandoned." Chia, like few others, proves that cummings was only partially correct. And we should be glad that although Chia may not have "finished" this work that has consumed him for over four years, we are the beneficiaries of his refusal to abandon the project. Not all translators are like fighting bulls or protagonists of tragedies — destined to failure and extinction; some few are noble because of attempting the impossible, without being fools.

I, too, cannot "abandon" this "Foreword" without giving my opinion about which are Chia's most successful efforts. #23, "Dead Deer," could be an original modern poem in English — so subtle and delicate, yet so direct. #71, "Wild Grapes," poignantly expresses the plight of so many women, trapped in lamentable marriages, no matter where or when in human history. #87, "Lift Your Gown," has lovely ambiguity, while being playful, especially in comparison to other English versions. #99, "Sun at the East," rings true in its elemental simplicity. #113, "Big Rat," eloquently lambastes the parasites who live off near-slave labour, today and eons ago. #118, "Wedding Night," discreetly, yet almost comically, portrays the enthusiastic intimacy of newly-weds. And #129, "Reeds" is hauntingly other-worldly, dreamlike in its insistence on essence rather than substance. Perhaps because of its feeling of modernity and timelessness, "Reeds," is my favourite of the entire collection; it should be frequently anthologized as a beacon guiding readers to the rest of the *Shi Jing*.

These, and many more poems here, merit inclusion in English as a Second Language courses (as well as in Chinese as a Second Language), and in anthologies of world literature. (It is with these pedagogical functions in mind that Fu-Shiang Chia plans as a future adjunct to this volume a CD Rom which will present the poems and translations of the "Airs" in the voices of trained speakers in both Chinese and English.) As China rises to global eminence in this century, its cultural heritage is becoming part of the necessary education of people around the globe, and for some time to come, English will primarily be the medium through which it is accessed. Thus, although all works important to a new, global culture must be regularly re-translated in order for cross-cultural understanding and multi-cultural cohesion to be assured, this work of Fu-Shiang Chia seems destined for a long, vital life.

---

[1] Apparently many versions in modern Chinese have appeared, though likely none have had the same set of principles applied to them as the ones Chia chose to guide his work, in both Chinese and in English — principles which will be elucidated later in this "Foreword."

The first known translation of the *Shi Jing* into English was **Jacob Lee**'s in his *The Chinese Classics*, published from 1861-1871 in Hong Kong. The earliest version I have consulted is **James Legge**'s *The She King or the Book of Poetry*. *The Chinese Classics*, vol. 4, 1871 (rpt. 1898) (place and publisher, unknown). In 1960 it was reprinted by Hong Kong University Press, and again in an edition by Wen Zhi Zhe chu pan she (Taiwan, 1971). The Legge text consulted here was an electronic, machine-readable version created by Xuepen Sun and Xiaoqiuan Zeng at the University of Virginia, publicly accessible at URL:http://etext.lib.virginia.edu/chinese (1998).

Ezra Pound's complete 1936 (?) translation — *Shih-ching*: *The Classic Anthology Defined by Confucius* — has been reprinted numerous times by Harvard University Press since its initial publication there in 1954.

Arthur Waley's *The Book of Songs: The Ancient Chinese Classic of Poetry* first appeared in 1937 (parts having been published as early as 1919), and has been several times re-edited by Grove Press, most recently in 1996. Waley's bibliography, updated by Joseph R. Allen in recent Grove editions, lists:

Bernhard Karlgren's *The Book of Odes*: Chinese Text, Transcription, and Translation as published in 1950 in Stockholm by the Museum of Far Eastern Antiquities. The date of its original publication is unknown; however, its "Guide to Pronunciation" is cited by Ezra Pound in his 1936 translation.

Most recently, *The Book of Songs*: A Chinese Selection of Ancient Poems (Chinese-English), ed. **Yea, Mong**, translated by **Dai, Nai-Xien** and **Yang, Xian** came out in 2001 from the Foreign Language Publishing Company, Beijing. It contains only 40 of the 160 "Airs of the States" — sufficient, however, to warrant comparative translation study.

[2] The only possible contenders for this distinction are the Hebrew Old Testament's "Song of Solomon" — a religious lyric — and the *Rig Veda* — ancient Sanskrit hymns — religious poems. But the *Shi Jing* is unchallenged as the oldest extant collection of written, *secular* lyrics.

[3] A few examples from English translators' treatment of erotic elements in the "Airs" should suffice to illustrate these points.

"Air" #29 is about seduction and abandonment....

Legge's late Victorian version betrays the squeamishness one might predict, by nearly obscuring the matter altogether: "...the man, / With virtuous words, but not really good./ ...Would he then allow me to be forgotten?" **Waley**'s approach is hardly more direct, and he employs the mildly archaic verb "requited": "Better if he had not requited me./.../ How should he be true?/ He requited me, but did not follow up." **Pound** shows unusual reserve: "...his like of evil reputation?/ ...forgetting love?" Chia remains delicate, but far more direct: "How can such a person exist? He has no moral sense./ ...he has forgotten me completely./ ...He is not true to me."

"Air" #45, on the same subject, receives similar treatment. **Legge**: "He was my only one;/ And I swear that till death I will not do the evil thing." **Waley**: "He swore that truly he was my mate,/ And till death would not fail me./ ...That a man could be so false!" **Pound**, using the word "bull" (blatantly sexual), pulls back into utter obscurity, using — for the sake of making a rhyme — the word "traist," a word unknown to modern English: "My bull till death he were,/.../ Shall no one be traist?!" **Yea, Dai** and **Yang**, in 2001, do not come close to the poem's clear expression of sexual transgression: "Too much indignity I've been treated with./ .../ My heart stained with sorrow,/ Cannot be washed clean like dirty clothes." **Chia**, typically, suggests human and moral complexity: "The ... man ... is my dearest./ I swear I will never change my mind./ Heavens, mother! Why don't you understand?"

"Air #23, **Legge** reached the limits of Victorian boldness: "There is a young lady with thoughts natural to the spring,/ And a fine gentleman would lead her astray." **Waley**, for once, heads right into the bush: "There was a lady longing for the spring;/ A fair knight seduced her." **Pound** also calls a spade a spade: "A melancholy maid in spring is luck for lovers./ ... / dead as doe is maidenhood." **Yea, Dai** and **Yang** rise at least to suggest passion: "A girl is longing for love,/ A fine fellow tempts her." **Chia**, rather than rely on the graphic final stanza to make seduction obvious, suggests it subtly in advance: "A sensual young maiden, / ... / An oak tree deep in soft woods" — a clearly coital image.

自序

"多识鸟兽草木之名"是诗经余绪吗?

贾福相
加拿大英属哥伦比亚省盐泉岛
2007年11月

《论语·阳货篇》子曰:"诗可以兴,可以观,可以群,可以怨。迩之事父,远之事君。多识于鸟兽草木之名"。这是说诗经有三大功用。第一:训练联想力、观察力、合群力、批评力。第二:教人孝敬父母、忠于君国。第三:多多认识一些动植物,多多接近自然。两千多年来,学诗经的人多数引用这几句话。近几年出版的诗经白话译本作者在序言或导言中都提到这句话,而且多数对第一和第二作了引申,唯有对第三句却草草略过。屈万里在《诗经选注》(1995年,正中书局,页2)中写道:"至于多识鸟兽木之名,那不过是次要的事。"糜文开在《诗经欣赏与研究》(1977年,三民书局,页139)书中专文《论语与诗经》也说:"至于多识于鸟兽草木之名,只是诗学的余绪。"有些译者甚至把第三句完全忽略了。每次读到这里我总有种莫名的纳闷,不单是生物学家的关系,我内心的诗人不禁疑惑,为甚么鸟兽草木是余绪? 那么不重要?

我读诗经匆匆十余年了,过去四年把国风160篇译成白话中文和英文。我的经验以为诗经之所以千年不衰多少与"鸟兽草木之名"有关,生物美化了诗的语言,美化了诗的篇章,如果没有鸟兽草木之名,国风就大大失色了。十五国风首篇《关雎》与最后一篇《狼跋》,起首是鸟,结尾是狼,中间纵横多姿的158篇多处引用了动植物的名字。

诗经的赋、比、兴,奠定了中国诗作方法:赋,直书其事;比,明喻或以物喻志;兴,隐喻或因物起兴。明喻如卫风的《硕人》篇第二章"手如荑荑,肤如凝脂,领如蝤蛴,齿如瓠犀,螓首蛾眉,巧笑倩兮,美目盼兮。"28个字,用了两种植物四种动物作了六个比喻。这篇硕人被清代诗学大儒姚际恒称为"千古颂美人者,无出其右,是为绝唱"。隐喻如《氓》篇中以"桑之未落,其叶沃若。"是说年轻的桑叶,又嫩又绿又新鲜,形容初婚的少妇(因此将她与柔软蚕丝做联想)。后来丈夫别恋,变得憔悴无神,又以"桑之落矣,其黄而陨。"是说桑叶枯黄,纷纷飘雪,来形容被抛弃后的落寞情形。如果译者擅自改动诗中名物,势必也将改写诗中之意,使诗意前后不连贯,因此名物不可谓不重要。

当起首的风景和文本没有直接关系时是"兴",如讽刺贪官的《伐檀》首章:"叮叮砍青檀哟,檀木放在河岸上哟,河水清清有微波哟",伐檀是兴,与其后诗文关系不大,主旨在于批评官员贪腐,但两者连在一起成了美丽诗篇。檀木独特的气味与下阶层的庶民百姓较为亲近,与诗中所述的上位者形成对比。若任意以其他树木起兴,诗的力道将会大大削弱,再次说明草木鸟兽名称之重要。

另有许多篇章写景仅仅数言,却道出了深深情意,如《蒹葭》开头二句:"蒹葭苍苍,白露为霜",好一片肃杀秋景,清朝学者王国维的"景语即情语"当始于斯。芦苇比起其它植物都更适于烘托秋天的愁绪,秋天是芦花最璀璨也最近凋零的季节。

国风160篇最长的是《七月》,共八章,第四章的前七句是"四月秀葽,五月鸣蜩。八月其获,十月陨萚。一之日于貉,取彼狐狸,为公子裘。"译成白话可以是:"四月狗尾草结子,五月知了唧唧啼。八月庄稼收成时,十月黄叶飘飘离。十一月出外去打猎,捉到狐狸剥了皮,好为公子作皮衣。"诗人用了29个字,讲了七个月的农耕和行猎,但不是流水帐而是韵律自然,每一个提及的名物皆重要,标记着农民的年历,《七月》一诗被许为"天下至文"。

其实人间哪一样艺术作品能离开鸟兽草木?诸如绘画、音乐、舞蹈、诗歌都是艺术家响应了自然的色彩、声音、动作的节奏纷纷多样,从中又观察出矛盾性和不稳定性,由点、线、面而波而圆,充塞天地,形成永不休止的大块文章,正如孔子所言一般。

1962年美国生物学家瑞秋卡森发表了她划时代的名著《寂静

的春天》,讨论杀虫剂对自然生态的影响,当时英国的赫胥黎爵士深有所感地说:"如果我们的春天也寂静了,二分之一的英国文学也会随之消逝。"人活着就要吃饭,就要穿衣,就要住房子,就要美化环境,拒绝毒害,哪一样不需要动物和植物?哪一样不需要生物多样?自然生物是人类赖以维生的资源,鸟兽草木是我们的灵魂,正如他们是诗经的灵魂一般,是3000年文学的血液,怎么会是次要?怎么会是余绪?

Preface

Is "To Learn the Names of Birds, Beasts, Grasses and Trees..." Unimportant?

Fu-Shiang Chia
Saltspring Island, British Columbia, Canada
November, 2007

More than twenty three centuries ago, in the chapter "Yang-huo" of Confucius' book, *Rien-Yu*, the great sage told his students that the *Shi Jing* had three functions: 1) to help us to think, to observe, to live with others and to make good judgments; 2) to help us to respect our parents and the state; and 3) to help us to learn the names of birds, beasts, grasses and trees. Ever since then these teachings have almost always been quoted by *Shi Jing* scholars. However, in the introductions or prefaces of recently translated versions of the *Shi Jing*, translators have paid a great deal of attention to Confucius' first two points, and much less to his third point. Mr. Ch'u, Wan-li, in his heavily annotated presentation of the *Shi Jing* (Taipei: Cheng-Chung Publishing Company, 1995; page 2), wrote: "As for the 'names of birds, beasts, grasses and trees', they are of secondary importance." Mr. Mi, Wenkai, in his special article "*Shi Jing* and Confucius" in *Shi Jing: Appreciation and Study* [co-authored by his wife, Fei, Pu-xian (Taipei: Three Peoples Book Company, 1977; volume 4, page 139)], proclaimed the same opinion: "As for 'learning the names of birds, beasts, grasses and trees', these are unimportant for the study of the *Shi Jing*." There are still other translators who have ignored Confucius' third function entirely. Every time I have read such comments, I have become quite puzzled. The poet in me, not just the biologist, has wondered why these names are "unimportant"?

I have been studying the *Shi Jing* for more than ten years. Over the last four years I have spent countless hours translating the 160 poems of the "Airs of the States" into modern Chinese and English. In my judgment, the fact that the *Shi Jing* still holds the interest of readers after thousands of years must be related to the names of plants and animals because such names have beautified the language and hence the poetry. If we remove or change the names of plants and animals, the poetry is no longer the same. "Kingfisher" (# 1), the first of the poems of the "Airs of the States," and the final poem, "Wolf Walking" (# 160), frame the entire book with a bird and a beast. The other 158 poems are filled with plant and animal names.

The *Shi Jing* established three main styles of writing to follow in Chinese poetry: "fu" (narrative), "bi" (similes or explicit comparisons) and "xing" (metaphors or implied comparisons). For an example, see the poem "Madam Zhuang-jiang" (# 57); within fifty words (twenty eight characters) of the second stanza, the poet names two plants and four animals as *bi* (similes) to describe the lady's fingers, skin, neck, teeth, forehead and eyebrows, and this poem was praised by Mr. Yao, Chi-heng of the Ching dynasty as the best of all poems describing the appearance of a woman. As for metaphor, "Cloth Peddler" (# 58, line 23), compares a newly-wed woman with a soft and tender mulberry tree (thus associating her with the soft delicacy of silk). Further on in the poem (line 28), after being abandoned, she is "brown and broken," like an old mulberry tree. If translators were to change the names of any of these biological entities, the meanings of the poems they are in would change utterly and would even become incoherent. Therefore, the names *are* important.

The scenery or setting at the beginning of a poem sometimes

seems to have little to do with the poem's major meanings or effects. For example in the poem "Chopping Down Sandalwood Trees" (# 112), the opening three lines:

> Kan, kan, kan, chopping down the sandalwood trees,
> Laying them along the river bank.
> The water is clear with small ripples

seem to have apparently little to do with the rest of the poem, which denounces the corruption of officials. Nevertheless, the juxtaposition of the two (*xing*, implied comparison) is necessary for the beauty of the poem's effect. The lovely pungency of incense from sandalwood is related to the common worker, in contrast to the ugliness of the rulers who dominate the remainder of the poem. If any other tree were chosen at random to open the poem, the poem's effectiveness would have been significantly diminished. Again, the name is important.

In some of the poems, the description of scenery involving the biological world is hardly incidental—as, for example in "Reeds" (# 129, lines 1 and 2): "White infinity of reed plumes./ White frost forms" — the opening lines of which describe an autumn scene. As Wang, Kuo-wi wrote during the Ching dynasty, "the language of scenery is the language of emotion." Few plants would be as appropriate as reeds for eliciting the feelings associated with autumn, the season when they are most beautiful and close to death.

The longest of the 160 "Airs" is "The Seventh Month" (# 154), which has eight stanzas. In the fourth stanza, the first seven lines read:

> Foxtails flower in April.
> Cicada calls in May.
> Autumn is our harvest time.

Yellow leaves fall in October.
In November we hunt
Fox fur for our young lord's coat.

In twenty nine words (twenty characters) the poet has described farming and hunting within a seven month period, and this is not merely a random cataloguing of events and things. The poem names things which follow a specific, natural rhythm; these names are important, a mnemonic almanac for peasant folk. The poem has been considered by many critics and scholars as the best of its kind.

In fact, there is almost no art which can be divorced from the natural world. Arts such as music, dance and poetry all respond to the colours, sounds, motions and rhythms of nature, just as Confucius tried to teach us.

In 1962, Rachel Carson published her famous book *Silent Spring*, a monumental ecological study focused on the effects of pesticides on nature. At that time the British Lord Julian Huxley observed that if pesticides were to kill off the birds in England as they had in America, silencing the spring in the homeland of so many wonderful poets, half of English literature would disappear. If we are to survive as a species, we have to eat, have dwellings, clothes to wear and a beautiful environment free from poisons. None of our needs can be available without plants and animals, whose names we should know. We need biodiversity. Nature's creatures are necessary for humanity's survival, and birds, beasts, grasses and trees are our soul, as they are the soul of the *Shi Jing* and the blood of 3,000 years of literature. How could they be "unimportant"?

导言

 3000多年前,黄河下游诸省:陕西、山西、河南、山东、河北都在周朝境内,全国物饶民聪,但政治紊乱,战争连连。在这种又安康又混乱的时代里,在群山之谷,在群河之畔,人民以诗言志,以诗抒情,唱出了诗经的305篇。2600年后仍保留得完完整整,岂不是中国文化的奇迹?

 诗经有风、雅、颂三部分,笔者费时五年把国风160篇译成白话、译成英文,是我从事研究生活以来最大的一件工程。

(一) 我为什么译诗经?

 译诗的动机是希望今人可以欣赏中国最早的诗篇,也希望西方人可以窥视一些中国古老的灿烂文化。但这么几年下来,使我孜孜不倦而致发愤忘食的动力则是为古人说今话的大喜悦,而我读诗的方法是摆脱非以文学为目的之传统注疏的影响。[1]

 七岁入私塾,我常被诗中的名句如:"桃之夭夭,灼灼其华"或"青青子衿,悠悠我心"或"风雨如晦,鸡鸣不已"所吸引,在大学和研究所时读的是理科,对诗经少有涉猎,后来教书40年,忙了40年,只有在长途旅行的时候才偶然带本手边仅有的诗经(1964年,台湾出版)与我作伴,退休后闲散在家重习旧爱,译诗对我是一种圆梦、是一种深入学习、也是对自己能力的挑战。

(二) 我如何译诗经?

 2002年6月,我在爱德蒙顿市的《光华报》辟一专栏"食桑吐丝"集,每周译诗一篇,才知道译诗的困难。"食桑吐丝"是余英时先生形容翻译大家严复的态度,桑叶被蚕吃下后要完全消化,再经过诸多发酵作用而转化成丝。邶风的"小戎"篇译了三年,修修改改

---

[1] 请参考诗作《桥》与附录《夜读蒹葭》。

十几遍,也曾去台湾参观过秦代的兵车,脱稿后仍不满意。

"关雎"一篇也是一改再改花了三年。手边的参考书当中,有六人把雎鸠译为水鸟,可是水鸟有一百多种。有二人译为鸭子,种类也多。有四人不译仍保留雎鸠,有九人译为鱼鹰(包括颜重威著《诗经里的鸟类》)。我看过不少吃鱼的鸟类没有一种"关关"鸣叫,而鱼鹰(osprey)是一种鹰类,雄壮威大,高高地站在树巅,这种鸟形容江湖武士可以,形容一个窈窕女子就有些不太合适了,鱼翠却是种体小艳丽的食鱼鸟,飞行时贴着水面一上一下,如采荇菜的少女,姿势美妙。以大部分鸟类而言,雄鸟的羽毛比雌鸟更为美丽,但是鱼翠鸟却恰好相反,因此鱼翠雌鸟非常适合用于形容貌美的年轻女子,因此作者才用雎鸠起兴,寄相思于这位少女而致失眠,于是我决定译雎鸠为鱼翠(kingfisher)。

我不是文学科班出身,没有诗序、郑笺、朱熹及清代训诂的包袱,我读诗经像看一个赤裸的婴儿,或啼哭或微笑,凭生之经验和直觉为他/她画像。古字古意不懂就猜,猜的训练我倒是源远流长。二次大战初期,我七八岁的时候,夜晚常常为母亲在灯下读章回小说,很多字看不懂,母亲是文盲,我们就猜来猜去,把故事弄懂了才停止。其实历代许多诗经学人也是东猜西猜,累积成书。诗经作者无名,编者不详,谁也不能肯定作者的原意。

我的专业是生物学,对诗经中的花花草草,水中的鱼,空中的鸟,地上的昆虫和走兽都有些了解,也都有感情,我相信诗经作者在比兴中用草木鱼虫之名的时候也有亲切的感情。国风中只有少数几篇没有引用动植物的名字,粗略数了一下,其中提到动植物的名字有412次,草类143次,树类122次,哺乳类69次,鸟类52次,昆虫25次,两栖类1次。

译诗过程我是捧着原文一读再读,想了又想,自己以为懂了就试着翻译,完成初稿,放在案头一周后再修改,同时也参考手中的二十几种参考书,脱稿后在《光华报》发表。本来计划2005年冬付梓出版,碰巧我生了一场病,躺在病榻上重读旧稿,发现有些译诗为了贴近信、达、雅的原则把诗意弄丢了,于是决心重译,也请了李福井先生校对中文,我的妻子雪瑞,好友亚诺尔教授校对英文,文藻学院郑惠雯老师中英文都校,也负责打字整理,我作最后校对。特别值得一提的是,过去几年亚诺尔和我常常咖啡一杯促膝长谈,每篇诗都不放过(他在大学教近代诗28年,常以译本理解原诗),这样我不但学会了一些英译的技巧,也学了一些英诗。

(三)国风的地域

十五国风中,周南、召南和王风是指地区不是国名,每区都可能包括几个小诸侯国,都在河南境内。周南又包括湖北的汉水流域,召南又包括甘肃的天水流域,其他十二国风都是诸侯国名,边界虽不清楚,大致说来,邶风、鄘风、卫风都在河南。这三国到后来都成了卫国。郑风、陈风和桧风也在河南,秦风最西在甘肃,齐风和曹风在山东,魏风和唐风在山西,豳风在陕西。所以十五国风中三个地区六个诸侯国都在河南,两个在山西,两个在山东,一在陕西,一在甘肃,这些地域的风俗习惯和方言比较接近,虽然风土人情三千年变化很大,但昔日的语言和故事仍有蛛丝马迹可寻,如此,译诗我又沾了生在山东长在山东的光。

(四)作者和编者

最早的国风诗作很可能出现在商周之交,3000多年了。最后的一篇据考证是陈风的"株林",也有2600多年了,所以国风160篇费时六百年来搜集,占地数千里,这些诗歌如何编辑成书呢?最可靠的推测是,周天子和诸侯国王喜欢歌舞,他们常常派些小官敲着梆子或者摇着铃铛到乡下口耳相传地采集歌谣,这些小官叫风人或行人,他们把采来的诗歌交给诸侯的乐官,乐官们自由编选,并在诸侯宫里演奏,他们又把编选的诗歌交给周天子的太师,太师再重新编选,加上乐谱作为授乐的教科书,也在天子宫殿里演出。当然乐官和太师也自己写诗,所以诗经一方面来自民谣,一方面来自乐官,从千万篇中选择了305首。

(五)小史

春秋中叶当孔子周游列国,广收三千弟子的时候,诗三百就存在而且成书了,并且是孔子重要的教科书,发展为经典,他说诗"可以兴,可以观,可以群,可以怨。迩之事父,远之事君。多识于鸟兽草木之名。"这是说诗经有三大功用。第一:训练联想力、观察力、合群力、批评力。第二:教人孝敬父母、忠于君国。第三:多认识一些动植物,多接近自然。秦朝(221—205B.C.)一把大火,许多书籍灰飞烟灭,西汉(206 B.C.—24 A.D.)废除挟书令,因为诗经中有许多是口耳相传,很快被恢复,出名者有三大家:鲁诗、齐诗和韩诗。这三家诗都是用当时的隶书写成,所以又叫今文诗,后来又出了第四家毛诗,毛诗是用篆字写成,是为古文诗,之后的诗经版本就是毛诗传下来的。到了东汉(25—220 A.D.)出了位大学问家郑玄,他兼通古文今文,为毛序作笺,又有位卫宏为毛诗写序,全诗经的序叫大序,每一篇的序叫小序,小序就是题解,诗序最大的贡献是归纳出诗六义:风、雅、颂、赋、比、兴,前三者是诗经分类,后三者是写诗的体裁与表现方法,绵绵三千余年今人写诗仍离不开这三个规范。郑笺和诗序使毛诗一枝独秀,其他的三家却相继式微了。唐代(618—907 A.D.)诗经学人虽多,但一直是追随孔子、郑玄和诗序的道统,无多创意,只有陆机专心整理了诗经中的名物,贡献很大。到了宋朝(960—1279 A.D.)朱熹以革命的手法使诗经脱离了千年道统,再拉回到文学的天地,之后数百年都是朱熹的信徒,到了清朝(1644—1911 A.D.)学者们崇尚训诂和考证,也有几位诗经大家如方玉润和姚际恒又革了朱熹一命,把诗经与文学拉得更近了些。民国(1912 A.D.—)五四运动后在打倒孔家店的口号下,许多文人如胡适之、傅斯年、闻一多、俞平伯诸人都有自己的看法,有些人把在大学授课的笔记发表,这段时间有几位国外学者开始翻译诗经,但是他们缺乏中国古典文学的造诣,译诗与原文距离相当远。近50年来,台湾许多大学中文系都有诗经课,也成立了硕士、博士班,这样许多与诗经有关的论文或教科书也问世了。十年来大陆古书新译也非常盛行,2000年我在北京大学附近的一家书店,一次就买了16本不同的诗经今译,但有些仅是选译,并非全译。

（六）结语

目前坊间诗经译本林林总总，有的只有原文和注释，有的有原文、注释和题解，更有的有注释、题解、今译、评语和古韵。注释多是你抄我抄大家抄，抄两千多年来很多人积累的研究成果，多数人都同意汉代的小序是削足适履，错得离谱。但在今译的题解中又常常把诗序搬出来重复一遍，再重新否定，自己写题解。其实今人题解就是今人的小序，旧瓶内装了金门高粱、葡萄酒或茅台，端看译者背景和程度，每一篇题解都清清楚楚地告诉读者诗意是如此如此，牵着鼻子，强人所难。其实诗应该是要感觉，每人了解不一，诗意自异，这才是诗的真精神。当然读诗不可捕风捉影，乱来一通。所谓精读是要了解作者当时的情况，要懂得诗的形象和作用，也要了解诗人写诗时心中的读者是谁，所谓通读也是要有规有矩，不要距离诗意太远，我主张读者应该亲自去反复领会，领会文字的优美、婉约、含蓄和音乐；领会诗句的意象和意境；领会篇章的结构和多样。把诗还给诗经，还它以丰富的生命。

Introduction

Over 3,000 years ago the lower part of the Yellow River, including Shannxi, Shanxi, Henan, Shandong and Hebei Provinces, was all in the territory of the Zhou dynasty. It was a fertile land with well-educated people, but the politics of the age were chaotic, and wars incessant. During this wealthy period of upheaval, the people living in the hills and valleys and along the banks of rivers expressed their hopes, dreams and daily reality in poems, bequeathing them to us as the 160 "Airs of the States" in the *Shi Jing*. After 2,600 years, these poems/songs remain in perfect order. Is this not a miracle of Chinese literature?

The *Shi Jing* consists of three parts: "Airs of the States," "Odes," and "Hymns." I have spent the last half-decade translating the 160 poems of the "Airs of the States" into modern Chinese as well as into English. This is the largest enterprise I have ever undertaken in my entire scholarly life.

1) Why did I translate the *Shi Jing*?

My motive was the hope that Chinese people today can appreciate the oldest poems in Chinese. I also hoped that westerners might appreciate these fine examples of ancient Chinese literature. But during this long period of translating, the strongest force that motivated me was the great happiness I felt in returning their voices to ancient poets.[1] By "returning their voices," I mean to see them through a lens unclouded by many volumes of traditional, largely

---

[1] Refer to my poem, "Bridge," p. 016, following "Acknowledgements" (above). See also "Appendix: Evening Reading of 'Reeds'," pp. 360ff, below.

non-literary "scholarship."

When I was seven years old, I entered a private academy in my village in Shandong province. There I was attracted by famous lines from the *Shi Jing* such as: "A young peach tree, with flowers aflame" (poem #6), or "Man with the blue collar, I have been thinking of you" (#91), and "Through another night of wind and rain, roosters remain restless" (#90). When I was an undergraduate and graduate student in universities, I was majoring in science, and rarely had a chance to read the *Shi Jing*. Later, while I was busying myself for forty years as a university professor — teaching, doing research and being active in administration, it was only when I was traveling long distances that I would take out my only copy of the *Shi Jing* to keep me company, one that had been published in Taiwan in 1964. After my retirement I began to read the *Shi Jing* again, so this translation of the book is the fulfillment of an old dream. An indepth study of the Chinese classics, in preparation for this task, and the translation itself were great challenges to my own abilities.

2) How did I translate the *Shi Jing*?

Beginning in June 2002, I wrote a column in the weekly *Chinese Journal* (Edmonton, Canada), under the title "From Mulberry Leaves to Silk," in which I translated one poem per week. That is when I began to realize how difficult it is to do translations. "From Mulberry Leaves to Silk" is a phrase borrowed from Professor Yu Ing-shi, who was describing the attitude of the most famous Chinese translator in history, Yangfu. Mulberry leaves, when eaten by silk worms, have to be completely digested by going through a long series of enzymatic actions, which eventually transform them into silk. The poem "Small War-Chariot" (#128) in the "Airs of Yong," took me three years to translate. It had to be edited more than ten times. To complete the task, I even went to Taiwan to examine a replica of a Chin dynasty war chariot in the Library of the National Chiao Tung University.

Even now that I have finished, I am still not happy with the result.

Translation of the poem "Kingfisher" (#1, in "Airs of Zhou-nan") lasted for three years. In the references available to me, I examined twenty one translations of the bird name "ju-jiou" (four into English and seventeen into modern Chinese), finding that six people translated "jujiou" as "waterbird," but there are more than 100 species of water birds. Two people translated it as "duck," yet there are many species of ducks. Four persons did not translate it, keeping the original Chinese name. Nine people translated it as "fish hawk." I have observed and read about a number of birds which feed on fish. Not one makes the noise "Guan, guan," the first two characters of the first poem of the *Shi Jing*. "Fish hawk" and "osprey" are the most common English translations of the "jujiou" in the poem, but these are eagle-like birds, strong predators which prefer to stay on the tops of trees. Such birds are properly compared with a soldier, but not with a young girl gathering water fringe. The kingfisher, on the other hand, is a relatively small and beautiful fish-eating bird. When it flies, it keeps just above the water, up and down; its motions, size and beauty resemble the young woman in the first poem, who is collecting water fringe left and right in the stream. Among most birds, the male's plumage is more beautiful than the female's. The opposite is true with the kingfisher. Therefore the female kingfisher is more appropriate for describing a beautiful young woman. It is possible that a kingfisher inspired the poet (or his persona), who offered his love to this young woman, a love so urgent that he could not sleep. So I decided to translate "ju-jiou" as kingfisher.

I am not trained in the field of literature. I have never read the original "Preface" to the *Shi Jing*, nor have I read Cheng's commentaries and Zhuxi's interpretations from the East Han and Song dynasties. Furthermore, I am not well-versed in the philological and etymological studies from the period of the Ching dynasty. When I read the *Shi Jing*, I look at it as if observing a naked baby, smiling or crying. My portrayal of this baby and my interpretation of its utterances are based on my own life experience and intuition. The old meanings of some words may have escaped me, so often I have had to make guesses. How so? I was trained for a long time to make educated guesses. During the first part of the Second World War, when I was seven or eight, I often read romantic stories by candlelight for my mother. Many words were new to me. My mother was illiterate, so the two of us tried to guess the meaning of troublesome words until we felt confident that we understood the story. The reality is, I believe, that many *Shi Jing* scholars and translators have also made many guesses and these have accumulated throughout the years by repetition in many books. We don't honestly know the names of the poets or the editors of these precious poems, and no one can be confident about the poems' original meanings.

My profession is biology. Thus it is to be expected that I have some knowledge — as well as feelings — about grasses, flowers, trees, fish in the water, birds in the air, insects and animals on the earth. I believe that when the poets who wrote these poems invoked the names of grasses, leaves, birds, insects and other natural beings, they also had knowledge and intimate feelings about them. In the "Airs of the States," only a few poems contain no names of animals or plants. Through a rough calculation I found 412 plant or animal names mentioned: 143 herbs; 122 trees; 69 mammals; 52 birds; 25 insects and 1 amphibian. Why would an ancient poet be any less precise than a modern poet when naming an element of our natural environment? To adopt this attitude when translating would be tantamount to taking no care at all to distinguish a carriage from a chariot or a boat from a raft. We owe our ancient poets respect, and this obliges us to take care with the names they gave to natural objects and beings.

My process of translation involves holding the original text in front of me, reading it again and again, thinking about it over and over and deferring translation until I think I understand what I am going to take from one language to another. When done with a draft, I put it in a drawer for at least a week. While it is there, I consult the more than twenty reference works I have on the *Shi Jing* in my study. Then I rework my translation before submitting it for publication in the *Chinese Journal*.

    My original plan was to deliver this manuscript of translations of the totality of the "Airs of the States" to the publisher in the winter of 2005. But I became ill during this period. On my sick bed I read my translations one more time and realized that I had often been too loyal to the three basic principles of translation: fidelity, readability and beauty, yet sometimes losing that indescribable essence of what is called poetry. So I decided to retranslate all of the poems. At the same time, I asked Mr. Li Fu-jing's help in proofreading the Chinese sections. My wife, Sharon, and my good friend Professor Stephen Arnold, proofread the English. Miss Heather Cheng from Wenzao College in Kaohsiung, Taiwan, proofread both the Chinese and English. She has also been responsible for the typing and organization of the manuscript. I, myself, have been responsible for the final proofreading. It should also be especially noted that Stephen Arnold and I have spent many hours talking and arguing over many cups of coffee, never letting a single poem go without feeling it had been justly treated. (Arnold taught modern poetry in universities for more than a quarter century, often using translation as an aid to understanding the original.) In this way I not only learned some translation skills, I also studied much poetry in English from many countries.

3) Localities of the "Airs of the States"

Among the fifteen sections of "Airs of the States," "Airs of Zhao-nan" and "Airs of Wang" are the names of districts and not the names of States. Each one of them consisted of parts of several small states, but all were in the province of Henan. Zhou-nan includes part of Hubei of the Han River district. Zhao-nan includes part of Gansu of the Tian River district. The remaining twelve are the names of States whose borders are not clear. In general, the "Airs of Bei," the "Airs of Yong," and the "Airs of Wei" are all from the present province of Henan. The "Airs of Zheng," "Airs of Chen" and "Airs of Kuai" are also from the province of Henan. The "Airs of Qin" are from the furthest point west, in the province of Gansu. The "Airs of Qi" and the "Airs of Cao" are from the province of Shandong. The "Airs of Wey" and the "Airs of Tang" are from the present province of Shanxi. The "Airs of Bin" are from the province of Shannxi. Therefore, within the fifteen groupings of "Airs of the States," three districts and six states are in Henan, two in Shandong, one in Shannxi and one in Gansu. The customs and dialects of these provinces are rather similar, even though a great many changes have taken place in 3,000 years. The language and stories of old are sometimes still traceable. As a translator, I have the advantage of having been born — and having grown up — in Shandong.

4) Authors and Editors of the *Shi Jing*

The oldest poems of the "Airs of the States" are usually dated around 3,000 years ago, from the beginning of the Zhou dynasty. The last, most recent poem, is believed to be #144 ("Zhu-lin"), 2,600 years old. Therefore the 160 poems in the "Airs of the States" were collected over a period of about half a millenium from across an area over 1,000 kilometers wide. How were the poems selected and edited? The most probable scenario derives from the love of singing and dancing in the courts of the King of Zhou and the Lords of the various States. They often sent "*Feng* People" (or "Walking People") — low ranked officials (usually illiterate men over sixty years old, and women over fifty, who had excellent memories) —to walk through villages, ringing bells or sounding drums, to gather people from whom they would collect folk songs. The songs were then transmitted to the Music Officer in their individual States. These Music Officers would select and edit texts, which would be presented in concert within the State palaces. Finally, they submitted the collected songs to the Grand Music Officer who resided at the King's palace. These Grand Music Officers would reselect songs and edit their texts again, for use as teaching texts. Of course the *Feng* People, the Music Officers and the Grand Music Officers could write poems themselves. Therefore the sources of the *Shi Jing* are twofold: one, from folksongs, and two, from officials of the State. The 305 poems that make up the corpus of the *Shi Jing* were likely selected from among thousands.

5) Brief History of the *Shi Jing*
During the middle period of the "Autumn" and "Spring" periods, when Confucius was visiting many States, and when he already had more than 3,000 disciples, the *Shi Jing* already existed. It is also the most important textbook for his teachings. From it, he developed "*Jing*," the rules of governing. He said there were three major functions of "*Shi*" ("poems"): 1) training in: expression of feelings; observation; comradeship or team spirit; and critical thinking; 2) to teach people how to respect their parents and be loyal to the State; and 3) the teaching and learning of the names of animals and plants, and how to get closer to nature. During the Qin dynasty (221 — 205 BC), all books were ordered to be burned. When the Western Han dynasty (206 BC — 24 AD) rescinded the book burning orders, the *Shi Jing*, being folksongs, was quickly and easily recovered from the people's memories. Three interpretive schools of the *Shi Jing* became established in three books, written in the vernacular of the time: *Lu shi*, *Qi shi* and *Han shi*, collectively called the "modern language" *Shi Jing*. Later a fourth book, written with the ancient characters appeared; it was the *Mao shi*, and was called the "Old language shi."

Many of the books published today about the *Shi Jing* are based on the text and interpretations of the *Mao shi*.

During the East Han dynasty (25 — 220 AD), there was a great scholar, Cheng Xian, who knew both the current and ancient languages, who wrote the "Commentaries" for the *Mao shi*. About the same time, another scholar, Wei Hung, wrote the "Preface" to the *Shi Jing*. His preface for the entire book is called the "Greater Preface," and the preface for each poem was called the "Little Preface." The "Little Prefaces" are, in fact, analyses of the meanings of the poems. The major contribution made by the "Preface" was to call attention to six elements of the *Shi Jing*: "The Airs of the States," "Odes" and "Hymns" (the *Shi Jing*'s three sections) and the three styles of writing or methods of expression: "*fu*" (narrative), "*bi*" (similies or explicit comparisons) and "*xing*" (metaphor or implied comparisons). After 3,000 long years, modern Chinese poets still cannot escape the three styles of *fu*, *bi* and *xing*. Cheng's commentaries and Wei's "Preface" ensure the perpetuation of the *Mao shi*. The other three books (*Lu shi*, *Qi shi* and *Han shi*) have slowly disappeared.

During the Tang dynasty (618 — 907 AD), there were a number of people who commented on the *Shi Jing*, but they were all followers of the traditions of Confucius, of Cheng's commentaries, and Hung's "Preface." There was little new contribution, except by the poet Lu Ji, who concentrated on explaining the names of flora and fauna. During the Song dynasty (960 — 1279 AD), Mr. Zhuxi, another great scholar, revolutionized the meanings of the *Shi Jing* by removing it from the tradition of moral discussion and returning it to the realm of literature. For centuries, most people who studied the *Shi Jing* were basically disciples of Zhuxi. During the Qing dynasty (1644 — 1911 AD), scholars concentrated mainly on philology, but there were some brilliant commentators who revolutionized the previous understanding of the *Shi Jing* by bringing it back much closer to the study of literature as literature. During the Republics (1911 — today), many scholars such as Hu Shi, Fu Si-ning, Weng Yi-duo and others have expressed their own opinions about the *Shi Jing* by publishing lecture notes from their teachings. At the same time, several western scholars began to translate the *Shi Jing*, but most of them have lacked an in-depth understanding of the Chinese classics. Their translations remain at some distance from the original text.

During the past fifty years, many universities in Taiwan have developed departments of Chinese literature. They have also established Masters and Doctoral programs, and many theses and textbooks related to the *Shi Jing* have been published. In mainland China, translation of the Chinese classics has been very popular during the past decade. In the year 2000, I went to a bookstore near Beijing University, where I bought sixteen (some partial, not complete) translations of the *Shi Jing* into modern Chinese.

6) Concluding Remarks

Currently there are many translations of the *Shi Jing* into modern Chinese available on the market. Some contain only the original texts and explanations of old terms. Some contain original texts, definitions of terms and exegetical remarks. Still others contain the original text, explanations of terms, exegetical commentary, translations into modern Chinese, critiques and ancient rhymes. The explanations of terms in these tomes are largely copied from each other, as are "research results," borrowed from the accumulation of 2,000 years of scholarship. All *Shi Jing* scholars of today agree that the "Little Preface" of the East Han dynasty "cut the toes to fit the shoes," *i.e.* its points are nearly all wrong, and it is mainly a recounting of stories and historic events that have nothing to do with the poems. "Scholarly" commentaries accompanying many contemporary translations do little more than recycle the "Little Preface," before disputing it. The translators then write their own ideas about the poems, but basically in the same vein as found in the "Little Preface." The same old bottle is refilled with different liquor. The differences between these "interpretations" derive from the backgrounds of the translators. Each discussion of a poem spells out clearly to the reader what the poem is supposedly meant to mean. The translators are leading readers by the nose to interpretations they want them to make. It does not seem to occur to them that a poem is meant to be felt, to evoke feelings and perceptions.

The true spirit of poetry is to provoke different meanings in different readers. Of course one cannot read a poem as if catching wind and shadows, a purely idiosyncratic reading which is irrelevant to the poem's original meaning. There are "demanded" readings, and they require study, contemplation and the understanding of contexts, intended audiences, forms and functions. Only then can a "good" reading become possible. Less rigorous readings are acceptable, but they still require a reader's imagination to be guided by the poem's literary elements, and not by purely personal associations. I believe the reader should carefully study a poem, try to understand the beauty, the music, the plural meanings of words, the imagery and the meanings generated between the lines. The reader must pay attention to the structure of the poem, and to the plurality of its contributing, literary features. By approaching the *Shi Jing* in this manner, we will return it to the realm of poetry, restore its rich life and potential, and make it a bridge between the ages and between cultures.

Fu-Shiang Chia
February, 2008

后记

写完"导言"后总有种"意犹未尽"的感觉,几件未曾提及的事记录于下:

(一)译诗时我手边的参考书共有25种,4种英文译本(于加拿大购得)。21种中文今译(于台湾、香港、内地购得),其中有些是选译,也有几本是研究报告。诗篇的安排顺序各书都一致,原文中如有差异时,以屈万里的《诗经诠译》(台北:联经出版社,2002)为准,诗中标点符号我自己负责,错误之处一定不少,请诸读者指正。

(二)能够阅读诗经原文的读者应该会注意到,白话中译和英译不完全相同,但互为补偿,主要是为求表达畅通,有时英译反而较贴近原文,而与白话中文较不相似。有时很自然地,则是白话中文较接近原文。所以和大多数译者一样,我常用"译者的自由"下笔,譬如卫风《氓》(#58)第四章最后两句,中文译为"我是始终如一,你却三心二意",这句用了一、二、三,有些神来之笔的喜悦,同一句译成英文"It is your mind, not mine, that waxes, wanes and waivers."第四和第六个字以m开始,最后三个字皆以wa开始,另有一种妙处。

Postscript

After completing the "Preface" and "Introduction" to this volume, I still felt I had not written all I wanted to say. The following are but two of those left-over things:

1) I had twenty five reference books during work on this translation, of which four are in English (purchased in Canada), twenty one are Chinese translations of classical *Shi Jing* texts (purchased in Taiwan, Hong Kong and in mainland China). Among the Chinese translations, some are selections from the *Shi Jing*, and some are original research done on it. The sequence of poems in the direct translations is identical. When there were differences in the original, classical verse, I followed the order detailed in Ch'u Wan-li's Interpretation of the *Shi Jing* (Taipei: United Literary Publishing Company, 2002). I am responsible for the punctuation in my translations, for which I would be pleased to receive corrections from readers (via the publisher).

2) Readers who can read the original classical language *Shi Jing* will note that my translation into modern Chinese and my translation into modern English are not always literally similar. Variations derive mainly from attempts to be faithful to the idiomatic aspects of the two modern languages. Thus at times my English translation is closer to the classical Chinese than to the modern Chinese. At other times, and more naturally, the modern Chinese is closer to the classical. I have, like most translators, exercised a certain poetic license. For example, in poem number 58 ("Cloth Peddler"), the last two sentences of the fourth stanza (in classical Chinese; in English it is the third stanza), I have translated into modern Chinese as (literally) "I am always one from beginning to end; it is you who change your mind twice and three times." In this sentence I used the numbers one, two and three. I was pleased with myself because the three numbers have idiomatic, proverbial references (which would be absent in English). The same sentence, translated into English, reads: "It is your mind, not mine, that waxes, wanes and waivers," alliterating the fourth and sixth and the last three words, employing a device common in English poetry to achieve the same ends.

周南

Airs of Zhou-nan

1—11

诗经·国风——英文白话新译

关雎

关关雎(jū)鸠,在河之洲。窈窕淑女,君子好逑。
参差(cēn cī)荇(xìng)菜,左右流之。窈窕淑女,寤寐求之。
求之不得,寤寐思服。悠哉悠哉,辗转反侧。
参差荇菜,左右采之。窈窕淑女,琴瑟友之。
参差荇菜,左右芼(mào)之。窈窕淑女,钟鼓乐之。

鱼翠

鱼翠关关唱,黄河小岛上。
有个姣好的女子,一个男人追求伊。

高高低低的水荇菜,或左或右的流动着。
有个姣好的女子,男人梦着她。

得不到她的青睐,日日夜夜相思着。
漫漫悠悠长夜,翻来覆去睡不着。

高高低低的水荇菜,或左或右的采撷着。
女子和男士,如琴如瑟的相爱着。①

高高低低的水荇菜,或左或右的采撷着。
洞房花烛了,撞钟敲鼓的庆祝着。

---

① 琴瑟为乐器,状似古筝,有七弦和二十五弦二种,通常一起演奏。

《周南》关雎

Kingfisher

Kingfisher sings "Guan guan" along the river bank.
A gentleman pursues a lovely young maiden.

Water fringe, long and short, sways left and right.
The gentleman drifts, dreaming of the young beauty.

Courts, but engages her not, thinks of her day and night,
Such a long, long night, tossing and turning.

Water fringe, long and short, gathering left and right.
The lovely young maiden's and suitor's stars align
like *qin* and *se* [1] - in seamless harmony.

Water fringe, long and short, coupling left and right.
The radiant maiden marries; drums throb and bells peal.
Ecstasy!

---

[1] Seven and twenty-five stringed zither- or lute-like instruments, always played together.

诗经·国风——英文白话新译

葛覃

葛之覃(tán)兮,施(yì)于中谷,维叶萋萋。
黄鸟于飞,集于灌木,其鸣喈喈(jiē)。

葛之覃兮,施于中谷,维叶莫莫。
是刈(yì)是濩(huò),为絺(chī)为绤(xì),服之无斁(yì)。

言告师氏,言告言归。薄污我私,薄浣(huàn)我衣。
害(hé)浣害否,归宁父母。

葛麻

葛麻蔓蔓延延,布满山谷之间;
密密叶子好茂盛,黄莺飞舞其中,
停在灌木丛,歌声婉啭动听。

葛麻蔓蔓延延,布满山谷之间;
密密叶子好葱绿,砍了下来用水煮,
纺成粗布细布,制成舒适衣服。

去向师傅请假,"回家洗裙裾,回家洗内裤"。①
不是完全洗衣服,回家也要看父母。

---

① 女人月经染血的内裤,就是奴隶也得允许清洗。

《周南》葛覃

Cloth-Vine

The cloth-vine spreads — across the middle of the valley.
So prosperous; the leaves, luxuriant.
A gold finch alights on a bushy perch
To warble a poignant air.

The cloth-vine spreads — across the middle of the valley.
So prosperous; the leaves, luxuriant.
Boil them for fibers fine, fibers coarse.
Weave them into garment cloth.

I ask my master for leave
To go home.
"I want to wash my skirt and underwear."[①]
In truth, I want to see my parents.

[①] Women (even slaves) were allowed to wash underwear soiled during their monthly periods.

诗经·国风——英文白话新译

卷耳

采采卷耳,不盈顷筐。
嗟我怀人,寘(zhì)彼周行。

陟彼崔嵬(cuī wéi),我马虺隤(huī tuí)。
我姑酌彼金罍,维以不永怀。

陟彼高冈,我马玄黄。
我姑酌彼兕觥(sì gōng),维以不永伤。

陟彼砠(jū)矣,我马瘏(tú)矣。
我仆痡(fū)矣,云何吁矣!

卷耳

女:"采卷耳呵,采卷耳,半天也采不到一浅筐。
　　惦记着我的意中人,把浅筐放在大道旁。"

男:"爬上那座石山,我的马儿已腿酸。
　　满满斟了金杯酒,借酒浇愁。"

　　"爬上那座小山岗,我的马儿已受伤。
　　满满斟了犀杯酒,借酒浇愁。"

　　"爬上那座小土山,我的马儿疲不堪。
　　我的仆人步行也艰难,何时才能不长叹!"

《周南》卷耳

Cocklebur

Woman:
    "Plucking, plucking cockleburs;
    I cannot fill this shallow bucket.
    Missing him so, I cannot go on...
    I'll leave the bucket by the roadside."

Man:
    "Climbing up this rocky hill...
    My horse tires.
    I'll fill my golden wine cup...
    To escape my misery in drink.

    Climbing up this high mountain...
    My horse falls ill.
    I'll fill my ivory wine cup...
    Submerging my pain in wine.

    Climbing up this high dirt hill...
    My horse trembles.
    My companion can no longer walk...
    Alas, alas, I am in agony."

诗经·国风——英文白话新译

樛木

南有樛(jiū)木,葛藟(lěi)累(léi)之。乐只君子,福履绥之。
南有樛木,葛藟荒之。乐只君子,福履将之。
南有樛木,葛藟萦(yíng)之。乐只君子,福履成之。

弯曲的树

南方有棵弯曲的树,野葡萄攀附着,
那位快乐好人,福禄跟着他。

南方有棵弯曲的树,野葡萄覆盖着,
那位快乐好人,福禄扶助他。

南方有棵弯曲的树,野葡萄环绕着,
那位快乐好人,福禄成就他。

《周南》樛木

Crooked Tree

Wild grapes climb a southern crooked tree.
Happy is the good man; fortune follows him.

Wild grapes cover a southern crooked tree.
Happy is the good man; fortune honours him.

Wild grapes surround a southern crooked tree.
Happy is the good man; fortune completes him.

诗经·国风——英文白话新译

螽斯

螽斯（zhōng sī）羽，诜诜（shēn shēn）兮，宜尔子孙，振振兮。
螽斯羽，薨薨（hōng hōng）兮，宜尔子孙，绳绳（shéng shéng）兮。
螽斯羽，揖揖（qì qì）兮，宜尔子孙，蛰蛰（zhí zhí）兮。

纺织娘

纺织娘歌唱，闪闪翅膀，
祝你多子多孙啊，体面又健康。

纺织娘歌唱，闪闪翅膀，
祝你多子多孙啊，昌盛又兴旺。

纺织娘歌唱，闪闪翅膀，
祝你多子多孙啊，绵绵又吉祥。

《周南》螽斯

Grasshopper

The grasshopper sings by rubbing its wings.
Bless all your children; may they enjoy health and wealth.

The grasshopper sings by rubbing its wings.
Bless all your children; may they prosper and be courageous.

The grasshopper sings by rubbing its wings.
Bless all your children; may they know fame and humility.

诗经·国风——英文白话新译

桃夭

桃之夭夭,灼灼其华。之子于归,宜其室家。
桃之夭夭,有蕡(fén)其实。之子于归,宜其家室。
桃之夭夭,其叶蓁蓁(zhēn zhēn)。之子于归,宜其家人。

桃树

年轻的桃树,花开如焰;女子出嫁了,夫家之欢。
年轻的桃树,果实累累;女子出嫁了,夫家之禄。
年轻的桃树,枝叶蓁蓁;女子出嫁了,夫家之欣。

《周南》桃夭

Quince Tree

A young quince tree, with flowers aflame.
The lovely maiden marries, bringing comfort
   to her new home.

A young quince tree, with delicious fruits laden.
The lovely maiden marries, bringing fortune
   to her new home.

A young quince tree, with lush leaves festooned.
The lovely maiden marries, bringing happiness
   to her new home.

诗经·国风——英文白话新译

兔罝

肃肃兔罝(jū),椓(zhuó)之丁丁(zhēng zhēng)。
赳赳武夫,公侯干城。

肃肃兔罝,施于中逵(kuí)。
赳赳武夫,公侯好仇。

肃肃兔罝,施于中林。
赳赳武夫,公侯腹心。

兔网

布置捕兔网,叮叮栽木桩;赳赳武士们,国家栋梁。

布置捕兔网,参差在路旁;赳赳武士们,保卫家乡。

布置捕兔网,座落林中央;赳赳武士们,领袖心房。

《周南》兔罝

Rabbit Nets

Set up the rabbit nets, knocking the pegs into the ground.
Valiant warriors, defenders of the realm.

Set up the rabbit nets, where roads cross.
Valiant warriors, government counselors.

Set up the rabbit nets, in the forest's heart.
Valiant warriors, protectors of our governor.

诗经·国风——英文白话新译

芣苢

采采芣苢(fú yǐ),薄言采之;采采芣苢,薄言有之。
采采芣苢,薄言掇(duō)之;采采芣苢,薄言捋(lè)之。
采采芣苢,薄言袺(jié)之;采采芣苢,薄言襭(xié)之。

车前草

车前草,车前草,一边谈心一边采;
车前草,车前草,一边唱歌一边采。

车前草,车前草,丢在地上捡起来;
车前草,车前草,弄断枝茎摘下来。

车前草,车前草,放在裙子兜起来;
车前草,车前草;装在口袋回家来。

《周南》芣苢

Plantain

Gathering plantain, plucking while talking;
Gathering plantain, plucking while singing.

Gathering plantain, picking it from fields;
Gathering plantain, snapping it from stems.

Gathering plantain, placing it in aprons;
Gathering plantain, bringing it home in waist pockets.

诗经·国风——英文白话新译

汉广

南有乔木,不可休思。汉有游女,不可求思。
汉之广矣,不可泳思!江之永矣,不可方思!

翘翘错薪,言刈(yì)其楚。之子于归,言秣(mò)其马。
汉之广矣,不可泳思!江之永矣,不可方思!

翘翘错薪,言刈其蒌(lóu)。之子于归,言秣其驹。
汉之广矣,不可泳思!江之永矣,不可方思!

汉水宽广

南方有棵大树,不可在树下休息。
汉水有位女子,不可向她追觅。
汉水太宽,游泳渡河难。
江水太长,不能木筏航。

薪柴乱糟糟,最好砍荆条。
汉水女子要出嫁,快把马儿喂饱。
汉水太宽,游泳渡河难。
江水太长,不能木筏航。

薪柴乱糟糟,最好砍蒌蒿。
汉水女子要出嫁,快把马儿喂饱。
汉水太宽,游泳渡河难。
江水太长,不能木筏航。

《周南》汉广

Broad Han River

A large tree in the south, tenders me no shade.
The young maiden of the Han River, so difficult to pursue.
The Han is too broad to swim across,
The Yang-zi too long to travel by wooden raft.

Firewood is tangled but plenty;
    I choose to cut the thorn bush.
The Han maiden is ready to marry —
    I had better feed my horse.
The Han is too broad to swim across,
The Yang-zi too long to travel by wooden raft.

Firewood is tangled but plenty;
    I choose to cut the Lü grass.
The Han maiden is ready to marry —
    I had better feed my horse.
The Han is too broad to swim across,
The Yang-zi too long to travel by wooden raft.

诗经·国风——英文白话新译

汝坟

遵彼汝坟,伐其条枚。未见君子,惄(nì)如调(zhōu)饥。
遵彼汝坟,伐其条肄(yì)。既见君子,不我遐弃。
鲂(fáng)鱼赪(chēng)尾,王室如毁。虽则如毁,父母孔迩(ěr)。

汝水岸

她:"沿着汝水岸,砍些灰楸作木柴,
　　没有看到他,饥肠如火烧。

　　沿着汝水岸,砍些灰楸作木柴,
　　已经见到他,不再分离吧!"

他:"鲂鱼的尾巴赤红,国家大事纷争,
　　谁管得这些大事,身边父母要待奉。"

Ru River Banks

She:
"I walked along the River Ru,
  chopping bean trees for firewood.
I did not see him; my longing burned
  like morning hunger.

Walking along the River Ru,
  chopping bean trees for firewood.
Now I have seen him we shall never separate."

He:
"The bream's tail is red, the King's affairs chaotic.
I cannot help the King's business;
  I merely want to care for my parents."

诗经·国风——英文白话新译

麟之趾

麟之趾,振振公子,于嗟(xū jiē)麟兮!
麟之定,振振公姓,于嗟麟兮!
麟之角,振振公族,于嗟麟兮!

麒麟①之趾

公侯,你的儿子,伟岸神奇,像麒麟的足趾。
是的,他简直就是麒麟呀!

公侯,你家的子孙,奋发英勇,像麒麟的额顶。
是的,他们简直就是麒麟呀!

公侯,你氏族的子孙,英风飒飒,像麒麟的肉角。
是的,他们简直就是麒麟呀!

① 麒麟是传说中的神兽,代表高贵和吉祥,全身有鳞,独角。

《周南》麟之趾

Chi-lin's[①] Foot

My lord, your son, noble and courageous,
　　favours the Chi-lin's foot.
Sir, your son is indeed the Chi-lin itself.

My lord, your descendant boys, brave and bright,
　　favour the Chi-lin's forehead.
Sir, they are the Chi-lin themselves.

My lord, your kindred male heirs, diligent and honourable,
　　favour the Chi-lin's horn.
Sir, they are indeed the Chi-lin themselves.

[①] Chi-lin: a legendary deer-like animal which signifies nobility, dignity and prosperity.

召南
Airs of Zhao-nan
12—25

诗经·国风——英文白话新译

鹊巢

维鹊有巢,维鸠居之。之子于归,百两(liàng)御之。
维鹊有巢,维鸠方之。之子于归,百两将之。
维鹊有巢,维鸠盈之。之子于归,百两成之。

喜鹊巢

喜鹊造了巢,布谷搬进来。①
年轻的姑娘要出嫁,百辆马车来等她。

喜鹊造了巢,布谷住进来。
年轻的姑娘要出嫁,百辆马车来迎她。

喜鹊造了巢,布谷住下来。
年轻的姑娘要出嫁,百辆马车来接她。

---
① 布谷鸟照顾其他鸟类幼鸟乃是一种吉兆;即"异族通婚"(跨越种族)是桩好事。

《召南》鹊巢

Magpie Nest

Magpies build nests; cuckoos move in.①
A young woman marries; a hundred wagons await her.

Magpies build nests; cuckoos move in.
A young woman marries; a hundred wagons receive her.

Magpies build nests; cuckoos move in.
A young woman marries; a hundred wagons welcome her.

---

① It is propitious for a cuckoo to raise another's young; i.e. exogeny (cross-clan) marriage is good.

诗经·国风——英文白话新译

采蘩

于以采蘩,于沼于沚(zhǐ)。
于以用之,公侯之事。

于以采蘩,于涧之中。
于以用之,公侯之宫。

被(pī)之僮僮(tóng tóng),夙夜在公。
被之祁祁(qí,qí),薄言还归。

采蒿菜

去哪里采蒿,在水潭和小岛。
去哪里用蒿,在诸侯的祭台。

去哪里采蒿,在山谷的水潦。
去哪里用蒿,在诸侯的祖庙。

头上饰一高髻,日夜诉求。
礼完,卸下祭衣,回家休息。

《召南》采蘩

Collecting Mugwort

Where to collect mugwort — in the ponds and on isles.
What to do with mugwort — it's for her lord's affairs.

Where to collect mugwort — in the valley streams.
Where to offer mugwort — at her lord's ancestral hall.

She wears a tall headdress to revere our lord's ancestors.
Once done, she removes her ceremonial robes,
Slowly returning to her rooms.

诗经·国风——英文白话新译

草虫

喓喓(yāo yāo)草虫,趯趯(tì tì)阜螽(fù zhōng)。
未见君子,忧心忡忡;
亦既见止,亦既觏(gòu)止,我心则降。

陟(zhì)彼南山,言采其蕨。
未见君子,忧心惙惙(chuò chuò);
亦既见止,亦既觏止,我心则说(yuè)。

陟彼南山,言采其薇。
未见君子,我心伤悲;
亦既见止,亦既觏止,我心则夷。

蟋蟀

蟋蟀唧唧的叫,蚱蜢突突的跳。
很久没有见到你,心焦烦恼;
如今又见了,如今又依了,我就完全放心了。

走到南山坡,采蕨作菜吃。
很久没有见到你,相思痴迷。
如今又见了,如今又依了,我就满心欢喜了。

走到南山坡,去采野豌豆,
很久没有见到你,内心伤悲;
如今又见了,如今又依了,我就满心平安了。

《召南》草虫

Crickets

Crickets were singing, grasshoppers jumping.
Not having seen you for so long a time, my heart was suffering.
Now I have seen you, now I have held you,
It is a time for rejoicing.

I went to South Hill, picking plump fiddlehead ferns for food.
Not having seen you for so long a time, I was forlorn.
Now I have seen you, now I have held you,
I am totally enthralled.

I went to South Hill, gathering wild beans for food.
Not having seen you for so long a time, my heart was grieving.
Now I have seen you, now I have held you,
Peace again engulfs my heart.

诗经·国风——英文白话新译

采蘋

于以采蘋,南涧之滨;于以采藻,于彼行潦(háng lǎo)。
于以盛之,维筐及筥(jǔ);于以湘之,维锜(qí)及釜(fǔ)。
于以奠之,宗室牖(yǒu)下;谁其尸之,有齐季女。

采野菜

南边涧水旁,采采田字草;
潺潺溪水滂,采采杉叶藻。

草和藻采到了,用筐用筥来装好;
细火的锅和鼎,恭恭敬敬来烹调。

可以祭奠了,在宗庙的窗下;
谁是主祭呢?齐国的少女呀。

《召南》采蘋

Harvesting Ceremonial Vegetables

Gone to collect cross-leaved vegetables
From the southside stream;
Gone to collect fox-tail vegetables
From the rivulet.

Vegetables harvested
In a basket and a scuttle —
Cooked with great respect
In a three-legged kettle,

Made ready for offering
Beneath the temple window.
Who shall lead the service?
The young maiden from the Qi nation.

诗经·国风——英文白话新译

甘棠

蔽芾(bì fèi)甘棠,勿翦勿伐,召(shào)伯所茇(bá)。
蔽芾甘棠,勿翦勿败,召伯所憩。
蔽芾甘棠,勿翦勿拜,召伯所说。

杜梨树

茂盛的杜梨树,不要翦它,不要砍它,
召伯曾在树下住宿过。

绿荫的杜梨树,不要翦它,不要伐它,
召伯曾在树下乘凉过。

高大的杜梨树,不要翦它,不要毁它,
召伯曾在树下讲道过。

《召南》甘棠

Pear Tree

Please don't fell the lush pear tree,
Under which Shao-bo once slept.

Please don't harm the sweet pear tree,
Beneath which Shao-bo once lay.

Please don't cut the great pear tree,
Under which Shao-bo once preached.

诗经·国风——英文白话新译

行露

厌浥(yàn yì)行露。岂不夙夜,谓行多露。

谁谓雀无角,何以穿我屋?谁谓女(rǔ)无家,
何以速我狱?虽速我狱,室家不足!

谁谓鼠无牙,何以穿我墉(yōng)?谁谓女无家,
何以速我讼?虽速我讼,亦不女从!

露水

露水浓重。早起去官府,哪怕湿了衣服。

谁说雀儿没有角,怎会穿破我房屋?谁说我嫁不出,
急着要置我入狱?就是逼着我入狱,娶我理由仍不足。

谁说老鼠没有牙,怎会穿过我窗户?谁说我嫁不出,
急着逼我去官府?就是官府去诉讼,我是仍然不依从。

《召南》行露

Evening Dew

The evening's dew weighs low.
I'm eager to leave for court,
Having no fear I'll soak my clothes.

Who said a bird has no beak?
    How else can it peck through my wall?
Who said I can't find a husband,
    without forcing me to court?
Even if I go to court, I shall never concede.

Who said a rat has no teeth?
    How else can it gnaw through my wall?
Who said I can't find a husband,
    without threatening me with jail?
Even if I'm sent to jail, I shall never marry you.

诗经·国风——英文白话新译

羔羊

羔羊之皮,素丝五紽(tuó)。退食自公,委蛇(wēi yí)委蛇!
羔羊之革,素丝五緎(yù)。委蛇委蛇,自公退食!
羔羊之缝,素丝五总(zǒng)。委蛇委蛇,退食自公!

羔羊皮袍

那位公侯,穿了羔羊皮袍——以白丝缝绕。
走出公庭,回家用餐。自由自在,风度翩翩。

那位公侯,穿了羔羊皮袍——以白丝缝绕。
走出公庭,回家用餐。自由自在,从容安闲。

那位公侯,穿了羔羊皮袍——以白丝缝绕。
走出公庭,回家用餐。自由自在,悠悠闲闲。

《召南》羔羊

Lamb Skin Coat

Look! The Lord wears a lamb skin coat, sewn with white silk.
He leaves the palace on his way home for dinner,
So relaxed and graceful in manner.

Look! The Lord wears a lamb skin coat, sewn with white silk.
Leaving the palace on his way home for dinner,
So relaxed and graceful in manner.

Look! The Lord wears a lamb skin coat, sewn with white silk.
Leaving the palace on his way home for dinner,
So relaxed and graceful in manner.

18

诗经·国风——英文白话新译

殷其靁

殷其靁(léi),在南山之阳。
何斯违斯,莫敢或遑(huáng)？
振振君子,归哉归哉！

殷其靁,在南山之侧。
何斯违斯,莫敢遑息？
振振君子,归哉归哉！

殷其靁,在南山之下。
何斯违斯,莫敢遑处？
振振君子,归哉归哉！

雷声轰轰

雷声轰轰,在南山之阳。
为什么你远去他乡？匆匆忙忙？
辛勤的夫君呀,归来吧;归来！

雷声轰轰,在南山之侧。
为什么你远去他地？不得休息？
辛勤的夫君呀,归来吧;归来！

雷声轰轰,在南山之下。
为什么你远去他乡？匆匆忙忙？
辛勤的夫君呀,归来吧;归来！

《召南》殷其靁

Thunder Rumbles

Thunder rumbles on the South Hill's sunny slope.
Why are you so far away? Why do you always hurry?
My diligent husband, come back — oh, come back to me!

Thunder booms at the South Hill's foot.
Why are you so far away? Why don't you return to rest?
My diligent husband, come back — oh, come back to me!

Thunder roars at the South Hill's edge.
Why are you so far away? Why do you always hurry?
My diligent husband, come back — oh, come back to me!

诗经·国风——英文白话新译

摽有梅

摽(piǎo)有梅,其实七兮;求我庶士,迨其吉兮。
摽有梅,其实三兮;求我庶士,迨其今兮。
摽有梅,顷筐塈(xì)之;求我庶士,迨其谓之。

梅子熟了

梅子熟了,三成落了地;
爱我的男人呀,不要再迟疑。

梅子熟了,七成落了地;
爱我的男人呀,正是好日子。

梅子熟了,装进了筐里;
爱我的男人呀,快来娶我为妻。

《召南》摽有梅

Falling Mei Plums

The mei plums are ripe; one third have fallen to the ground.
My handsome man, why do you wait....

The mei plums are ripe; two thirds have fallen to the ground.
My dearest man, today is the day.

The mei plums are ripe — all in the basket now.
My precious man, hurry to make me your wife.

诗经·国风——英文白话新译

小星

嘒(huì)彼小星,三五在东。
肃肃宵征,夙夜在公。
寔(shí)命不同!

嘒彼小星,维参(shēn)与昴(mǎo)。
肃肃宵征,抱衾(qīn)与裯(chóu)。
寔命不犹!

小星①

在东方,三五小星,朦朦胧胧,
为了公事疾疾匆匆,还要赶夜路。
唉,我的命实在不同。

在东方,参星,昴星,亮晶晶,
背了自己行李,还要赶夜程。
唉,我的命实在不幸。

---

① 参星与昴宿星。

《召南》小星

Small Stars[1]

Three small stars and five twinkle in the eastern sky.
I have to race through the night on the king's business.
Alas, thus passes my life; not so for others.

Shen Star, Mao Star twinkle in the eastern sky.
I have to march quickly in the night,
    carrying my own bed rags.
Alas, thus transpires my life; not so for others.

---
[1] Orion's Belt and the Pleiades.

诗经·国风——英文白话新译

江有汜

江有汜(sì),之子归,不我以!
不我以,其后也悔。

江有渚(zhǔ),之子归,不我与!
不我与,其后也处。

江有沱(tuó),之子归,不我过!
不我过,其啸也歌。

江有潟湖

江水流入潟湖,你弃我而去,不再管我!
不再管我,你会后悔失措。

江中有小岛,你与我分手了,孤单一人!
一人,怎么生活。

江水有支溪,你与我分离,昼夜相思!
相思,只有长叹饮泣。

《召南》江有汜

River Lagoon

The river has a lagoon.
You are gone.
You care for me no longer, no longer.
You will regret it.

The river has a little isle.
You have left.
I am alone, alone.
How shall I carry on?

The river has tributaries.
You have departed.
I am depressed, depressed.
I can only cry aloud.

诗经·国风——英文白话新译

野有死麕

野有死麕(jūn),白茅包之;有女怀春,吉士诱之。
林有朴樕(pú sù),野有死鹿;白茅纯束,有女如玉。
"舒而脱脱(duì duì)兮! 无感(hàn)我帨(shuì)兮!
无使尨(máng)也吠!"

野地死獐

野地里有头死獐,茅草整齐的包着;
有位怀春的少女,体面的男子追求她。

林地里有棵栎树,野地里有头死鹿;
茅草巧巧的捆成一束,怀春少女美如玉。

"慢一点儿,这样已很舒服!
不要碰我裙裾!
也不要让狗吼!"

《召南》野有死麕

Dead Deer

A dead deer in the field,
    shrouded in white grass;
A sensual young maiden,
    courted by a gentleman.

An oak tree deep in soft woods,
    a dead deer in the field,
    swaddled in downy white,
The maiden — precious as a piece of jade.

"This moment — wonderful!
    Don't be in such a rush!
    Please don't touch my skirt!
    Don't make the dog bark!"

诗经·国风——英文白话新译

何彼襛矣

何彼襛矣！唐棣(táng dì)之华(huā)！
曷(hé)不肃雝(yōng)？王姬之车。
何彼襛矣！华如桃李！平王之孙？齐侯之子。
其钓维何？维丝伊缗(mín)。齐侯之子，平王之孙。

多么艳丽哟

多么艳丽哟，唐棣的花叶，
多么肃穆哟，王姬的嫁车。

多么艳丽的花哟，红是桃白是李，
齐侯的公子娶了平王的孙女儿。

那珍贵的钓竿哟，鱼线是白丝，
平王的孙女嫁了齐侯的公子。

《召南》何彼襛矣

So Beautiful

The cherry blossoms — so beautiful!
Wang-ji's wedding carriage — so glorious!

The pear and peach blossoms — so beautiful!
His Lord Ping's granddaughter is marrying
    the son of Lord Qi.

The precious fishing pole — a bright silk line.
King Ping's granddaughter marries Lord Qi's son.

诗经·国风——英文白话新译

驺虞

彼茁者葭(jiā),壹发五豝(bā),于嗟乎,驺虞(zōu yú)!
彼茁者蓬,壹发五豵(zōng),于嗟乎,驺虞!

驺虞

芦苇茂盛郁郁,一箭射中五头野猪,
了不起呵,驺虞!

野菊茂盛郁郁,一箭射中五头小猪,
了不起呵,驺虞!

《召南》驺虞

Zou-yu

Forest of luxurious reeds — one arrow hit five pigs!
Zou-yu, sir, you are great!

Meadow of opulent daisies — one arrow hit five pigs!
Zou-yu, sir, you are great!

邶风
Airs of Bei
26—44

诗经·国风——英文白话新译

柏舟

泛彼柏舟,亦泛其流。耿耿不寐,如有隐忧。
微我无酒,以敖以游。

我心匪鉴,不可以茹。亦有兄弟,不可以据。
薄言往愬(sù),逢彼之怒。

我心匪石,不可转也。我心匪席,不可卷也。
威仪棣棣(dì dì),不可选也。

忧心悄悄,愠于群小。觏(gòu)闵既多,受侮不少。
静言思之,寤辟(bì)有(yǒu)摽(piǎo)。

日居月诸,胡迭而微?心之忧矣,如匪澣(huàn)衣。
静言思之,不能奋飞。

柏木小舟

一条柏木小舟,在河中漂流。
睁着眼睛不能睡,有难言的隐忧。
并非我没有好酒,并非我不想遨游。

我的心不是铜镜,事事都可照分明。
我也有同胞兄弟,他们对我都不理。
我曾向他们求助,他们却对我发怒。

我的心不是石头,可以随便转移。
我的心不是草席,可以随便卷起。
我有自己的骨气,不能随便屈膝。

我悲伤担心,为那些小人嫉恨。
受尽了他们侮辱和轻视。
静下来仔细想想,仍是捶胸悲戚。

太阳啊!月亮啊!为什么这样交替昏暗?
我是如此忧伤,像一堆待洗的脏衣裳。
静下来仔细想想,希望飞去他乡。

《邶风》柏舟

Cedar Boat

A small cedar boat floats on the river.
Grief gnaws at me in sleepless shiver.
It is not because I have no wine,
Nor want the needs for play.

My heart is not a copper mirror, to reflect all that's shone.
I have brothers, but they don't support me.
I've tried to explain to them,
But nothing abates their ire.

My heart is not a stone which can be turned.
My heart is not a straw mat which can be folded.
I have my dignity, my standards.
I cannot bow to the wicked.

I am hated by evil people.
I suffer this plight alone.
I have tried to remain calm and think.
Still, I strike my chest in anger.

O Sun! O Moon! Why are you so blind?
My heart, with sorrow stained,
Cannot be cleaned like dirty clothes.
I have tried to remain calm and think —
I wish I could fly away.

诗经·国风——英文白话新译

绿衣

绿兮衣兮,绿衣黄里。心之忧矣,曷维其已!
绿兮衣兮,绿衣黄裳。心之忧矣,曷维其亡!
绿兮丝兮,女所治兮。我思古人,俾无訧(yóu)兮!
絺(chī)兮绤(xì)兮,凄其以风。我思古人,实获我心。

绿衣

绿衣,绿衣,绿色外表,黄色里子。
内心悲凄,何时才停止?

绿衣,绿衣,绿色上装,黄色下裳。
内心凄凉,何时才能忘?

绿色丝线,是你亲自治染。
思念你,亡妻,是谁的过失?

葛布粗粗细细,凉风又起。
思念你,亡妻,永在我心里。

《邶风》绿衣

Green Coat

Green coat, green coat, green coat has a yellow lining.
The sorrow in my heart, when will it cease?

Green coat, green coat, green coat —
    dressed with a yellow apron.
The sorrow in my heart, when can it be forgotten?

Green silk, green silk, prepared by your hands.
Missing you, my deceased wife; whomever can one blame?

Fine fabric, coarse cloth, cold wind blowing again.
Missing you, my deceased wife — I am a shell,
    housing only love for you.

诗经·国风——英文白话新译

燕燕

燕燕于飞,差池(cī chí)其羽。
之子于归,远送于野。
瞻望弗及,泣涕如雨。

燕燕于飞,颉(xié)之颃(háng)之。
之子于归,远于将之。
瞻望弗及,伫立以泣。

燕燕于飞,下上其音。
之子于归,远送于南。
瞻望弗及,实劳我心。

仲氏任只,其心塞渊。
终温且惠,淑慎其身。
先君之思,以勖(xù)寡人。

小燕子

小燕子飞舞,参差尾羽。
妹妹出嫁,送她到城下。
眼看她背影逝去,泪下如雨。

小燕子飞翔,忽下忽上。
妹妹出嫁,送她到坡旁。
眼看她背影消逝,路边饮泣。

小燕子飞翔,高低哀唱。
妹妹出嫁,送她到南郊。
眼看她背影消逝,心碎魂离。

她值得信任,诚恳温文,
贤慧柔顺,处世谨慎。
她常说:"思念先君",鼓励我这寡德人。

《召南》驺虞

Zou-yu

Forest of luxurious reeds — one arrow hit five pigs!
Zou-yu, sir, you are great!

Meadow of opulent daisies — one arrow hit five pigs!
Zou-yu, sir, you are great!

《邶风》燕燕

Swallow

Swallow flies, darting left and right.
I escort my betrothed sister to the city gate,
Gazing after her until she dissolves from view;
My tears cascade like rain.

Swallow flies, hovering up and down.
My sister leaves to be married; I ache to see her go.
I gaze after her until she's long disappeared;
I weep rivers at the roadside.

Swallow flies, crying high and low.
My sister leaves to be married; I escort her to the south field.
I gaze after her until she's long lost to sight,
My heart in shards.

She is true, tender and diligent.
She is gentle, kind and generous.
To bolster me, she has often said:
"Be true to our late father."

诗经·国风——英文白话新译

日月

日居月诸,照临下土。
乃如之人兮,逝不古处。
胡能有定? 宁不我顾。

日居月诸,下土是冒。
乃如之人兮,逝不相好。
胡能有定? 宁不我报。

日居月诸,出自东方。
乃如之人兮,德音无良。
胡能有定? 俾也可忘。

日居月诸,东方自出。
父兮母兮,畜(xù)我不卒。
胡能有定? 报我不述。

太阳与月亮

太阳啊!月亮啊!照临大地。
怎么会有这种人?我发誓不跟他在一起。
他的心犹豫不定,对我完全不照应。

太阳啊!月亮啊!照临国土。
怎么会有这种人?我发誓不再爱他了。
他的心犹豫多疑,对我完全不珍惜。

太阳啊!月亮啊!升自东方。
怎么会有这种人?没有品格和天良。
他的心游游晃晃,把我完全遗忘。

太阳啊!月亮啊!升自东方。
父亲啊!母亲啊!我真不应该离开你。
他为人朝三暮四,完全不讲道理。

《邶风》日月

Sun and Moon

O Sun! O Moon! Shining over the earth below.
How can such a person exist? I swear I will leave him soon.
His mind is always shifting; he does not care about my
    feelings.

O Sun! O Moon! Shining over the land below.
How can such a person exist? I swear I will leave him soon.
His mind is always shifting; he does not respond to my
    attention.

O Sun! O Moon! Rising in the east.
How can such a person exist? He has no moral sense.
His mind never settles; he has forgotten me completely.

O Sun! O Moon! Rising in the east.
O father! O mother! I should never have left you.
His mind never settles; to me he is untrue.

诗经·国风——英文白话新译

终风

终风且暴,顾我则笑。谑浪笑敖,中心是悼。
终风且霾(mái),惠然肯来。莫往莫来,悠悠我思。
终风且曀(yì),不日有曀。寤言不寐,愿言则嚏(zhì)。
曀曀其阴,虺虺(huī huī)其雷。寤言不寐,愿言则怀。

风暴

风暴,风暴,他老是对我傻笑。
如此轻佻,如此莫名其妙,我是又悲伤又苦恼。

阴阴沉沉的风雨,他高兴了就来,不高兴了就走,
有时数天无消息,惹得我悲伤又着急。

灰灰蒙蒙的风雨,太阳刚刚出来,
匆匆又隐去,躺在床上不能睡,相思憔悴。

湿湿漉漉的风雨,雷声不断的急催,
睁着眼睛不能睡,漫漫梦寐。

《邶风》终风

Storm

A storm. A storm. He looks at me, slyly smiling.
Why's he so casual and lacking in manners?
I am sad, confused.

The storm is dark. He comes and goes unannounced.
I do not hear from him for days.
I am sad, confused.

The blustery gloom blots out the sun.
I cannot sleep;
His image clouds my mind.

Thunder ignites through the clouds and wind.
I cannot sleep;
His image swamps my mind.

诗经·国风——英文白话新译

击鼓

击鼓其镗(tāng),踊跃(yǒng yuè)用兵。土国城漕,我独南行。
从孙子仲,平陈与宋。不我以归,忧心有忡(chōng)。
爰(yuán)居爰处?爰丧其马?于以求之?于林之下。
死生契阔,与子成说。执子之手,与子偕老。
于嗟(xū jiē)阔兮,不我活兮。于嗟洵(xún)兮,不我信兮。

鸣击战鼓

战鼓咚咚,踊跃用兵。
有人挖战壕,有人筑围城。我却奉命南征。

跟了将军孙子仲,平定了陈和宋。
战事结束,不能回家,内心忧愤忡忡。

独留异域,我的马儿又失踪。
到哪里找我呢,野树林中。

离家时,握住她的手,立约发誓,
"白首偕老,永不分离"。

唉!唉!日悠悠,路遥远,
生活如此困难,
再不能实践我的誓言!

《邶风》击鼓

War Drums

The war drums boom thunder. Weapons in hand, battle-ready.
Warriors digging foxholes; warriors building walls.
I alone was ordered to join the south-bound march.

General Sun Zi-zhong led us, conqueror of Chen and Song.
But when the war was over, my return was not allowed,
Left behind in anger, left behind in pain.

I am a refugee in the south; I have also lost my horse.
Where can I be found?
Abandoned in deep woods.

When I left home,
I clasped her hand and said:
"We shall grow old together!"

We are now so far apart; we parted long ago.
Oh, what a life is this!
Our promise cannot be kept.

诗经·国风——英文白话新译

凯风

凯风自南,吹彼棘心;棘心夭夭,母氏劬(qú)劳。
凯风自南,吹彼棘薪;母氏圣善,我无令人。
爰有寒泉,在浚(jùn)之下;有子七人,母氏劳苦。
睍睆(xiàn huǎn)黄鸟,载好其音;有子七人,莫慰母心。

暖风

暖风南边吹来,吹动年轻枣树;
枣树洋洋茁长,母亲辛苦备尝。

暖风南边吹来,幼树长成木柴;
母亲生养慈爱,可惜我不成材。

那里有清泉,浚城之边;
兄弟七人成长,母亲忍受饥肠。

黄莺婉转啼鸣,歌声优美清新;
兄弟七人,不能安慰母亲的心。

《邶风》凯风

Warm Wind

A warm southerly gusts through a young jujube grove.
Jujubes grow swiftly, while ceaselessly my mother toils.

A warm southerly swells, maturing jujubes into fuel.
Mother's love is a fathomless well — I fear I am unworthy.

Where is the pure spring in the city of Jun?
Seven brothers have grown up; mother's drudgery
    knows no end.

A gold finch sings a tender, moving melody.
None of the seven brothers comforts our mother's heart.

诗经·国风——英文白话新译

雄雉

雄雉于飞,泄泄(yì yì)其羽。我之怀矣,自诒(yí)伊阻。
雄雉于飞,下上其音。展矣君子,实劳我心。
瞻彼日月,悠悠我思。道之云远,曷云能来?
百尔君子,不知德行?不忮(zhì)不求,何用不臧(zāng)?

雄野鸡

雄野鸡飞翔,闪闪翅膀。
思念远方的他,自郁自伤。

雄野鸡飞翔,上下其响。
为了远方的他,内心悲怆。

看看月亮,看看太阳,忘不了。
遥遥的远方,何时再回到我身旁?

中央那些大人物,没有好心肠。
我要你不贪功,不害人,一本善良。

《邶风》雄雉

Cock Pheasant

Cock pheasant flaps his wings in flight.
He is far away, fighting the war,
Leaving me alone in misery.

Cock pheasant flies, his wings resounding round.
Missing him so,
I melt in molten tears.

Look at the sun — look at the moon.
He is so, so far away —
I yearn for his return.

All those important leaders have no heart.
But do your duty, my own true love.
Harm no one, be safe, at peace.

诗经·国风——英文白话新译

匏有苦叶

匏(páo)有苦叶,济有深涉。深则厉,浅则揭(qì)。
有渳济盈,有鷕(yǎo)雉鸣。济盈不濡轨,雉鸣求其牡(mǔ)。
雝雝(yōng yōng)鸣雁,旭日始旦。士如归妻,迨冰未泮(pàn)。
招招舟子,人涉卬(áng)否。人涉卬否,卬须我友。

葫芦叶黄了

葫芦的叶子变黄了,济河的渡口水深了。
水深,和衣渡过,水浅,提起裤脚。

济河渡口水盈盈,听听那野鸡啼鸣。
河水淹不到车轴,雌鸡呼唤配偶。

雁声划过秋空,东方旭日初升。
你要是迎我为妻,不要等到解冰。

船夫频频招手,别人过河,我不走。
别人过河,我不走,等我的男人到渡口。

《邶风》匏有苦叶

Gourd with Yellow Leaves

Gourd leaves turning yellow.
The Ji River crossing brims its banks.
When it is deep, wade across in your clothes.
When shallow, raise your trouser legs.

Water runs swiftly at the fords.
Hark! The pheasants crow.
Water climbs up the wagon spokes.
The pheasant hen calls her mate.

The song of wild geese fills the air,
As dawn breaks in the east.
If you desire to marry me,
Don't wait for winter's ice to thaw.

The boatman signals departure's nigh.
Others are on board, not me.
Others are on board, not me.
I wait here for my man.

诗经·国风——英文白话新译

谷风

习习谷风,以阴以雨。黾(mǐn)勉同心,不宜有怒。
采葑采菲(fěi),无以下体。德音莫违,及尔同死。

行道迟迟,中心有违。不远伊迩,薄送我畿。
谁谓荼苦?其甘如荠(jì)。宴尔新昏,如兄如弟。

泾以渭浊,湜湜(shí shí)其沚(zhǐ)。宴尔新昏,不我屑以。
毋逝我梁,毋发我笱(gǒu)。我躬不阅,遑恤我后。

就其深矣,方之舟之。就其浅矣,泳之游之。
何有何亡(wú),黾勉求之。凡民有丧,匍匐救之。

不我能慉,反以我为雠。既阻我德,贾用不售。
昔育恐育鞫(jú),及尔颠覆。既生既育,比予于毒。

我有旨蓄,亦以御冬。宴尔新昏,以我御穷。
有洸(guāng)有溃,既诒我肄。不念昔者,伊余来墍(xì)。

《邶风》谷风

Valley Wind

From the peaceful valley a strong wind blows.
A moment of cloud, a moment of rain.
I have obeyed all your wishes, why are you so angry with me?
When you cook turnips and daikons, the leaves are edible,
But the important part is the root.
Don't forget your oath: "We shall remain together till death."

I walk one step; stop one step. I really don't want to leave.
I hoped you would walk with me a little further,
Yet at the doorstep you turned back.
Who said the sow thistle is bitter? It is sweeter than licorice.
You have just wed a young wife, inseparable from her —
Even for an eye-blink.

The River Jing appears muddy because of the River Wei.
But some places of Jing remain clear.
You feast on your new marriage, not even your shadow
    visits my bed.
Tell her not to touch my fish dam. Tell her not to open
    my fish trap.
Oh, why should I worry about such matters while
I can hardly care for myself?

诗经·国风——英文白话新译

谷风

大风呼呼,吹自山谷;一会儿云,一会儿雨。
我是什么都顺着你,何必对我发怒。
吃芜菁和萝卜,叶子虽有用,重要的是根啊!
不要忘记你发过的誓:"生死不分离!"

走一步,停一步,多么不想离去。
陪我多走几步嘛?走到门口就回头。
谁说苦菜味道苦,怎比我内心酸楚。
你刚刚娶了新妻子,亲密似漆不分离。

渭水使泾水显得浑浊,但有些地方仍清澈。
你刚刚娶了新妻子,不再与我同床睡。
告诉她不要碰我捕鱼坝,告诉她不要开我捕鱼篓。
算了吧,自顾尚且不暇,何必管那么多。

水深的时候用筏渡过,水浅的时候和衣游过。
家中穷困潦倒,是我一人撑着。
朋友们有了灾难,是我一人帮着。

你不但不念万恩,反而视我为仇人。
忘了我一切好处,当我为卖不出的旧货。
我们生活渐渐宽裕,你就把我看成毒物。

我蓄了些美味的盐干菜,原来准备过冬。
你有了新老婆,只拿我来填空。
毒打谩骂来势汹汹,逼我一人作苦工。
想想昔日恩爱,怎可无动于衷?

《邶风》谷风

When the water was deep, I rafted through.
When the water was shallow, I swam across.
During our years of poverty together,
I coped alone.
When our friends knew dire trouble,
It was I, who on my knees, gave them help.

Not only have you ignored my virtues,
You have turned on me as on an old foe.
Forgetting all the things I have done,
You treat me like a rejected petty purchase.
We finally lived in comfort,
Yet now I am likened to a poisonous weed.

I prepared delicious preserved food for our winter's rainy days,
Yet now you feast with your new relations.
While I serve only for your needs,
You force me to work as your slave.
So tempestuous in words and deeds,
You have forgotten our loving days of old.

诗经·国风——英文白话新译

式微

式微,式微！胡不归？
微君之故,胡为乎中露？

式微,式微！胡不归？
微君之躬,胡为乎泥中？

晚了

天色已晚,天色已晚,为什么还不回去？
要不是为了你,怎么会犹豫中途？

天色已晚,天色已晚,为什么还不回去？
要不是为了你,怎么会陷身沟渠？

《邶风》式微

It's Late

It's late — it's late! Why do you not come home?
If it were not for my love for you,
I would not be wandering the road alone.

It's late — it's late! Why do you not come home?
If it were not for my love for you,
I would not be struggling in this muddy mire.

诗经·国风——英文白话新译
旄丘

旄(máo)丘之葛兮,何诞之节兮!叔兮伯兮,何多日也?
何其处也?必有与也!何其久也?必有以也!
狐裘蒙戎,匪车不东。叔兮伯兮,靡所与同。
琐兮尾兮,流离之子。叔兮伯兮,褎(yòu)如充耳。

旄丘

旄丘上的葛藤,何其茂盛。
我的兄弟们呵,为什么遗弃我这样久?

为什么让我老在等,一定有原因呵。
为什么这样久,一定有理由呵。

我的狐皮袍已破烂,救济还未来。
我的兄弟们呵!我们不是同盟吗?

可怜呀!卑微呀!我只是个浪子吗?
我的兄弟们呀!你们却在那里生活优裕。

《邶风》旄丘

Mao Hill

On Mao Hill, ivy grows in profusion.
Oh, brothers, why so long — why is there no message?

Why do you leave me alone? There must be reasons.
Why is it taking so long — there must be reasons.

My fox fur coat is worn; I have no replacement.
Oh, brothers, are we not partners?

I am so insignificant, a mere drifter.
Oh, brothers — you are home enjoying the good life.

诗经·国风——英文白话新译

简兮

简兮简兮,方将万舞。
日之方中,在前上处。

硕(shí)人俣俣(yǔ yǔ),公庭万舞。
有力如虎,执辔如组。

左手执钥(yuè),右手秉翟(dí)。
赫如渥赭(wò zhě),公言锡爵。

山有榛(zhēn),隰(xí)有苓(líng)。
云谁之思?西方美人。
彼美人兮,西方之人兮。

壮丽

如此壮丽,如此辉煌,盛大的舞蹈就要开始了。
日正当中;他是舞队的领袖。

如此强壮,舞步在宗庙的中庭。
活跃如虎,他手舞缰绳如丝绫。

左手执笛,右手举着雉羽。
脸色发亮如红土,诸侯赐他一杯酒。

山上有榛树,湿地有甘草。
他思念的是位西方美女,
一位西方的美女哟,是他心中的爱慕。

《邶风》简兮

So Glorious

So glorious, so beautiful —
A grand dance, about to begin.
It is noon. He is the leader of the troupe.

A great dancer in the temple courtyard,
Powerful as a tiger,
He holds the reins like silk ribbons.

A flute in his left had, a pheasant feather in his right;
His tanned face, the colour of red earth.
The lord offers him a drink.

Hazelnut tree on the hill. Licorice patch down below.
He is thinking of a beautiful woman in the west —
In the west, a beautiful woman for whom he pines.

诗经·国风——英文白话新译

泉水

毖(bì)彼泉水,亦流于淇(qí)。
有怀于卫,靡日不思。
娈(luán)彼诸姬,聊与之谋。

出宿于泲(jǐ),饮饯于祢(nǐ)。
女子有行,远父母兄弟。
问我诸姑,遂及伯姊。

出宿于干,饮饯于言。
载脂载舝(xiá),还车言迈。
遄(chuán)臻(zhēn)于卫,不瑕有害。

我思肥泉,兹之永叹。
思须与漕(cáo),我心悠悠。
驾言出游,以写(xiè)我忧。

泉水

泉水溪流入淇河,远离了故乡卫国。
乡愁每天加多,思念我的同宗姊妹们,
曾常与她们嬉乐。

曾在沛城住夜,曾在祢城饯别,
女孩子出嫁,远离父母和兄弟,
辞别了诸姑和大姊。

也曾在干城住宿,也曾在言城饯别,
车轴快些加油,调转马头,
赶回卫国,会有问题吗?

怀念泉水溪,久久叹息,
相思须城和曹城,恨悠悠,
只好驾车出游,解除心中愁。

《邶风》泉水

Spring Water

Spring water flows into the River Qi.
I left my homeland Wei; I miss it every day.
I remember all my cousins, sweet;
    I talked with them frequently.

We lodged one night at Ji, and toasted farewell at Ni.
When a girl marries, she parts with her parents and brothers;
She says goodbye to her aunts and elder sisters.

We lodged as well at Gan and toasted again at Yan.
I have greased my wagon axle and the wheel pins.
I want to hurry back to Wei — is this wrong?

I am homesick for spring water; I sigh long and deep.
I miss Xu and Cao; their memory swells my sorrow.
I want to ride away on my wagon; I want to forget this misery.

诗经·国风——英文白话新译

北门

出自北门,忧心殷殷。
终窭(jù)且贫,莫知我艰。
已焉哉！天实为之,谓之何哉！

王事适(zhí)我,政事一埤(pí)益我。
我入自外,室人交徧(biàn)谪(zhé)我。
已焉哉！天实为之,谓之何哉！

王事敦我,政事一埤遗(wèi)我。
我入自外,室人交徧摧我。
已焉哉！天实为之,谓之何哉！

北门

走出北门,忧心苦闷,
我的官阶又低生活又贫困,谁会知道我的艰辛。
算了吧！一切是天意呵,还有甚么好说。

官家事逼着我,地方差事压着我,
回到家,亲戚又责怪我,
算了吧！这是天意呵,还有甚么好说。

官家事逼着我,地方问题压着我,
回到家,亲戚又折磨我。
算了吧！这是天意呵,还有甚么好说。

《邶风》北门

North Gate

In misery I walk through the Northern Gate.
My rank is low and I am poor; no one knows my straits.
Alas, all is heaven's will; what can I say....

Government affairs pressure me; all sorts of business awaits.
When I return home, relatives' harangues give no respite.
Alas, all is heaven's will; what can I say....

Government affairs oppress me; all sorts of problems conspire.
When I return home, relatives burden me with ire.
Alas, all is heaven's will; what can I say....

诗经·国风——英文白话新译

北风

北风其凉,雨(yù)雪其雱(páng)。
惠而好(hào)我,携手同行。
其虚其邪(xú)? 既亟(jí)只且(zhǐ jū)!

北风其喈(jiē),雨雪其霏。
惠而好我,携手同归。
其虚其邪? 既亟只且!

莫赤匪狐,莫黑匪乌。
惠而好我,携手同车。
其虚其邪? 既亟只且!

北风

北风凛冽,大雪飞扬。
女:"亲爱的,握住我的手,一块走吧。"
男:"别太匆忙,再想一想。"
女:"情势已经很坏,不能再等待。"

北风呼呼,大雪茫茫。
女:"亲爱的,握住我的手,快回家吧。"
男:"别太匆忙,再想一想。"
女:"情势已经很坏,不能再等待。"

男:"没有狐狸不红,没有乌鸦不黑。"
女:"亲爱的,握住我的手,快些上车吧。"
男:"别太匆忙,再想一想。"
女:"情势已经太坏,不能再等待。"

《邶风》北风

North Wind

Cold north wind, thick blowing snow — a blizzard!
She: "My dear man, hold my hand and let us run."
He: "Slow down please; do not be in such haste."
She: "No, the situation is urgent; we cannot wait."

Cold north wind, thick blowing snow — a blizzard!
She: "My dear man, hold my hand and let's go home."
He: "Slow down please; do not be in such haste."
She: "No, the situation is urgent; we cannot wait."

He: " There is not a fox which is not red;
      There is not a crow which is not black."
She: "My dear man, hold my hand and let's get in the carriage."
He: "Slow down please; do not be in such haste."
She: "The situation is urgent; we cannot wait."

诗经·国风——英文白话新译

静女

静女其姝，俟(sì)我于城隅；
爱而不见，搔首踟蹰。

静女其娈(qí luán)，贻我彤(tóng)管；
彤管有炜(wěi)，说怿(yuè yì)女(rǔ)美。

自牧归(kuì)荑(tí)，洵美且异；
匪女之为美，美人之贻！

静美的姑娘

那位静美的姑娘，在城角等我；
找不到她，抓头抓腮徘徊着。

那位静美的姑娘，送我一管红箫；
那管细细的红箫，像她一样娇巧。

她从野外带给我一束白茅，又香又苗条；
因为是她送的，这束白茅特别好！

《邶风》静女

A Fair Maiden

A fair maiden awaited me at the city gate.
I could not find her, looking, pacing, scratching my head.

A fair maiden gave me a red clarinet;
Such a pretty clarinet, as lovely as the maiden.

From the field a fair maiden brought me a bundle
Of beautiful grass. Her gift, so very special.

诗经·国风——英文白话新译

新台

新台有泚(cǐ),河水弥弥。燕婉之求,蘧篨(qú chú)不鲜(xiǎn)。
新台有洒(cuǐ),河水浼浼(měi měi)。燕婉之求,蘧篨不殄(tiǎn)。
鱼网之设,鸿则离之。燕婉之求,得此戚施。

新楼台

河边筑了座新楼台,河水涛涛淹淹。
只想找个好男子,偏偏嫁了个丑陋汉。

新楼台巍巍壮观,河水涛涛漫漫。
只想找个好男子,偏偏嫁了个丑陋汉。

设下一张捕鱼网,却只捉了只呆头鹅。
一心要嫁好男子,丈夫却是个驼背的癞蛤蟆。

《邶风》新台

New Tower

A new tower by the swift Yellow River.
Though seeking a handsome mate,
　　she marries an ugly toad.

The new tower is so magnificent, by the swift water's side.
She's seeking a handsome mate,
　　but she is marrying an ugly toad.

She casts a large fishing net, and catches a silly goose.
She dreams of a handsome mate,
　　but she is marrying a hunch-backed toad.

诗经·国风——英文白话新译

二子乘舟

二子乘舟,泛泛其景。愿言思子,中心养养(yǎng yǎng)!
二子乘舟,泛泛其逝。愿言思子,不瑕有害!

两人乘小舟

两人乘了条小船,远去了,无岸无边。
思念你们,慌慌难安。

两人乘了条小船,逝去了,遥遥远远。
朋友呵,祝福你们安全。

《邶风》二子乘舟

Two Men in a Small Boat

Two of you left in a small boat,
Into the waves, far from sight.
Thinking of you, I am distressed.

Two of you left in a small boat,
Into the fog, out of sight.
Dear friends, I pray for your safety.

鄘风
Airs of Yong
45—54

诗经·国风——英文白话新译

柏舟

泛彼柏舟,在彼中河。
髡(dàn)彼两髦(máo),实维我仪,之死矢靡(mǐ)它(tuō)。
母也天只！不谅人只！

泛彼柏舟,在彼河侧。
髡彼两髦,实维我特,之死矢靡慝(tè)。
母也天只！不谅人只！

柏木小舟

那条柏木小舟,在河中悠悠飘流。
船上那位长发男人,是我男友,
我发誓,对他的爱至死不渝,
母亲啊,老天啊,为什么不了解我的心意？

那条柏木小舟,在河边荡漾飘流。
船上那位长发男人,是我男友,
我发誓,对他的爱至死不渝,
母亲啊,老天啊,为什么不了解我的心意？

《鄘风》柏舟

Cedar Boat

In the middle of the river a small cedar boat sails leisurely.
The long-haired man in the boat is my dearest.
I swear I will never change my mind.
Heavens, mother! Why don't you understand?

Along the river bank a small cedar boat sails leisurely.
The long-haired man in the boat is my beloved.
I swear I will never change my mind.
Heavens, mother! Why don't you understand?

墙有茨

墙有茨(cí)，不可埽(sǎo)也。
中冓(gòu)之言，不可道也。
所可道也，言之丑也。

墙有茨，不可襄也。
中冓之言，不可详也。
所可详也，言之长也。

墙有茨，不可束也。
中冓之言，不可读也。
所可读也，言之辱也。

墙头有蒺藜

墙头上的蒺藜，不可扫除呀。
睡房里的私话，勿与外人道呀。
道了出去，太丑陋呀。

墙头上的蒺藜，不可拔掉呀。
睡房里的私话，说不清楚呀。
要说清楚，长如裹脚布呀。

墙头上的蒺藜，不可清理呀。
睡房里的私话，不可喧嚷呀。
嚷了出去，太丢人呀。

《鄘风》墙有茨

Burdock on the Wall

Prickly burdock on the wall — don't remove them all.
Private conversations in the bedroom —
Don't repeat them to outsiders.
If you do, ugly rumours will follow.

Spiny burdock on the wall — don't destroy them all.
Private conversations in the bedroom —
Don't repeat them to strangers.
If you do, they're as long and rank as foot-binding rags.

Thorny burdock on the wall — don't clear them all.
Private conversations in the bedroom —
Don't reveal them to others.
If you do, humiliation will follow.

诗经·国风——英文白话新译

君子偕老

君子偕老,副笄(jī)六珈。
委委佗佗(tuó tuó),如山如河,象服是宜。
子之不淑,云如之何?

玼(cǐ)兮玼兮,其之翟(dí)也。
鬒(zhěn)发如云,不屑髢(dí)也。
玉之瑱(tiàn)也,象之揥(tì)也。
扬且(jū)之皙也,胡然而天也?胡然而帝也?

瑳(cuō)兮瑳兮,其之展也。
蒙彼绉絺(chī)，是绁袢(xiè fán)也。
子之清扬,扬且之颜也。
展如之人兮,邦之媛也!

白头偕老

嫁给君王白头偕老,她头上有六种宝石。
举止从容舒展,山一样稳重,河一样自然,
披着绣花长袍,亮丽美艳。
谁知命不好,谣言中伤,怎么办?

穿了绣着鸟羽的礼服,高贵美艳。
长发如云,不须假发装扮,
纯玉重耳,象牙发饰,皮肤细腻,美目流盼。
是帝女啊,是天仙!

美丽啊!罩袍盖住细纱内衫,是她应时夏装。
眼睛含情明亮,额角白皙丰满。
真有这样美女吗?是我们国家公主啊!

《鄘风》君子偕老

Married for Life

Married to her lord for life — her headdress displays six jewels.
Her behaviour — stately as a mountain, graceful as a river.
Exquisite in her embroidered robe.
But alas! She suffers from rumour's fangs.
What can one say about this?

How splendid she appears in her peacock feather print coat.
Her hair — black as a dark cloud — she needs no false locks.
Her ear-plugs — pure jade; her comb — precious ivory.
She is heaven's daughter,
And the goddess of our land!

Her elegant overcoat covers inner garments of cloth yet finer.
Clear eyes.
Full, smooth brow.
How can such a beauty exist?
Truly, our national princess.

诗经·国风——英文白话新译

桑中

爰(yuán)采唐矣,沫(mèi)之乡矣。
云谁之思?美孟姜矣。
期我乎桑中,要我乎上宫,
送我乎淇之上矣。

爰采麦矣?沫之北矣。
云谁之思?美孟弋矣。
期我乎桑中,要我乎上宫,
送我乎淇之上矣。

爰采葑(fēng)矣?沫之东矣。
云谁之思?美孟庸矣。
期我乎桑中,要我乎上宫,
送我乎淇之上矣。

桑林中

去哪里采菟丝呢?沫城的乡野呵。
知道我在想谁吗?孟家的美女呵。
她等我在桑林中,邀我去上宫。
回来,送我到淇水之东。

去哪里采小麦呢?沫城之北呵。
知道我在想谁吗?孟家的美女呵。
她等我在桑林中,邀我去上宫。
回来,送我到淇水之东。

去哪里采芜菁呢?沫城之东呵。
知道我在想谁吗?孟家的美女呵。
她等我在桑林中,邀我去上宫。
回来,送我到淇水之东。

《鄘风》桑中

In the Mulberry Field

Where to gather soy sponger? Outside the City of Mei.
Whom am I missing? The pretty maiden of the Mengs.
She waited for me in the mulberry field.
She went with me to Shang-gong.
She accompanied me to the east bank of the River Qi.

Where to gather wheat? North of the City of Mei.
Whom am I missing? The pretty maiden of the Mengs.
She waited for me in the mulberry field.
She went with me to Shang-gong.
She accompanied me to the east bank of the River Qi.

Where to gather turnip? East of the City of Mei.
Of whom am I thinking? The pretty maiden of the Mengs.
She waited for me in the mulberry field.
She went with me to Shang-gong.
She accompanied me to the east bank of River Qi.

诗经·国风——英文白话新译

鹑之奔奔

鹑(chún)之奔奔,鹊之强强(qiáng qiáng)。
人之无良,我以为兄?
鹊之强强,鹑之奔奔。人之无良,我以为君?

鹌鹑奔走

鹌鹑成双成对的走,喜鹊成双成对的飞。
那个人没有天良,他却是我的兄长。

喜鹊成双成对的飞,鹌鹑成双成对的走。
那个人没有天良,他却是我的君王。

《鄘风》鹑之奔奔

Quail Walk

Quail walk in pairs.
Magpies fly in pairs.
That man has no conscience,
Yet he is my brother.

Magpies fly in pairs.
Quail walk in pairs.
That man has no conscience,
Yet he is my lord.

诗经·国风——英文白话新译

定之方中

定之方中,作于楚宫。
揆之以日,作于楚室。
树之榛(zhēn)栗,椅桐梓漆,爰伐琴瑟。

升彼虚矣,以望楚矣。
望楚与堂,景山与京。
降观于桑,卜云其吉,终然允臧。

灵雨既零,命彼倌人。
星言夙驾,说(shuì)于桑田。
匪直也人,秉心塞渊,骐(lái)牝(pìn)三千。

定星①在空

定星出现在十一月的夜空,卫文公在楚丘兴建宫室,
用日影测好方向,他开始建筑房子。
在周围种了榛树和栗树,又种了楸、桐、梓和漆,
供应木材作琴瑟。

卫文公登上高高的废墟,遥望楚丘和堂城,
遥望高地和山岭,走下废墟去访问民间的桑田,
一切都是好风水,自始至终多吉利。

瑞雨及时沛沛,他吩咐车夫快准备,
日出前要出发,探望桑田和农家。
有远见,有计划,心肠好,智谋高,他有大马三千。

---

① 定星为营室星。

《鄘风》定之方中

Ding Star[1] in the Evening Sky

Ding Star hung in November's evening sky.
Lord Wen began to build his palace in Chu;
Calculating according to the direction of the sun's shadows,
He also built houses.
Next he planted hazelnut and chestnut trees,
Plus chu, tong, zi and varnish trees on the premises,
To provide wood someday for musical instruments.

Lord Wen ascended Chu's tall ruins
To view the city,
Its hills and ridges,
Descending to inspect
The mulberry fields.
The feng shui is good — he knows.
This is the place for prosperity.

Timely rains fell; Lord Wen commanded the coachman
To prepare to leave before dawn,
To visit the mulberry fields and peasants.
A dutiful visionary,
An honest man,
With a good set of plans.
The Lord will have strong mares — three thousand!

---

[1] Ding Star: A star which indicates a propitious time to build.

诗经·国风——英文白话新译

蝃蝀

蝃蝀(dì dōng)在东,莫之敢指。女子有行,远父母兄弟。
朝隮(jī)于西,崇朝其雨。女子有行,远兄弟父母。
乃如之人也,怀昏姻也。大无信也,不知命也!

彩虹

彩虹挂在东天,无人敢指指点点。
女孩子长大了要嫁人,远离兄弟父母。

早晨彩虹在西边,整个上午下雨天。
女孩子长大了要嫁人,远离兄弟父母。

就是这样么,女孩子大了要嫁人呵。
为什么要妇德妇从?为什么要父母之命?

《鄘风》蝃蝀

Rainbow

A rainbow in the East; we are taught not to point at it.
A girl grows up, naturally wanting to be married,
Leaving her parents and brothers.

A rainbow in the West; it rains the whole morning.
A girl grows up, naturally wanting to be married,
Leaving her parents and brothers.

Is this not so for a grown-up girl? She just wants to be married.
Why should she submit to conventional rules?
Why should she obey her parents?

诗经·国风——英文白话新译

相鼠

相鼠有皮,人而无仪。人而无仪,不死何为?
相鼠有齿,人而无止。人而无止,不死何俟(sì)?
相鼠有体,人而无礼。人而无礼,胡不遄(chuán)死?

看那老鼠

看那老鼠也有皮,有人却没有威仪。
如果没有威仪,为什么还不去死?

看那老鼠也有牙齿,有人却没有容止。
如果没有容止,死呀,还要等到几时?

看那老鼠也有四肢,有人却没有礼义。
如果没有礼义,还不快快去死?

《鄘风》相鼠

Look at the Rat!

Look at the rat!
Even a rat has skin.
Some people have no manners.
A man without manners might just as well die.

Look at the rat!
Even a rat has teeth.
Some people have no grace.
A man without grace might just as well die.

Look at the rat!
Even a rat has limbs.
Some people have no dignity.
A man without dignity should die, forthwith!

诗经·国风——英文白话新译

干旄

孑孑干旄(máo)，在浚之郊。
素丝纰(pí)之，良马四之。
彼姝者子，何以畀(bì)之？

孑孑干旟(yú)，在浚之都。
素丝组之，良马五之。
彼姝者子，何以予之？

孑孑干旌(jīng)，在浚之城。
素丝祝之，良马六之。
彼姝者子，何以告(gù)之？

牛尾旗

牛尾旗飘飘，公侯的座车到了浚城之郊。
旗边绣着白丝；拉车有良马四匹。
要访的女子高贵秀丽，应该送她什么礼？

隼鸟旗飘飘，公侯的座车来到浚城门桥。
旗边镶着白丝；拉车有良马五匹。
要访的女子高贵秀丽，应该送她什么礼？

玉彩旗飘飘，公侯的座车来到浚城街道。
旗边绣着白丝；拉车有良马六匹。
要访的女子高贵秀丽，应该送她什么礼？

114

《鄘风》干旄

Ox-Tail Banner

An ox-tail banner waves its white silk embroidery
Above the Lord's wagon as he arrives
Outside the city of Jun.
Four horses draw the wagon as he comes
To see a noble, beautiful lady.
What should he offer her as a gift?

A falcon banner waves its white silk braids
Over the Lord's wagon as he arrives
At the gate of the city of Jun.
Five horses draw the wagon as he comes
To see a noble, beautiful lady.
What should he offer her as a gift?

A rainbow banner stitched with white silk waves its colours
Over the Lord's wagon as he enters
The streets of Jun.
Six steeds draw the wagon as he comes
To see a noble, beautiful lady.
What should he offer her as a gift?

诗经·国风——英文白话新译

载驰[①]

载驰载驱,归唁(yàn)卫侯。
驱马悠悠,言至于漕。
大夫跋涉,我心则忧。

既不我嘉,不能旋反。
视尔不臧,我思不远。

既不我嘉,不能旋济。
视尔不臧,我思不閟(bì)。

陟彼阿(ē)丘,言采其蝱(máng)。
女子善怀,亦各有行。
许人尤之,众穉(zhì)且狂。

我行其野,芃芃(péng péng)其麦。
控于大邦,谁因谁极?
大夫君子,无我有尤。
百尔所思,不如我所之。

[①] 这篇诗是中国第一位女诗人穆姬所作,她原是卫国的公主,嫁给许国穆公,所以又称许穆夫人,后来卫为狄所灭,她父亲卫懿公战死。穆姬二兄复国,设都在漕,是为载公。载公死,她的三哥文公继位,设都在楚丘(参看《定之方中》)。

《鄘风》载驰

My Wagon Flies[①]

Behind my horse my wagon flies
To console my brothers in the Capital.
A long, long journey brings me here, where
A minister from Xu has come to stop me.
Though defiant, I am worried and afraid.

The Xu officials claim I am wrong,
    but my mind shall not be changed.
Their ideas lack light; less practical than my techniques.
They don't support my actions, but I am not returning;
Compared with all their ideas,
Mine is much better wrought.

I ascend a hilltop to gather toad-lilies to relieve my sorrow.
Women are naturally more sentimental,
But there is reason in their convictions.
The Xu officials all blame me.
They're so shallow and childish.

I pass the farmlands of Wei, their infinite shocks of gold.
I shall petition the large states for justice;
    perhaps one will help us.
All you officials from Xu, please understand that I am right.
Hundreds or more of your infantile plans lack
    the maturity and might of mine.

[①] This poem was written by the woman poet Mu-ji about 2,600 years ago. She was the princess of Wei, married to the Lord of Xu. Thus she is also known as Madam Xu-mu. When Wei was conquered by Di, her father Lord Yi of Wei was killed. Her second brother re-established Wei as Lord Di in Cao, but soon died and was succeeded by her third brother as Lord Wen in Chu (see # 50, "Ding Star in the Evening Sky", pp.108-109, above).

117

诗经·国风——英文白话新译

马车疾驰

马车在大路上疾驰,赶回卫国慰藉我的兄弟。
路遥遥,车行行,来到了祖国的漕城。
许国官员来阻拦,使我忧伤又为难。

许国官员尽排我的不是,我也不会变主意。
他们那些坏办法,不比我的更远大。

他们不赞成我的行动,我也不要转回程。
比起他们的鬼主张,我的计划更周详。

登上一座小山丘,采些贝母解忧愁。
女人自来多善感,她们也会有意见。
许国官员不拥护,真是肤浅又胡涂。

奔驰在祖国的田园,黄金麦浪连连。
我要去找大国评评理,他们会有好主意。
讨厌的许国官员,不要再和我为难。
你们的千条策略,也不比我的更完全。

118

卫风
Airs of Wei
55—64

诗经·国风——英文白话新译

淇奥

瞻彼淇奥(yù),绿竹猗猗(yī yī)。
有匪君子,如切如磋,如琢如磨。
瑟兮僩(xiàn)兮,赫兮咺(xuān)兮。
有匪君子,终不可谖(xuān)兮!

瞻彼淇奥,绿竹青青。
有匪君子,充耳琇莹,会(kuài)弁(biàn)如星。
瑟兮僩兮,赫兮咺兮。
有匪君子,终不可谖兮!

瞻彼淇奥,绿竹如箦(zé)。
有匪君子,如金如锡,如圭如璧。
宽兮绰兮,猗(yǐ)重较(chóng jué)兮。
善戏谑兮,不为虐兮!

淇水之湄

看那淇水之湄,绿竹依依,
有位文采斐然的男子工作努力,
有如大匠雕骨器时的用心,琢玉石时的仔细,
那样悠闲,那样雅致,那样磊落,那样威仪,
如此风流潇洒的男人,我永也不忘记。

看那淇水之滨,一片青青竹林。
有位文采斐然的男子衣饰华丽,
帽上宝石闪闪,精细明亮的垂耳,
那样悠闲,那样雅致,那样磊落,那样威仪,
如此风流潇洒的男人,我永也不忘记。

看那淇水之湾,一片竹林漫漫,
有位文质彬彬的男人,是金是银,
那么宏伟,那么闲逸,斜倚着他车厢上的扶手,
谈吐风趣,温文有礼。

《卫风》淇奥

The Bank of the River Qi

Behold the bank of the River Qi,
Where undulant bamboo forests dance.
A handsome man, intently working,
    As a great master carving a piece of ivory,
    As a great artist sculpting a piece of jade.
Relaxed, confident, dignified and stately....
Such an elegant man! How can I ever forget him?

Observe the shore of the River Qi
Against the green bamboo blanket.
A handsome man, elegantly dressed.
    The adornments of his ears glitter;
    The gems on his cap burnish the light.
Relaxed, confident, dignified and stately....
Such an elegant man! How can I ever forget him?

Consider the edge of the River Qi.
The bamboo forest, luxuriant.
There he stands, a handsome man,
    Pure as gold,
    Precious as diamonds.
Leaning on the rails of his chariot,
He speaks with wit, always without condescending.

诗经·国风——英文白话新译

考槃

考槃(pán)在涧,硕(shí)人之宽;独寐寤言,永矢弗谖(xuān)。
考槃在阿(ē),硕人之薖(kē);独寐寤歌,永矢弗过。
考槃在陆,硕人之轴;独寐寤宿,永矢弗告。

铜盘

涧水旁击盘而歌,隐者无忧无惧。
独言独语,乐土乐土。

山坡上击盘而歌,隐者无牵无挂。
独饮独饭,到处是家。

山丘上击盘而歌,隐者自在从容。
独睡独醒,乐趣几人能懂?

《卫风》考槃

Brass Gong

Singing alone beside a mountain creek,
    his brass gong marking tempo.
The wise gentleman has no worry and no fear.
Talking to himself, answering himself.
Happy land, happy land.

Singing alone at the foot of a hill,
    accompanied by his brass gong.
The wise gentleman has left human affairs behind.
Cooking by himself, eating by himself, with no fixed abode.
Peace has found his soul.

Singing alone on a rocky mound, tapping his brass gong.
The wise gentleman steeps in tranquility.
Sleeping by himself, waking by himself.
This happiness: how many people can comprehend?

诗经·国风——英文白话新译

硕人

硕(shí)人其颀(qí),衣锦褧(jiǒng)衣。
齐侯之子,卫侯之妻。
东宫之妹,邢侯之姨,谭公维私。

手如柔荑(tí),肤如凝脂。
领如蝤蛴(qiú qí),齿如瓠犀(hù xī)。
螓(qín)首蛾眉,巧笑倩兮,美目盼兮。

硕人敖敖,说(shuì)于农郊。
四牡有骄,朱幩(fén)镳镳,翟茀(dí fú)以朝。
大夫夙退,无使君劳。

河水洋洋,北流活活(guō)。
施罛(gū)濊濊(huò huò),鱣(zhān)鲔发发(bō bō),
葭(jiā)菼(tǎn)揭揭。
庶姜孽孽,庶士有朅(jiē)。

美人庄姜

有女庄姜,丰满颀长,锦衣外披了纱氅。
齐侯的女儿,卫侯的妻子。
东宫太子的妹妹,邢侯的小姨,姐姐是谭公的娇妻。

纤纤手指似芦苇的新芽,白皙皮肤如凝固羊脂。
细长脖子如天牛幼虫,洁白整齐的牙齿似葫芦的种子。
秋蝉方额,淡淡蛾眉,
笑时酒窝伴着甜甜的唇,回顾时眸子明亮又亲近。

有女庄姜,丰满颀长,她的座车停在近郊。
四匹雄马健壮,马衔红带飘扬,车上插了雉羽。
参见卫侯:"大夫们,早些退朝,莫使我夫太辛劳。"

黄河之水洋洋,浩浩荡荡,流向北方。
撒下鱼网水花四溅,捕了满网的鲤和鲔,岸边芦苇青青荡荡。
陪嫁女子亮丽健康,护车武士英勇强壮。

《卫风》硕人

Madam Zhuang-jiang

Madam Zhuang-jiang,
Curvaceous and tall,
Over her embroidered coat
Draped a shawl.
The daughter of Lord Qi, wife of Lord Wei.
Younger sister of the crown prince,
Sister-in-law of Lord Xing.
Another sister married Lord Tan.

Her fingers, slender as shoots of reeds.
Her skin, white and soft as lard.
Her neck, long and delicate as the ox-beetle's larva.
Her teeth, even and white as gourd seeds.
Her forehead, full and square as that of a cicada.
Her eyebrows, light as the eye marks of a moth.
Sweet dimples frame her teasing smile.
When she glances, behold her limpid, intimate eyes.

Madam Zhuang-jiang, curvaceous and tall,
Her carriage rests by the farm beyond the city wall.
Four horses strong and sleek,
Red silk trappings on their bits.
Pheasant feathers decorate her carriage curtains.
She arrives at her Lord's court:
"You noble ministers, please retire early.
Do not fatigue my Lord!"

The Yellow River surges mightily,
Flowing toward the North.
Fishnets thrown into the river,
Yield bountiful bass and carp.
Reeds grow profusely
On the river bank.
Her bridesmaids are splendidly attired;
Her guards are skilled and strong.

氓

氓(máng)之蚩蚩(chī chī),抱布贸丝。匪来贸丝,来即我谋。
送子涉淇,至于顿丘。匪我愆期,子无良媒。
将子无怒,秋以为期。

乘彼垝(guǐ)垣,以望复关。不见复关,泣涕涟涟。
既见复关,载笑载言。尔卜尔筮,体无咎言。
以尔车来,以我贿迁。

桑之未落,其叶沃若。于嗟鸠兮!无食桑葚。
于嗟(xū jiē)女兮!无与士耽。士之耽兮,犹可说也。
女之耽兮,不可说也。

桑之落矣,其黄而陨。自我徂(cú)尔,三岁食贫。
淇水汤汤(shāng shāng),渐车帷裳。女也不爽,士贰其行。
士也罔极,二三其德。

三岁为妇,靡(mǐ)室劳矣。夙兴夜寐,靡有朝矣。
言既遂矣,至于暴矣。兄弟不知,咥(xī)其笑矣。
静言思之,躬自悼矣。

及尔偕老,老使我怨。淇则有岸,隰(xí)则有泮(pàn)。
总角之宴,言笑晏晏。信誓旦旦,不思其反。
反是不思,亦已焉哉!

《卫风》氓

Cloth Peddler

A smiling peddler
Came to my house,
Wanting to exchange cloth for silk.
He did not intend an exchange....
He wanted to discuss marriage.
I crossed the River Qi with him.
When we parted at the Dun village, I said:
"I do not mean to delay the wedding date,
But your gifts do not suffice.
Please do not be angry with me.
Let's decide on an autumn date."

Climbing up a dirt wall —
Looking toward Fu-kuan.
I cannot see you;
Tears flood my face.
When I see you coming,
I begin happily chattering.
You have consulted
The tortoise shells,
And have found a propitious date.
Come with your wagon —
Take me and my dowry.

When the young mulberry tree is soft and tender,
Oh, doves, doves, do not be greedy for mulberries.
Oh, girls, girls, do not fall for a man too easily.
When a man falls in love, he can forget in a day.
When a girl falls in love, she falls for years and years.
When the mulberry tree turns old,
    it becomes brown and broken.

诗经·国风——英文白话新译

布贩子

棉布贩子笑嘻嘻,抱了布匹来换丝。
其实不是来换丝,是来与我谈婚事。
送你过了淇河水,到了顿丘才分离。
不是故意延婚期,是你没有好婚礼。
你也不要发脾气,就把婚期订秋季。

登上一堵土墙,遥望复关方向。
不见你来,泪沾衣裳。
见你来啦,嘻笑扬扬。
你已占了卜筮,择定了好日子。
驾车来吧,人和嫁妆跟着你。

年轻的桑树,又绿又娇嫩。
斑鸠鸟啊,不要贪吃桑葚!
年轻女子啊,不要贪恋男人。
男人爱了,随时忘记。
女人爱了,爱一辈子。

桑树枯黄,支离憔悴。
嫁到你家,贫苦受罪。
你把我送回娘家。
淇河的水沸沸,溅湿了我车帷。
我是始终如一,你却三心二意。

嫁到你家三年,
任劳任怨——不得休闲。
现在家境好转,
你就变了脸——丑恶凶悍。
自己兄弟不知情节,讥笑我罪有应得。
安静下来细细想,暗自悲伤。

你曾说:"白头偕老不分离。"
自己誓言已忘记。
淇水有岸,沼地有边。
记得少年时,欢欢喜喜。
算了吧,往事不再追忆。

《卫风》布贩子

Since we married, poverty has been our lot.
You sent me back to my brothers.
The waves in the River Qi surge high and violent,
    wetting my wagon curtains.
I have been faithful to you all along.
Your mind, not mine, waxes, wains and waivers.

For three years we have been married.
I have never complained about household chores.
I rise at daybreak,
Go to bed late at night.
I have never been idle for a moment.
In spite of the comfort we have finally achieved,
You have become rough and rude.
My own brothers do not know the truth;
They lay the blame for our problems on me.
To calm myself, I think again,
Weeping in cold silence.

I hoped to marry for life,
But can no longer endure your cruelty.
The River Qi has its banks;
The swamps have their edges.
Remembering when I was a little girl —
My life was filled with laughter.
Once you swore: "Let us grow old together."
You have betrayed your own oath,
Behaving like a tyrant.
Oh, there is no more to be said.
Stop thinking about the past.

诗经·国风——英文白话新译

竹竿

籊籊(dí dí)竹竿,以钓于淇。岂不尔思?远莫致之。
泉源在左,淇水在右。女子有行,远兄弟父母。
淇水在右,泉源在左。巧笑之瑳(cuō),佩玉之傩(nuó)。
淇水滺滺,桧楫(jí)松舟。驾言出游,以写(xiè)我忧。

竹竿

细细长长的竹竿,垂钓在淇水畔。
怎么能不想你呢?我们相隔如此遥远。

泉水在左边,淇河在右边。
你已出嫁,离开了家园。

淇河在右边,泉源在左边。
怀念你甜甜的微笑,你衣裙佩玉的哨哨。

淇水悠悠,载我独木舟。
驾车出走吧,远游忘忧。

《卫风》竹竿

Bamboo Pole

A slender bamboo pole, fishing in River Qi.
How I miss you; we parted long ago.

Spring well on my left, River Qi on my right.
You have married and left home for far away places.

River Qi on my right, spring well on my left.
I miss your smile's sweetness and the jeweled music
    of your skirt.

River Qi flows ceaselessly, carrying my wooden boat.
I withdrew in my chariot, trying to forget my sorrow.

诗经·国风——英文白话新译

芄兰

芄(wán)兰之支,童子佩觿(xī)。
虽则佩觿,能不我知?
容兮遂兮,垂带悸兮。

芄兰之叶,童子佩韘(shè)。
虽则佩韘,能不我甲(xiá)?
容兮遂兮,垂带悸兮。

萝藤

萝藤夹果成双对,小男儿配了腰角锥。①
虽然配了腰角锥,对我心情不明白。
装腔作势大人样,胆小心虚衣颤荡。

萝藤叶子成双对,小男儿戴了大板指。②
虽然戴了大板指,不敢和我表亲密。
装腔作势大人样,衣衫颤抖孩子气。

---

① 腰角锥为象牙吊饰,用来解开腰带结,象征男孩成年。
② 大板指为拇指形状的玉制或象牙套,射箭时使用;也象征男孩成年。

《卫风》芄兰

Pea Vine

Pea vine pods grow in pairs.
On his belt a child sports an awl. [1]
Though he wears it,
He does not understand me as would a mature lad.
So immature, pretending to be adult,
Yet trembles when he is close to me.

Pea vine leaves grow in pairs.
On his thumb a child sports a ring. [2]
Though he wears it,
He does not know how to please me.
So immature, pretending to be adult,
Yet trembles when he is close to me.

---

[1] An ivory adornment, used to untie girdle knots, symbol of adulthood.
[2] A thimble-like instrument of jade or ivory, used in archery; also a symbol of adulthood.

诗经·国风——英文白话新译

河广

谁谓河广？一苇杭(háng)之。谁谓宋远？跂(qì)予望之。
谁谓河广？曾(zēng)不容刀。谁谓宋远？曾不崇朝(zhāo)。

黄河宽阔

谁说黄河太宽阔？乘一枝苇草可渡过。
谁说宋国太遥远？立着脚尖看得见。

谁说黄河太宽大？一只小船也容不下。
谁说宋国太遥远？一个早晨到那边。

《卫风》河广

Wide River

Who said the Yellow River is too wide —
 it can be crossed on a blade of grass.

Who said the Song nation is too far —
 it can be seen when one's on tiptoe.

Who said the Yellow River is too wide —
 it cannot even hold a small boat.

Who said the Song nation is too far —
 it can be reached by a morning's journey.

诗经·国风——英文白话新译

伯兮

伯兮朅(qiè)兮,邦之桀兮。伯也执殳(shū),为王前驱。
自伯之东,首如飞蓬。岂无膏沐?谁适(dí)为容!
其雨其雨,杲杲(gǎo gǎo)出日。愿言思伯,甘心首疾。
焉得谖(xuān)草?言树之背。愿言思伯,使我心痗(mèi)。

丈夫

我的丈夫高大威风,是国家的英雄。
手持长矛,君王的阵前先锋。

自从丈夫去了东方,我不再对镜梳妆。
不是没有香水和面霜,因为他不在我身旁。

希望落一些小雨,偏偏火热大太阳。
日夜想念我的丈夫,悲伤断肠。

谁会给我"忘忧草"?我会种在中堂。
为什么我这样想你,衷心难忘。

《卫风》伯兮

My Husband

My husband is tall and strong, a hero of our land.
It's he who leads,
Long spear in hand,
The king's great fighting band.

Since he left me for the East,
My beauty I have not adorned.
Not because I lack perfumes and creams,
But because I am not with him — alone, forlorn.

Mocked by searing sun, I thirst for rain;
I miss him so, he who alone can slake
 my drought struck heart.
Who can give me "forget-anguish" grass
 to plant beside my house?
Why do I prefer this misery without balm,
 the ache of a heart alone?

诗经·国风——英文白话新译

有狐

有狐绥绥(suí suí),在彼淇梁。心之忧矣,之子无裳。
有狐绥绥,在彼淇厉。心之忧矣,之子无带。
有狐绥绥,在彼淇侧。心之忧矣,之子无服。

狐狸

有只狐狸慢慢走,在淇水的桥上。
她在默默思念呵,"那人有无新外套?"

有只狐狸慢慢走,在淇水河滩上。
她在默默担忧呵,"那人有无新腰带?"

有只狐狸慢慢走,在淇水的岸上。
她在默默发愁呵,"那人有无新袍子?"

《卫风》有狐

Fox

A fox ambles
On the Qi River bridge.
Her heart suffers —
"Does he have a new robe?"

A fox ambles
On the Qi River beach.
Her heart pains —
"Does he have a new sash?"

A fox ambles
On the Qi River bank.
Her heart breaks —
"Does he have a new coat?"

诗经·国风——英文白话新译

木瓜

投我以木瓜,报之以琼琚(jū);
匪报也,永以为好也。

投我以木桃,报之以琼瑶;
匪报也,永以为好也。

投我以木李,报之以琼玖(jiǔ)。
匪报也,永以为好也。

木瓜

送我一颗木瓜,给你一块佩玉;
不是交换礼物,是友谊的誓约。

送我一颗木桃,给你一块璧玉;
不是交换礼物,是友谊的誓约。

送我一颗李子,给你一块宝石;
不是交换礼物,是友谊的誓约。

《卫风》木瓜

Papaya

Give me a papaya, I'll give you an ornament of jade;
Not a gift exchange, just a pledge between friends.

Give me a peach, I'll give you a jade Bi piece;
Not a gift exchange, just a pledge between friends.

Give me a plum, I'll give you a gem stone;
Not a gift exchange, just a pledge between friends.

Prayer

王风
Airs of Wang
65—74

诗经·国风——英文白话新译

黍离

彼黍离离,彼稷(jì)之苗。行迈靡靡(mǐ mǐ),中心摇摇。
知我者谓我心忧,不知我者谓我何求。
悠悠苍天,此何人哉?

彼黍离离,彼稷之穗。行迈靡靡,中心如醉。
知我者谓我心忧,不知我者谓我何求。
悠悠苍天,此何人哉?

彼黍离离,彼稷之实。行迈靡靡,中心如噎。
知我者谓我心忧,不知我者谓我何求。
悠悠苍天,此何人哉?

黍穗

那片黍子一列列排着,那片高粱一列列站着,
步履沉重,我慢慢的走着,内心摇晃不安着,
知道我的人说:"他有忧愁",
不知道我的人问:"他在找寻什么?"
"苍天啊,苍天,什么事把我逼成这样?"

那片黍穗一列列仰着,那片高粱穗一列列望着,
步履沉重,我慢慢的走着,迷迷糊糊如醉汉,
知道我的人说:"他有忧愁",
不知道我的人问:"他在找寻什么?"
"苍天啊,苍天,什么事把我逼得这样?"

黍子熟了,穗子沉甸甸的垂着,
高粱熟了,穗子沉甸甸的立着,
步履沉重,我慢慢的走着,哽咽如噎,
知道我的人说:"他有忧愁",
不知道我的人问:"他在找寻什么?"
"苍天啊,苍天,是什么把我逼成这样?"

《王风》黍离

Millet

Millet seedlings grow in rows.
    Sorghum seedlings grow in rows.
Slowly I walk, with heavy steps. My heart races.
Those who know me say, "He is sad."
Those who do not know me ask, "What is he looking for?"
Oh, merciful heaven above —
What has forced me to become such a man?

Millet tassels stand in rows.
    Sorghum tassels stand in rows.
Slowly I walk with heavy steps, confused and far from sober.
Those who know me say, "He is sad."
Those who do not know me ask, "What is he looking for?"
Oh, merciful heaven above —
What has forced me to become such a man?

Ripe millet tassels bow in rows.
    Ripe sorghum tassels rise in rows.
Slowly I walk with heavy steps, my heart choking with pain.
Those who know me say, "He is sad."
Those who do not know me ask, "What is he looking for?"
Oh, merciful heaven above —
What has forced me to become a man like this?

诗经·国风——英文白话新译

君子于役

君子于役,不知其期,曷至哉?
鸡栖于埘(shí),日之夕矣,羊牛下来。
君子于役,如之何勿思!

君子于役,不日不月,曷其有佸(huó)?
鸡栖于桀,日之夕矣,羊牛下括(kuò)。
君子于役,苟无饥渴!

丈夫远征

丈夫远征去了,不知要多久?什么时候才回来呢?
黄昏又到了,鸡已回笼,牛羊已下山。
丈夫在远方,如何不思量。

丈夫远征去了,数不清的岁月呵,什么时候再相聚呢?
黄昏又到了,鸡已回笼,牛羊已下山。
丈夫在远方,祝福他无饥无寒勿受伤。

《王风》君子于役

My Husband Fights in the War

Far away my husband fights.
How long this war will last I do not know,
Nor when he'll return to me.
The sun is setting once again.
Chickens are returning to their pen;
Sheep and cattle descend from the hills.
Where is my husband?
How I yearn for him.

Far away my husband fights in the war.
I have lost count of the days he's been gone.
I do not know when we shall be rejoined.
The sun is setting once again.
Chickens are returning to their roost;
Sheep and cattle descend from the hills.
Where is my husband? I can only pray
He does not suffer hunger, thirst and chill.

诗经·国风——英文白话新译

君子阳阳

君子阳阳,左执簧;右招我由房,其乐只且(zhǐ jū)。
君子陶陶,左执翿(dào);右招我由敖,其乐只且。

君子喜洋洋

君子喜洋洋,左手持笙簧;
右手招我进房,欢乐似疯狂。
君子乐陶陶,左手持羽毛;
右手招我舞蹈,欢乐无限好。

《王风》君子阳阳

An Elated Gentleman

A gentleman, elated, holds a flute in his left hand;
With his right hand, beckons me to his room.
I am thrilled.

A gentleman, elated, holds a feather in his left hand;
With his right hand, invites me to dance.
I am delighted.

诗经·国风——英文白话新译

扬之水

扬之水,不流束薪。
彼其之子,不与我戍申。
怀哉怀哉,曷(hé)月予还归哉!

扬之水,不流束楚。
彼其之子,不与我戍甫。
怀哉怀哉,曷月予还归哉!

扬之水,不流束蒲。
彼其之子,不与我戍许。
怀哉怀哉,曷月予还归哉!

河水激扬

激扬的河水,漂不走一捆柴薪?①
我的意中人,不能与我在一起防卫申,
深深的思念,绵绵的思念。
何时才能回归家园?

激扬的河水,漂不走一捆荆楚?
我的意中人,不能与我在一起防卫甫,
深深的思念,绵绵的思念。
何时才能回归家园?

激扬的河水,漂不走一捆柳蒲?
我的意中人,不能与我在一起防卫许,
深深的思念,绵绵的思念。
何时才能回归家园?

---

① 此处所指为水占,将一捆木柴投入河流卜凶吉卦,木柴漂远为吉,反之为凶。

《王风》扬之水

Swift Water

Water flows swiftly — can it carry a bundle
 of firewood? ①
My love is not with me here, as I guard Shen.
I miss her, I miss her so —
When can I go home?

Water runs swiftly — can it carry a bundle
 of jujube branches?
My love is not with me here, as I guard Fu.
I miss her, I miss her so —
When can I go home?

Water flows swiftly — can it carry a bundle
 of willow branches?
My love is not with me here, as I guard Xu.
I miss her, I miss her so —
When can I go home?

---

① This poem likely refers to a local belief in fortune telling by water. Bundles of wood thrown into a stream foretold good fortune if they traveled far, and ill-fortune if they did not.

诗经·国风——英文白话新译

中谷有蓷

中谷有蓷(tuī)，暵(hàn)其干矣。
有女仳(pǐ)离，嘅其叹矣。
嘅其叹矣，遇人之艰难矣！

中谷有蓷，暵其修矣。
有女仳离，条其歗(xiào)矣。
条其歗矣，遇人之不淑矣！

中谷有蓷，暵其湿(qì)矣。
有女仳离，啜其泣矣。
啜其泣矣，何嗟及矣！

谷地里的益母草

谷地里有益母草，被太阳灼伤了。
有位女子被遗弃，唉声叹息。
唉声叹息，嫁错了人呵！

谷地里有益母草，被太阳晒焦了。
有位女子被遗弃，吞声饮泣。
吞声饮泣，嫁错了人呵！

谷地里有益母草，被太阳晒死了。
有位女子被遗弃，痛哭流涕。
痛哭流涕，后悔不及了呵！

《王风》中谷有蓷

Motherwort in the Valley

Motherwort in the valley, seared white by the sun.
An abandoned woman grieves —
She regrets wedding the wrong man.

Motherwort in the valley, scorched black by the sun.
An abandoned woman sobs —
She regrets marrying the wrong man.

Motherwort in the valley, slain by heaven's blaze.
An abandoned woman wails —
Wails inconsolably, knowing all is too late.

诗经·国风——英文白话新译

兔爰

有兔爰爰(yuán),雉离于罗。
我生之初,尚无为;
我生之后,逢此百罹。尚寐无吡(é)!

有兔爰爰,雉离于罦(fú)。
我生之初,尚无造;
我生之后,逢此百忧。尚寐无觉!

有兔爰爰,雉离于罿(tóng)。
我生之初,尚无庸;
我生之后,逢此百凶。尚寐无聪!

兔儿轻轻跳

兔儿轻轻的跳,野鸡落网了。
当我幼年,天下平安。
长大了,一片混乱。
睡吧!什么也不说了。

兔儿轻轻的跳,野鸡落网了。
当我幼年,天下平安。
长大了,处处劫难。
睡吧!什么也不看了。

兔儿轻轻的跳,野鸡落网了。
当我幼年,天下平安。
长大了,战祸连连。
睡吧!什么也不听了。

《王风》兔爱

A Rabbit Hops Gently

A rabbit hops gently; a pheasant is caught in a snare.
When I was born, all was quiet.
When I grew up, chaos engulfed the world.
Sleep! No need to talk any more.

A rabbit hops gently; a pheasant is caught in a snare.
When I was born, all was peaceful.
When I grew up, disasters prevailed.
Sleep! No need to see any more.

A rabbit hops gently; a pheasant is caught in a snare.
When I was born, things were harmonious.
Since I've been grown, we've known only war.
Sleep! No need to hear any more.

诗经·国风——英文白话新译

葛藟

绵绵葛藟(lěi)，在河之浒。
终远兄弟，谓他人父。
谓他人父，亦莫我顾！

绵绵葛藟，在河之涘(sì)。
终远兄弟，谓他人母。
谓他人母，亦莫我有！

绵绵葛藟，在河之漘(chún)。
终远兄弟，谓他人昆。
谓他人昆，亦莫我闻。

野葡萄

绵绵野葡萄，生在河水边。
远离了家园，叫异姓人为"父亲"。
虽然叫父亲，也得不到父子的温馨。

绵绵野葡萄，生在河水湄。
远离了家室，叫异姓人为"母亲"。
虽然叫母亲，也得不到母子的怜惜。

绵绵野葡萄，生在河水旁。
远离了家乡，叫异姓人为"兄长"。
虽然叫兄长，也得不到兄长的呵护。

《王风》葛藟

Wild Grapes

At the river's edge, wild grapes grow.
I left home long ago,
Calling a stranger "Father."
Even though I called him "Father,"
No affection I invited was ever requited.

On the river bank, wild grapes grow.
I left home long ago,
Calling a stranger "Mother."
Even though I called her "Mother,"
No love I gave was ever repaid.

On the river front, wild grapes bloom.
I left home long ago,
Calling a stranger "Brother."
Even though I called him "Brother,"
No warmth I craved he ever gave.

诗经·国风——英文白话新译

采葛

彼采葛兮,一日不见,如三月兮。
彼采萧兮,一日不见,如三秋兮。
彼采艾兮,一日不见,如三岁兮。

采蒿藤

她采蒿藤去了,一天见不到,仿佛三月了。
她采荻蒿去了,一天见不到,仿佛三季了。
她采艾菜去了,一天见不到,仿佛三年了。

《王风》采葛

Gathering Ge

She's gone to gather Ge;
I've not seen her for a whole day long —
As if three months had passed.

She's gone to gather Xao;
I've not seen her for a whole day long —
As if three seasons had passed.

She's gone to gather Ai;
I've not seen her for a whole day long —
As if three years had passed.

诗经·国风——英文白话新译

大车

大车槛槛(kǎn kǎn)，毳(cuì)衣如菼(tǎn)。
岂不尔思？畏子不敢。
大车啍啍(tūn tūn)，毳衣如璊(mén)。
岂不尔思？畏子不奔。
谷则异室，死则同穴。谓予不信，有如皦(jiǎo)日。

大车

大车坑坑的走了，你的雨衣荻绿色，
我要跟你同行，只怕你意志不坚决。

大车啍啍的走了，你的雨衣土黄色，
不是我不想跟你走，只怕你中途会变心。

活着不能同一房，死了跟你同一坟，
如果你不信我的话，白热太阳是证人。

《王风》大车

Large Wagon

"Klunk. Klunk. Klunk." There goes your wagon.
Your raincoat is reed-green.
I will miss you. I want to go with you,
But I fear you may change your mind.

"Creak. Creak. Creak." There goes your wagon.
Your raincoat is earthen brown.
I will miss you. I want to go with you,
But I fear you may abandon me.

Alive, we cannot live in the same room.
In death, we shall be buried in the same tomb.
If you doubt my sincerity,
Our witness is the white sun above.

73

诗经·国风——英文白话新译

丘中有麻

丘中有麻,彼留子嗟。彼留子嗟,将(qiāng)其来施施(shī shī)。
丘中有麦,彼留子国。彼留子国,将其来食。
丘中有李,彼留之子。彼留之子,贻我佩玖(pèi jiǔ)。

丘陵地有麻田

麻田在丘陵地,刘子嗟先生在哪里?
我的子嗟呀!他施施来迟。

麦田在丘陵地,刘子嗟先生在哪里?
我的子嗟呀!他会与我共食。

李子林在丘陵地,刘家有位俊男儿,
我的子嗟呀!他赠我块玉璧。

《王风》丘中有麻

Hemp Grows in the Hills

Hemp grows in the hills.
Where is Liu Zi-jie?
My dear Zi-jie.
Over there; slowly he walks to me.

Wheat field in the hills.
Where is Liu Zi-jie?
My dear Zi-jie.
He comes to dine with me.

Plums grow in the hills.
A handsome lad in Liu's family,
My dear Zi-jie.
He has given me a jade brooch.

郑风
Airs of Zheng
75—95

诗经·国风——英文白话新译

缁衣

缁(zī)衣之宜兮,敝予又改为兮。
适子之馆兮,还予授子之粲(càn)兮。

缁衣之好兮,敝予又改造兮。
适子之馆兮,还予授子之粲兮。

缁衣之席兮,敝予又改作兮。
适子之馆兮,还予授子之粲兮。

黑色制服

为你缝一套黑制服,穿旧了,我会再修补,
穿了制服去办公,等你回来,晚饭已在等。

黑制服合身又漂亮,穿旧了,我会再修装,
穿了制服去办公,等你回来,晚饭已在等。

黑制服舒适又流行,穿旧了,我会再裁缝,
穿了制服去办公,等你回来,晚饭已在等。

《郑风》缁衣

Black Uniform

I made you a black uniform;
When it has frayed, I shall make repairs.
Go to work in your uniform.
When you return, your dinner will be prepared.

Your uniform fits, handsomely cut.
When it has frayed, I shall make repairs.
Go to work in your uniform.
When you return, your dinner will be prepared.

Your uniform is smart and stylish.
When it has frayed, I shall make repairs.
Go to work in your uniform.
When you return, your dinner will be prepared.

诗经·国风——英文白话新译

将仲子

将(qiāng)仲子兮,无逾我里,无折我树杞(qǐ)。
岂敢爱之?畏我父母。
仲可怀也,父母之言,亦可畏也。

将仲子兮,无逾我墙,无折我树桑。
岂敢爱之?畏我诸兄。
仲可怀也,诸兄之言,亦可畏也。

将仲子兮,无逾我园,无折我树檀。
岂敢爱之?畏人之多言。
仲可怀也,人之多言,亦可畏也。

二先生

二先生,不要到我家,不要折断我柳树,
我并不在乎柳树,我是在乎父母。
我当然爱你,父母的话也要服从呀。

二先生,不要爬我墙,不要折断我桑树,
我并不在乎桑树,我是在乎兄长。
我当然爱你,兄长们的话也要听呀。

二先生,不要到我房门,不要折断我檀树,
我并不在乎檀树,我是在乎街人和邻居。
我当然爱你,我是怕蜚短流长呀。

《郑风》将仲子

Qiang Zhong-zi (Second Son)

My dear sir, do not come to my house.
Do not break my willow tree.
I do not care about the tree;
I do care about my parents.
Of course I love you,
But I have to obey my parents.

My dear sir, do not climb my wall.
Do not break my mulberry tree.
I do not care about the tree;
I do care about my brothers.
Of course I love you,
But I have to listen to my brothers.

My dear sir, do not come to my door.
Do not break my sandalwood tree.
I do not care about the tree;
I do care about others.
Of course I love you,
But I fear rumours more.

诗经·国风——英文白话新译

叔于田

叔于田,巷无居人。岂无居人?不如叔也,洵美且仁。
叔于狩,巷无饮酒。岂无饮酒?不如叔也,洵美且好。
叔适野,巷无服马。岂无服马?不如叔也,洵美且武。

我的阿哥打猎去了

我的阿哥打猎去了,巷中已无可交之人。
并非没有可交之人,只是无人像他一样强壮温存。

我的阿哥打猎去了,巷中已无喝酒之人。
并非没有喝酒之人,只是无人像他一样雄心豪饮。

我的阿哥去野外了,巷中已无骑马之人。
并非没有骑马之人,只是无人像他一样矫健英俊。

170

《郑风》叔于田

My Man is Out Hunting

My man is out hunting.
No one can be a friend in my lane.
It is not that no one can be a friend,
But none is as kind as he.

My man is out hunting.
No one can drink in my lane.
It is not that no one can drink,
But none has his capacity.

My man has gone to the wilds.
No one can ride a horse in my lane.
It is not that no one can ride,
But none can match his skill.

诗经·国风——英文白话新译

大叔于田

叔于田,乘乘马。执辔(pèi)如组,两骖(cān)如舞。
叔在薮(sǒu),火烈具举。襢(tǎn)裼(xī)暴虎,献于公所。
将叔无狃(niǔ),戒其伤女。

叔于田,乘(chéng)乘(shèng)黄。
两服上襄,两骖雁行(yàn háng)。
叔在薮,火烈具扬。叔善射忌,又良御忌。
抑磬控忌,抑纵送忌。

叔于田,乘乘鸨。两服齐首,两骖如手。
叔在薮,火烈具阜。叔马慢忌,叔发罕忌。
抑释掤(bīng)忌,抑鬯(chàng)弓忌。

阿叔出外打猎

阿叔出外去打猎,四匹骏马拉猎车。
手舞缰辔如缎带,两马车边步井然。
来到猎场,燃起猎火。赤背搏虎,献给公侯。
公侯:"小心啊,阿叔,留得健康,不要受伤。"

阿叔出外去打猎,四匹黄马拉猎车。
两马夹车辕,两马护车边。
如雁阵飞行,四马奔腾。
来到猎场,燃起猎火。箭术百发百中,驭马技艺湛精。
忽而勒马慢行,忽而放缰疾冲。

阿叔出外去打猎,四匹花马拉猎车。
两马夹车辕,两马护车边。
来到猎场,燃起猎火。猎车放慢,停止射箭。
箭入筒,弓入袋,缓缓回来。

172

《郑风》大叔于田

Shu is Out Hunting

Shu has gone out hunting. Four horses draw his cart.
He holds the reins as if playing with silk ribbons.
The two outside horses, racing dancers.
When he reaches the hunting field, a circle of fire is lit.
He leaves the cart, seizes a tiger with bare hands,
Presenting it to his lord.
Lord: "My man, be careful, you are needed for our wars."

Shu has gone out hunting, seated behind four yellow horses:
Two in the middle, two on the sides.
Like the wings of flying geese, they pull together.
When he reaches the hunting field, a circle of fire is lit.
His archery skill astonishes, matched only by his
    horsemanship.
The instant he reins his horses in, their pace begins to slack;
The second he relaxes them, his charges resume their flight.

Shu has gone out hunting. Four dappled greys draw his cart.
Two run in the middle;
Like his arms, two pull on each side.
When he reaches the hunting field, a circle of fire is lit.
Shu slows down; he shoots no more.
Returns the arrows to their quiver,
The bow into its case.
He returns home.

诗经·国风——英文白话新译

清人

清人在彭,驷介旁旁。二矛重英,河上乎翱翔。
清人在消,驷介麃麃(biāo biāo)。二矛重乔,河上乎逍遥。
清人在轴(zhú),驷介陶陶。左旋右抽,中军作好(zuò hǎo)。

清城的壮丁

清城的壮丁,驻防在彭城。
四匹披甲战马,两柄长矛交错,
沿着黄河岸,来回巡索。

清城的壮丁,驻防在消城。
四匹披甲战马,两柄长矛摇动,
沿着黄河岸,他们来回练兵。

清城的壮丁,驻防在轴城,披甲的战马疾跑,
武官左手持旗,右手抽刀,神采英武发号施令。

《郑风》清人

Men from Qing

Men from Qing guard the city of Peng.
Four horses wear bright armour.
Two red tasseled spears: one rises, the other dips,
Along the Yellow River, on a merry march.

Men from Qing guard the city of Xiao.
Four horses bear bright armour.
Two pheasant feathered spears wildly whip the air,
Along the Yellow River, on a joyful march.

Men from Qing guard the city of Zhu.
Four horses run beside the river.
In his left hand the commander holds a flag —
    in his right, a sword.
He beams in anticipation, eagerly issuing orders.

诗经·国风——英文白话新译

羔裘

羔裘如濡,洵(xún)直且侯。彼其之子,舍(shě)命不渝。
羔裘豹饰,孔武有力。彼其之子,邦之司直。
羔裘晏兮,三英粲兮。彼其之子,邦之彦兮。

羔羊皮袍

羔羊皮袍软绵绵,大方美观。
穿皮袍的那位君子,耿耿称职。

羊袍镶着豹皮袖,英雄服饰。
穿皮袍的那位君子,正直无私。

羊皮袍光滑丽艳,丝花绣边。
穿皮袍的那位君子,国家俊彦。

《郑风》羔裘

Lamb Skin Coat

A lamb skin coat, soft and smooth;
Its wearer, dutiful and loyal.

A lamb skin coat with leopard cuffs, a warrior's prize;
Any who's mantled thus, must be honest, must be just.

Embroidered with bright silk flowers,
This lamb skin coat adorns the leader of our land.

诗经·国风——英文白话新译

遵大路

遵大路兮，掺(shǎn)执子之袪(qū)兮，
无我恶(wù)兮，不寁(jié)故也。

遵大路兮，掺执子之手兮，
无我魗(chǒu)兮，不寁好也。

走在路上

沿着大路跟你走，牢牢拉住你袖口。
不要厌我而分手，岂可一旦不念旧。

沿着大路跟你走，紧紧抓住你的手。
不要弃我而远去，旧日恩情怎可丢。

《郑风》遵大路

Walking on the Street

Along the lane I walk with you,
Hanging onto your sleeve.
Please don't think I am unworthy;
Remember the good times.

Along the street I walk with you,
Gripping your hand tightly.
Please do not leave me, please my dear;
Remember how we were.

诗经·国风——英文白话新译

女曰鸡鸣

女曰鸡鸣,士曰昧旦。
子兴视夜,明星有烂。
将翱将翔,弋(yì)凫(fú)与雁。

弋言加之,与子宜之。
宜言饮酒,与子偕老。
琴瑟在御,莫不静好。

知子之来之,杂佩以赠之。
知子之顺之,杂佩以问之。
知子之好之,杂佩以报之。

鸡已啼叫

女:"鸡已啼叫。"
男:"天尚未晓。"
女:"快些起床。
　　明星煌煌,正是行猎时光,
　　射些鸭雁回家共享。"

女:"带了野味回来,我会为你烹煎。
　　一块饮酒,偕老白头。
　　鼓瑟弹琴①,美好安闲。"

男:"知道你对我体贴,送你一块玉佩。
　　知道你对我温顺,送你一块玉饰。
　　知道你对我爱惜,送你一块玉璧。"

---

① 一组乐器,通常一起演奏,参考"关雎"(鱼翠)一诗注释。

《郑风》女曰鸡鸣

Cocks Are Crowing

She:
    "Cocks are crowing...."
He:
    "But dawn has yet to break...."
She:
    "Please get up and look at the sky.
    The morning stars are shining;
    Good time for hunting.
    Go shoot some wild geese and ducks.
    When you bring the birds home,
    I will dress them
    And cook a meal for you.
    Together, until our hair turns white;
    I will play Qin, you will play Se,[①]
    Living in peace and harmony."
He:
    "You are so considerate.
    I will give you a piece of my girdle jade.
    You are so thoughtful.
    I will give you a piece of my girdle jade.
    You are so true.
    Here is a piece of jade, my heart."

[①] Paired instruments, always played together. See note to Poem #1, "Kingfisher", pp.2-3, above.

诗经·国风——英文白话新译

有女同车

有女同车,颜如舜华(huā)。
将翱将翔,佩玉琼琚。
彼美孟姜,洵美且都。

有女同行,颜如舜英。
将翱将翔,佩玉将将(qiāng qiāng)。
彼美孟姜,德音不忘。

同车女子

同车的有位女子,木槿花一般美丽。
马车狂奔疾驶,她裙上玉饰多姿。
她是美女孟姜啊,又文雅又标致。

同车有位女子,木槿花一样美丽。
马车疾奔飞翔,她裙上佩玉锵锵。
她是美女孟姜啊,她的声音令人难忘。

《郑风》有女同车

A Girl in Our Carriage

A girl sits in our carriage,
A vermillion hibiscus flower.
As our carriage dashes,
Crimson adornments on her skirt appear.
Graceful and elegant,
Meng-jiang, the beauty of our land.

A girl rides in our carriage,
A vermillion hibiscus bloom.
As our carriage dashes,
Her jade jewels jingle.
Graceful and elegant,
Meng-jiang, the beauty of our land.

诗经·国风——英文白话新译

山有扶苏

山有扶苏,隰(xí)有荷华(huā)。不见子都,乃见狂且(jū)。
山有乔松,隰有游龙。不见子充,乃见狡童。

山地有桑树

山地上有桑树,隰地里有荷花。
没有看到我帅哥男友,却碰到个可憎的恶徒。

山地上有高松,隰地里有红蓼。
没有看到我帅哥男友,却碰到个混帐的滑头。

《郑风》山有扶苏

Highlands Mulberries

Mulberry trees on the highlands,
Lotus flowers in the lowlands.
I did not see my handsome boyfriend,
But met a repulsive swine instead.

Lofty pines on the highlands,
Dragon flowers in the lowlands.
I did not see my handsome boyfriend,
But met a lumpish lout instead.

诗经·国风——英文白话新译

萚兮

萚(tuò)兮萚兮,风其吹女(rǔ)! 叔兮伯兮,倡予和(hè)女!
萚兮萚兮,风其漂女! 叔兮伯兮,倡予要(yāo)女!

黄叶

黄叶,黄叶——
秋风起,纷纷飘落,
亲爱的兄弟们,一起来唱歌,
我领头,你们跟着。

黄叶,黄叶——
秋风起,纷纷飘落,
亲爱的兄弟们,一起来唱歌,
你们领头,我来接着。

《郑风》萚兮

Autumn Leaves

Autumn leaves, autumn leaves —
They will fall when the wind blows.
My dear brothers, let us sing.
I'll set the tune for you to follow.

Autumn leaves, autumn leaves —
They will fly when the wind blows.
My dear brothers, let us sing.
You'll set the tune for me to follow.

诗经·国风——英文白话新译

狡童

彼狡童兮,不与我言兮。
维子之故,使我不能餐兮。

彼狡童兮,不与我食兮。
维子之故,使我不能息兮。

滑头男子

那个滑头男子,和我呕气,
不和我讲话了啊。
为了他的缘故,
食不下咽了啊。

那个滑头男子,和我呕气,
不与我吃饭了啊。
为了他的缘故,
不能喘气了啊。

《郑风》狡童

Silly Man

What a silly man he is.
He's not talked to me for days.
Because of this,
I cannot eat.

What a silly man he is.
For days he's not taken meals with me.
Because of this,
I can barely breathe.

诗经·国风——英文白话新译

褰裳

子惠思我,褰(qiān)裳涉溱(zhēn)。
子不我思,岂无他人？狂童之狂也且！

子惠思我,褰裳涉洧(wěi)。
子不我思,岂无他士？狂童之狂也且！

提起长衫

如果你爱我,就该提起长衫,渡过溱河来看我。
如果不爱我,难到没有别人吗？你真是个大傻瓜。

如果你爱我,就该提起长衫,渡过洧河来看我。
如果不爱我,难到没有别人吗？你真是个大傻瓜。

Lift Your Gown

If you love me, you'll lift your gown,
Cross the River Zhen and come see me.
If you don't love me, others will.
Don't be such a stubborn child.

If you love me, you'll lift your gown,
Cross the River Wei and come see me.
If you don't love me, others will.
Don't be such a stubborn child.

诗经·国风——英文白话新译

丰

子之丰兮,俟我乎巷兮,悔予不送兮。
子之昌兮,俟我乎堂兮,悔予不将兮。
衣锦褧(jiǒng)衣,裳锦褧裳。叔兮伯兮,驾予与行。
裳锦褧裳,衣锦褧衣。叔兮伯兮,驾予与归。

体面

你是如此体面,老是在巷口等我,
后悔分手时,没有对你说实话。

你是如此高雅,老是在门外等我,
后悔分手时,没有依依送你。

穿上锦服,披上罩衣。
可爱的男子,驾车来吧,我要和你在一起。

穿上锦服,披上罩衣。
可爱的男子,驾车来吧,我要嫁给你。

《郑风》丰

Handsome

At the corner of the street you would always wait for me,
So elegant.
I regret not telling you my secret.

At my house you would always wait for me,
So handsome.
I regret not saying goodbye to you.

I'll put on my new dress and my embroidered shawl.
My dear man, please come with your wagon
    and take me away.

I'll put on my new dress and my embroidered shawl.
My dear man, please come with your wagon
    and I will marry you.

诗经·国风——英文白话新译

东门之墠

东门之墠(shàn)，茹藘(rú lǘ)在阪。其室则迩，其人甚远。
东门之栗，有践家室。岂不尔思？子不我即。

东门外的土山

东门外有座小土山，山坡上有片茜草园，
他的家就在眼前，他的人却如此遥远。

东门外有棵栗树，栗子树下有家住户，
我想念他朝朝暮暮，他却不来与我相处。

《郑风》东门之墠

A Hill Outside the Eastern Gate

Beyond the Eastern Gate a hill rises.
Madder grows upon its slopes.
His home — so near,
His person — so far.

His house sits under the chestnut tree,
Outside the Eastern Gate.
I miss him so,
Yet he never comes to see me.

诗经·国风——英文白话新译

风雨

风雨凄凄,鸡鸣喈喈(jiē jiē)。既见君子,云胡不夷。
风雨潇潇,鸡鸣胶胶(jiāo jiāo)。既见君子,云胡不瘳(chōu)。
风雨如晦,鸡鸣不已。既见君子,云胡不喜。

风雨

凄风苦雨,雄鸡叫白了长夜。
又见到了你,怎不满心感谢。

风雨潇潇,雄鸡不停的叫。
又见到了你,我的相思病好了。

风雨漆漆,雄鸡一直在啼。
又见到了你,怎不满心欢喜。

《郑风》风雨

Wind and Rain

Roosters crow in the wind and rain.
Now that I have seen you, my worries have ceased.

While the storm rages on, the roosters continue crowing.
Now that I have seen you, my heart is healed.

Through another night of wind and rain,
    roosters remain restless.
Now that I have seen you, my heart rejoices.

诗经·国风——英文白话新译

子衿

青青子衿,悠悠我心。
纵我不往,子宁不嗣音?

青青子佩,悠悠我思。
纵我不往,子宁不来?

挑兮达(tà)兮,在城阙(què)兮。
一日不见,如三月兮!

你的衣领

青青衣领的男子,我一直在想你。
纵然我没去找你,你何不捎个信息?

青青佩玉的男子,我一直在想你。
纵然我没去找你,为何不来看我呢?

悠悠恍恍,独自徘徊,我在城楼一角等你。
一天不见,仿佛是三个月了啊。

《郑风》子衿

Your Blue Collar

Man with the blue collar,
I have been thinking of you.
Because I cannot go to you,
Why don't you send me a message?

Man with the blue sash,
I have been thinking of you.
Although I cannot go to you,
Why can't you come to see me?

I have been wandering here and there,
Waiting for you at the city gate.
A whole day without seeing you
Drags like three months passing.

诗经·国风——英文白话新译

扬之水

扬之水,不流束楚。
终鲜(xiǎn)兄弟,维予与女(rǔ)。
无信人之言,人实迋(guàng)女。

扬之水,不流束薪。
终鲜兄弟,维予二人。
无信人之言,人实不信。

山溪奔流

山溪奔流滔滔,带不走一捆荆条。①
我们无兄无弟,只有我和你。
不要听信谎言,不要被人欺骗。

山溪奔流滚滚,带不走一捆柴薪。
我们无兄无弟,只有我和你。
不要听信谎言,不要被人欺骗。

---

① 参见第68首《扬之水》(河水激扬)关于水占之说明。

《郑风》扬之水

Turbulent Water

The surging mountain streams
Cannot carry a bundle of hawthorn.①
We have no brothers,
Just you and me.
Do not believe the rumours.
Do not be deceived by others.

The swift mountain stream
Cannot carry a bundle of firewood.
We have no brothers,
Just you and me.
Do not believe the rumours.
Do not be deceived by others.

---

① See note to poem 68, "Swift Water," pp.150-151, above, about fortune telling by water.

诗经·国风——英文白话新译

出其东门

出其东门,有女如云。
虽则如云,匪我思存。
缟(gǎo)衣綦(qí)巾,聊乐我员。

出其闉闍(yīn dū),有女如荼(tú)。
虽则如荼,匪我思且(jū)。
缟衣茹藘(rú lǘ),聊可与娱。

走出东门

走出东门,女子们结队如云。
虽则结队如云,无一是我意中人。
意中人,白衣青巾,悦目赏心。

走出外廓,女子们结队如茅花。
虽则茅花芸芸,无一是我心上人。
心上人,白衣红巾,相处欢欣。

《郑风》出其东门

Walking Out the Eastern Gate

Outside the Eastern Gate, girls — flowering, downy clouds.
Although there are many, not one is my sweetheart.
My sweetheart — in a white dress and in a blue scarf —
She is the one I miss.

Beyond the city walls, girls — floating pampas plumes.
Although there are many, not one is my sweetheart.
My sweetheart — in a white dress and in a red scarf —
She is the one I love.

诗经·国风——英文白话新译

野有蔓草

野有蔓草,零露漙(tuán)兮。
有美一人,清扬婉兮。
邂逅相遇,适我愿兮。

野有蔓草,零露瀼瀼(ráng ráng)。
有美一人,婉如清扬。
邂逅相遇,与子偕臧。

青草蔓蔓

郊野青草蔓蔓,露珠湿亮涟涟。
有位姣好姑娘,眉目清秀甜甜。
我们偶然相遇,得偿终生心愿。

郊野青草蔓蔓,露珠洗亮颤颤。
有位姣好姑娘,眉目清秀甜甜。
我们偶然相遇,结下美满姻缘。

《郑风》野有蔓草

Green Grass

Green grass thrives in the wild,
    where dew drops glow like pearls.
There is a lovely maiden, so sweet, with diaphanous eyes.
We met accidentally; by surprise, this my dream fulfilled.

Green grass flourishes in the wild,
    where dew drops shimmer like pearls.
There is a beautiful maiden, so sweet, with deep pooled eyes.
By chance we met; such a lovely jolt, this my dream fulfilled.

诗经·国风——英文白话新译

溱洧

溱(zhēn)与洧(wěi),方涣涣兮。士与女,方秉蕑(jiān)兮。
女曰观乎？士曰既且(cú)。且(qiě)往观乎！
洧之外,洵讦(xū)且乐。
维士与女,伊其相谑,赠之以勺药(sháo yào)。

溱与洧,浏其清矣。士与女,殷其盈矣。
女曰观乎？士曰既且。且往观乎！洧之外,洵吁且乐。
维士与女,伊其将谑,赠之以勺药。

溱河与洧河

溱河与洧河,水流涣涣。少年情人们,手持香兰。
女："到溱河那边去吧！"
男："我已去过了。"
女："再去一次嘛,水旁是个好地方。"
男与女,打情骂俏,互赠一枝芍药。

溱河与洧河,水流淙淙。少年情人们,结伴踏青。
女："到洧河那边去吧！"
男："我已去过了。"
女："再去一次嘛,水旁是个好地方。"
男与女,打情骂俏,互赠一枝芍药。

《郑风》溱洧

The Zhen and Wei Rivers

Along the musical flow of the Zhen and Wei,
Young lovers walk and talk, holding orchids.
Girl: "Shall we go to the Zhen?"
Boy: "I have already been there."
Girl: "Let's go again, it's a heavenly place."
They stroll and tease, exchanging peonies.

Along the musical flow of the Zhen and Wei,
Young lovers walk and talk, holding orchids.
Girl: "Shall we go to the Wei?"
Boy: "I have been there already."
Girl: "Let's go again, it's a heavenly place."
They stroll and tease, exchanging peonies.

齐风
Airs of Qi
96—106

诗经·国风——英文白话新译

鸡鸣

"鸡既鸣矣,朝既盈矣。"
"匪鸡则鸣,苍蝇之声。"

"东方明矣,朝既昌矣。"
"匪东方则明,月出之光。"

"虫飞薨薨(hōng hōng),甘与子同梦。"
"会且归矣,无庶予子憎。"

鸡鸣

妻:"雄鸡啼叫,早朝的官员到齐了。"
夫:"不是鸡鸣,是苍蝇的嗡嗡。"

妻:"东方已白,早朝的官员挤满了。"
夫:"东方未亮,白的是月光。"

妻:"唉哟!天已大亮,群虫飞翔,
我也想伴你多躺一躺,但是,
就要散朝了,你要迟到受罚了。"

《齐风》鸡鸣

Cocks are Crowing

Wife: "The cocks are crowing; the King's council's begun."
Husband: "It's not cocks,
It's the buzzing sound of flies."

Wife: "The East glows white;
    the King's meeting's in session."
Husband: "The morn has not yet come;
It's the bright moonrise."

Wife: "Ai-yoo! It's morning; the insects are flying.
I too want to linger, wrapped in slumber with you….
You may lose your position, I fear,
    if you're late for the meeting."

诗经·国风——英文白话新译

还

子之还(xuán)兮,遭我乎峱(náo)之间兮。
并驱从两肩兮,揖我谓我儇(xuān)兮。

子之茂兮,遭我乎峱之道兮。
并驱从两牡兮,揖我谓我好兮。

子之昌兮,遭我乎峱之阳兮。
并驱从两狼兮,揖我谓我臧兮。

敏捷

你是如此敏捷哟,
我们相遇在峱山之间哟。
两马并驰,追逐两头野猪哟,
你作揖,夸我身手利落哟。

你是如此健美哟,
我们相遇在峱山道上哟。
两马并驰,追逐两头野獐哟,
你拱手,说我姿势优美哟。

你是如此强壮哟,
我们相遇在峱山之南哟。
两马并驰,追逐两头野狼哟,
你敬礼,说我身体完善哟。

《齐风》还

You are So Agile

You are so agile — O!
We met between the Nao Hills,
Riding together, chasing a brace of boars.
You greeted me saying, "You are so agile."

You are so nimble — O!
We met on the way to the Nao Hills,
Riding together, chasing two swift deer.
You saluted me, saying, "You are so daring."

You are so graceful — O!
We met on the south side of the Nao Hills,
Riding together, chasing a pair of wolves.
You bowed to me, saying, "You are so brave."

著

俟我于著乎而，充耳以素乎而，尚之以琼华乎而。
俟我于庭乎而，充耳以青乎而，尚之以琼莹乎而。
俟我于堂乎而，充耳以黄乎而，尚之以琼英乎而。

大门①

新郎等我在大门内哟咳，②
耳饰用的是白丝线哟咳，
丝线上挂着红玉花哟咳。

新郎等我在庭院中哟咳，
耳饰用的是青丝线哟咳，
丝线上挂着红玉花哟咳。

新郎等我在厅堂内哟咳，
耳饰用的是黄丝线哟咳，
丝线上挂着红玉花哟咳。

---

① 习俗中新郎和新娘在仪式未完成之前不得看见对方的脸。
② "哟咳"，舞蹈或歌唱时的语助词，无实义。

《齐风》著

Front Gate[①]

My bridegroom waited for me at the gate, hu-ar.[②]
White silk held his ear ornaments, hu-ar,
With small red jade flowers, hu-ar.

My bridegroom waited for me in the yard, hu-ar.
Black silk held his ear ornaments, hu-ar,
With small red jade flowers, hu-ar.

My bridegroom waited for me in the central hall, hu-ar.
Gold silk held his ear ornaments, hu-ar,.
With small red jade flowers, hu-ar.

[①] It was customary that the bride and bridegroom should not see each others' faces before the completion of the wedding ceremony.
[②] Hu-ar: dancing or singing gestures, having no specific meaning.

诗经·国风——英文白话新译

东方之日

东方之日兮,彼姝(shū)者子,在我室兮。
在我室兮,履我即兮。

东方之月兮,彼姝者子,在我闼(tà)兮。
在我闼兮,履我发兮。

东方之日

太阳在东方,有位姣好的姑娘,在我房内了。
在我房内了,站在我面前了啊。

月亮在东方,有位姣好的姑娘,在我卧室了。
在我卧室了,站在我席上了啊。

《齐风》东方之日

Sun in the East

Sun in the East.
An exquisite young woman
Comes to my house,
And now she stands before me.

Moon in the East.
An exquisite young woman
Comes to my room,
And now she stands by my bed.

诗经·国风——英文白话新译

东方未明

东方未明，颠倒衣裳。颠之倒之，自公召之。
东方未晞(xī)，颠倒裳衣。倒之颠之，自公令之。
折柳樊圃，狂夫瞿瞿(jù jù)。不能辰夜，不夙则莫(mù)。

东方天未亮

东方天未亮，急着穿衣裳，
里里外外，颠颠倒倒，因为公侯相召。

东方天未亮，急着穿衣裳，
里里外外，倒倒颠颠，因为公侯相召。

匆匆离家，撞倒柳树和篱笆，
守夜人不称职，不是太早就太迟。

《齐风》东方未明

The Eastern Sky is Not Yet Light

The eastern sky is not yet light.
Putting on clothes in a hurry —
Upside down, inside out.
The Lord is calling.

The eastern sky is still dark.
Putting on clothes in a hurry —
Upside down, inside out.
The Lord is calling.

Rushing out like a man gone mad,
Crashing into a tree and a fence.
The watchman is incompetent.
It is either too early or too late.

诗经·国风——英文白话新译

南山

南山崔崔,雄狐绥绥(suí suí)。
鲁道有荡,齐子由归。
既曰归止,曷又怀止?

葛屦(jù)五两,冠緌(ruí)双止。
鲁道有荡,齐子庸止。
既曰庸止,曷又从止?

蓺(yì)麻如之何? 衡从其亩。
取妻如之何? 必告父母。
既曰告止,曷又鞠止?

析薪如之何? 匪斧不克。
取妻如之何? 匪媒不得。
既曰得止,曷又极止?

南山

南山有峻岭,雄狐慢慢行。
去鲁的大道平坦宽大,文姜由此出嫁。
既然出了嫁,襄公啊,为什么还追求她?

草鞋成对,帽穗成双。
去鲁的大道平坦宽畅,文姜去鲁作新娘。
既然出了嫁,文姜啊,为什么还见情郎?

大麻如何种法,田内纵横列着。
如何去娶媳妇,定要告诉父母。
既然娶了文姜,桓公啊,为什么任她会情郎?

柴薪如何砍法,非用斧头不可。
媳妇如何娶法,非要媒人不可。
既然娶了文姜,桓公啊,为什么任她会情郎?

《齐风》南山

South Hills

Peaks rise beyond the south hills.
An indolent fox ambles by.
The highway in Lu
Is wide and straight.
The princess of Qi, Wen-chiang, marries.
Lord Qi, she has married Lord Lu;
Why do you still wish to see her?

Straw slippers in pairs,
Cap tassels in pairs.
The highway in Lu
Is wide and straight.
Wen-chiang, the princess of Qi, marries.
But, Wen-chiang, now you are married;
Why do you still wish to see him?

How do you plant hemp?
In parallel rows.
How do you find a wife?
Ask your parents.
Wen-chiang has married Lord Lu.
But Lord Lu, why do you let her return
To see her lover?

How do you cut firewood?
Use an axe.
How do you find a wife?
Ask a matchmaker.
But Lord Lu, Wen-chiang is your wife.
Why do you let her return
To see her lover?

诗经·国风——英文白话新译

甫田

无田(diàn)甫田(tián),维莠(yǒu)骄骄。
无思远人,劳心忉忉(dāo dāo)。
无田甫田,维莠桀桀。
无思远人,劳心怛怛(dá dá)。
婉兮娈(luán)兮,总角丱(guàn)兮。
未几见兮,突而弁(biàn)兮。

大块地

耕地不要耕大块地,莠草蔓生难处理。
要爱不要爱远方人,两地相思太伤神。

耕地不要耕大块地,莠草蔓生难处理。
要爱不要爱远方人,两地相思太伤神。

他曾是那样年轻俊秀,梳着两个小辫子。
很多年不见他,应该长大了——戴着成年皮帽子。

《齐风》甫田

A Large Field

Do not till a field too large,
The weeds will take it over.
Do not love a man from afar,
You will miss him miserably.

Do not till a field too large,
The weeds will take it over.
Do not love a man from afar,
You will miss him miserably.

He was once a handsome horn-haired boy.
I've not seen him for so many years.
He must have grown up —
Wearing an adult fur cap.

诗经·国风——英文白话新译

卢令

卢令令（líng líng），其人美且仁。
卢重环，其人美且鬈（quán）。
卢重鋂（méi），其人美且偲（cāi）。

猎犬颈铃响

猎犬颈铃响当当，
猎人英俊又善良。

猎犬颈上双重环，
猎人英俊发又鬈。

猎犬颈上三重环，
猎人英俊美须髯。

《齐风》卢令

Dog Bells Ringing

The bells on the hunting dog ring: "Dong, dong."
The hunter is handsome and kind.

The hunting dog wears two collars.
The hunter is handsome with curly hair.

The hunting dog wears three collars.
The hunter is handsome with a tidy beard.

诗经·国风——英文白话新译

敝笱

敝笱(gǒu)在梁,其鱼鲂(fáng)鳏(guān)。
齐子归止,其从如云。
敝笱在梁,其鱼鲂鱮(xù)。
齐子归止,其从如雨。
敝笱在梁,其鱼唯唯。
齐子归止,其从如水。

破鱼篓

破鱼篓在桥下,捉不住鳊和鲜。
文姜公主出嫁时,护从队伍多如云。

破鱼篓在桥下,捉不住鳊和鲟。
文姜公主出嫁时,护从队伍多如雨。

破鱼篓在桥下,鱼儿进出自由。
文姜公主出嫁时,护从队伍如水流。

Broken Fish Trap

A broken fish trap left under the bridge;
It can no longer catch bream and roach.
The Princess of Qi marries Lord Lu,
Her wedding party as thick as a cloud.

A broken fish trap left under the bridge;
It can no longer catch bream and roach.
The Princess of Qi marries Lord Lu,
Her wedding party moves like rain drops.

A broken fish trap left under the bridge;
Fish swim freely in and out.
The Princess of Qi marries Lord Lu,
Her wedding party flows like a river.

载驱

载驱薄薄,簟茀(diàn fú)朱鞹(kuò)。
鲁道有荡,齐子发夕。
四骊济济,垂辔沵沵(nǐ nǐ)。
鲁道有荡,齐子岂弟(kǎi tì)。
汶(wèn)水汤汤(shāng,shāng),行人彭彭(bāng,bāng)。
鲁道有荡,齐子朝翔。
汶水滔滔,行人儦儦(biāo biāo)。
鲁道有荡,齐子游敖。

轿车疾奔

轿车疾飞波波响,围了竹板和皮帐。
鲁国大路宽又广,文姜连夜赴约忙。

四匹黑马拉轿车,缰绳华丽又整洁。
鲁国大路宽又直,文姜赴约心欢喜。

汶河之水荡荡流,岸上行人急急走。
鲁国大路宽又直,文姜赴约多自由。

汶河河水滔滔流,岸上行人急急走。
鲁国大路平畅畅,文姜赴约心荡漾。

《齐风》载驱

Carriage Running Rapidly

The stately carriage runs rapidly, "Pa, pa" —
Curtained with bamboo and leather.
The highway in Lu is wide and straight.
Wen-chiang leaves at dusk for her rendezvous.

Four black horses pull the carriage,
Their reins shine bright with patent gloss.
The Highway in Lu is wide and straight.
Wen-chiang hurries to meet her intended.

The River Wen flows swiftly —
People hurry along the bank.
The Highway in Lu is wide and straight.
Wen-chiang thrills to meet her chosen one.

The River Wen flows swiftly —
People hurry along the bank.
The Highway in Lu is wide and straight.
Wen-chiang glides to her lover in ecstasy.

诗经·国风——英文白话新译

猗嗟

猗(yī)嗟昌兮,颀(qí)而长兮,
抑若扬兮,美目扬兮,
巧趋跄(qiāng)兮,射则臧兮。

猗嗟名兮,美目清兮,
仪既成兮,终日射侯,
不出正(zhēng)兮,展我甥兮。

猗嗟娈(luán)兮,清扬婉兮,
舞则选兮,射则贯兮,
四矢反兮,以御乱兮。

噢,啊

噢,啊,多么健壮哟!
身体修长,额角宽亮,双目生威哟!
行动敏捷,射击一流哟!

噢,啊,多么伟岸哟!
眉清目秀,射礼完毕,仍在练功哟!
百发百中,是齐国的好外甥哟!

噢,啊,多么体面哟!
额角发亮,舞技出群,射技高强哟!
箭箭中的,是抗敌的英雄哟!

Oh, Ah

Oh, Ah, how splendid he is —
Strong and tall,
Full browed — O.
Eyes blazing — O.
Moves like an athlete.
A champion archer — O.

Oh, Ah, how noble he is —
Eyes blazing — O.
After the end of the archery ceremony,
He keeps on practicing — O.
He is indeed
The good nephew of Qi — O.

Oh, Ah, how handsome he is —
An expert dancer.
A peerless archer — O.
Every arrow strikes the bull's eye.
He is indeed
A great war leader — O.

OH, AH

魏风
Airs of Wei
107—113

诗经·国风——英文白话新译

葛屦

纠纠葛屦(jù),可以履霜?
掺掺(xiān xiān)女手,可以缝裳?
要(yāo)之襋(jí)之,好人服之。

好人提提,宛然左辟(bì),
佩其象揥(tì),维是褊(biǎn)心,是以为刺。

草鞋

细薄的草鞋,怎么可以踏寒霜?
纤纤的手指,怎么可以缝衣裳?
我已弄好了腰身和衣领,妇人可以试新装。

妇人悠闲又舒适,左转右转摆姿势,
发上带了象牙饰,只是偏心又自私,
写这首诗,刺她一刺。

《魏风》葛屦

Straw Slippers

How can you walk on frosty ground with straw slippers?
How can you sew clothing with delicate fingers?
I have now finished the collar and waist.
Come, madam, try on your new dress.

Relaxed, at ease, with an ivory hair pin,
Round and round she turns, gazing in the glass.
Though pretty, she is vain, selfish and mean.
This poem is meant to stab her with wit.

诗经·国风——英文白话新译

汾沮洳

彼汾(fén)沮洳(jū rú)，言采其莫(mù)。
彼其之子，美无度。
美无度，殊异乎公路。

彼汾一方，言采其桑。
彼其之子，美如英。
美如英，殊异乎公行(háng)。

彼汾一曲，言采其藚(xù)。
彼其之子，美如玉。
美如玉，殊异乎公族。

汾水岸上

在汾水旁的湿地里，有位采模的女子。
那位女子，窈窕美丽，无人可比。
无人可比呵，她和官家女子殊不似！

在汾水岸上，有位采桑的女郎。
那位女郎，像花一样。
像花一样呵，官家女子比不上！

汾水之湄，有位采藚的女子。
那位女子，美如玉。
美如玉呵，官家女子不能比。

《魏风》汾沮洳

By the River Fen

On the lowland by the River Fen,
A pretty young maiden picks sorrel.
So lovely — no one can compare.
No one can compare,
She differs from the girls of nobility.

On the bank of the River Fen,
A young maiden picks mulberry leaves.
Pretty as a flower.
Pretty as a flower,
Different from the girls with wealth.

At the edge of the River Fen,
A young maiden picks water-plantain.
Beautiful as jade.
Beautiful as jade,
Unlike the girls of the minister's family.

诗经·国风——英文白话新译

园有桃

园有桃,其实之殽(yáo)。心之忧矣,我歌且谣。
不知我者,谓我士也骄。彼人是哉？子曰何其(jī)。
心之忧矣,其谁知之。其谁知之,盖(hé)亦勿思。

园有棘,其实之食。心之忧矣,聊以行国。
不我知者,谓我士也罔极。彼人是哉？子曰何其。
心之忧矣,其谁知之。其谁知之,盖亦勿思。

园地有桃树

园地里有桃树,桃子可以充饥。
内心烦恼忧戚,嘴里哼哼唧唧。
不认识的人说我狂痴,他们说错了吗？
自己也莫名所以,心中仍忧伤啊,谁会知道？
谁会知道？真是自寻烦恼！

园地里有枣树,枣子可以填肚。
内心烦恼忧苦,只在园内踱步。
不认识的人说我偏激,他们说错了吗？
别再独自唠叨,心中仍忧伤啊,谁会知道？
谁会知道？忘了岂不更好。

238

《魏风》园有桃

Peach Trees in the Garden

Peach trees in the garden,
Offering edible fruits.
My heart suffers;
I can only hum without sense.
People who do not know me say
I am too arrogant.
They are not wrong.
Why not stop complaining?
My heart aches; I am truly sad.
Who knows why?
Who knows why?
Stop this self-pity.

Jujube trees in the garden,
Laden with edible fruits.
My heart suffers;
I can only pace in the garden.
People who do not know me say
I am so eccentric.
They are not wrong.
Why not stop talking?
My heart aches; I am truly sad.
Who knows why?
Who knows why?
It is better to forget this misery.

陟岵

陟彼岵(hù)兮，瞻望父兮。
父曰："嗟予子，行役夙夜无已，
上慎旃(zhān)哉！犹来无止！"

陟彼屺(qǐ)兮，瞻望母兮。
母曰："嗟予季，行役夙夜无寐，
上慎旃哉！犹来无弃！"

陟彼冈兮，瞻望兄兮。
兄曰："嗟予弟，行役夙夜必偕(jiē)，
上慎旃哉！犹来无死！"

爬山

爬上座小秃山，遥望父亲。
父说："唉，儿呀，当兵早晚不得闲，
千万小心，安全的回来呀。"

爬上座小青山，遥望母亲。
母说："唉，儿呀，当兵睡不好觉，
千万小心，平安的回来呀。"

爬上座小山岗，遥望兄长。
兄说："唉，弟呀，当兵在战场，
千万小心，不要死在他乡呀。"

《魏风》陟岵

Climbing a Hill

Ascending a barren hill, looking afar to my father.
Father said: " My son, in the army you
    will be busy every day.
Be careful and return home safely."

Climbing up a treeless hill, looking afar to my mother.
Mother said: "My son, in the army
    you will have no time to sleep.
Be careful and return home safely."

Climbing up a rocky hill, looking afar to my brother.
Brother said: "My brother, life in the army is dangerous.
Be careful. Don't die in a foreign place."

诗经·国风——英文白话新译

十亩之闲

十亩之闲兮,桑者闲闲兮,行与子还兮。
十亩之外兮,桑者泄泄(yì yì)兮,行与子逝兮。

十亩悠闲

购得十亩薄田,种桑过日子,悠悠闲闲。
走吧!你和我回到田园。

桑田之外,还有桑田,作一对种桑侣伴,
走吧!我们一块回到林间。

《魏风》十亩之闲

Ten Acres of Leisure

I bought ten acres of wilderness.
Planted mulberry trees for pleasure.
Come! Let's retire into the wilderness.

There are more mulberry trees outside the ten acres.
Let's be happy,
Retiring into the wilderness.

诗经·国风——英文白话新译

伐檀

坎坎伐檀兮,寘(zhì)之河之干兮,河水清且涟猗。
不稼不穑(sè),胡取禾三百廛(chán)兮?
不狩不猎,胡瞻尔庭有县(xuán)貆(huán)兮?
彼君子兮,不素餐兮!

坎坎伐辐兮,寘之河之侧兮,河水清且直猗。
不稼不穑,胡取禾三百亿兮?
不狩不猎,胡瞻尔庭有县特兮?
彼君子兮,不素食兮!

坎坎伐轮兮,寘之河之漘(chún)兮,河水清且沦猗。
不稼不穑,胡取禾三百囷(qūn)兮?
不狩不猎,胡瞻尔庭有县鹑兮?
彼君子兮,不素飧(sūn)兮!

伐青檀

叮叮砍青檀哟,檀木放在河岸上哟,河水清清有微波哟,
栽秧收割你不作哟,为什么收粮三千担哟,
既不外出去打猎哟,为什么挂着野猪肉哟。
这些大人君子们,只会寄生吃白饭哟!

伐木叮叮作车辐哟,伐木放在河岸上哟,河水清清直直流哟,
耕种收割你不作哟,为什么收粮三万亩哟,
既不外出去打猎,为什么挂着野兽肉哟,
这些大人君子们,只能寄生吃白饭哟!

叮叮伐木作车轮哟,伐木放在河岸上哟,河水清清有微波哟,
插秧收割你不作哟,为什么收粮三百库哟,
既不外出去打猎哟,为什么挂着鹌鹑肉哟,
这些大人君子们,只会寄生吃白饭哟!

《魏风》伐檀

Chopping Down Sandalwood Trees

Kan, kan, kan, chopping down the sandalwood trees,
Laying them along the river bank.
The water is clear with small ripples.
You neither sow, nor reap.
How can you receive thirty thousand bushels of grain?
You do not go out to hunt.
How can you hang the meat of wild boars?
Oh, you, my Lord, you are a parasite on others!

Kan, kan, kan, chopping wood for wagon spokes,
Laying it along the river bank.
Ripples ruffle the clear water.
You neither sow, nor reap.
How can you receive grain from thirty thousand acres?
You do not go out to hunt.
How can you hang the meat of wild game?
Oh, you, my Lord, you are a parasite on others!

Kan, kan, kan, chopping wood for wagon wheels,
Laying it along the river bank.
Ripples wrinkle the clear water.
You neither sow, nor reap.
How can you receive three hundred tons?
You do not go out to hunt.
How can you have meat hung in your yard?
Oh, you, my Lord, you are a parasite on others.

诗经·国风——英文白话新译

硕鼠

硕鼠硕鼠,无食我黍！三岁贯女(rǔ),莫我肯顾。
逝将去女,适彼乐土。乐土乐土,爰(yuán)得我所？
硕鼠硕鼠,无食我麦！三岁贯女,莫我肯德。
逝将去女,适彼乐国。乐国乐国,爰得我直？
硕鼠硕鼠,无食我苗！三岁贯女,莫我肯劳(lào)。
逝将去女,适彼乐郊。乐郊乐郊,谁之永号(háo)？

大老鼠

大老鼠,肥老鼠,不要再吃我黍子了！
供养了你三年,从来不对我照顾。
我发誓要离开了,找一片乐土。
乐土啊,乐土,那是我平安的住处。

大老鼠,肥老鼠,不要再吃我麦子了！
供养了你三年,从来不对我感谢。
我发誓要离开了,找一个快乐国度。
乐国啊,乐国,那是我安身的角落。

大老鼠,肥老鼠,不要再吃我谷苗了！
供养了你三年,从来不安慰我。
我发誓要离开了,找一处快乐的荒郊。
乐郊啊,乐郊,那里不会有人哭号。

《魏风》硕鼠

Big Rat

Big rat, fat rat.
Stop devouring my millet.
For three years I have supported you,
But for me you take no care.
I swear I will leave you
To seek a happy place,
Happy place, happy place,
That is where I shall be.

Big rat, fat rat.
Please stop eating my wheat.
For three years I have slaved for you,
But to me you've shown no favour.
I swear I will leave you
To seek a happy state,
Happy state, happy state,
That is where I shall be.

Big rat, fat rat.
Stop eating my seedlings.
For three years I have cared for you,
Without comfort, without reward.
I swear I will leave you
To find a happy land,
Happy land, happy land,
Where no one suffers or weeps.

113

唐风
Airs of Tang
114—125

诗经·国风——英文白话新译

蟋蟀

蟋蟀在堂,岁聿(yù)其莫(mù)。今我不乐,日月其除。
无已大(tài)康,职思其居。好乐无荒,良士瞿瞿(jù)。

蟋蟀在堂,岁聿其逝。今我不乐,日月其迈。
无已大康,职思其外。好乐无荒,良士蹶蹶(guì guì)。

蟋蟀在堂,役车其休。今我不乐,日月其慆(tāo)。
无已大康,职思其忧。好乐无荒,良士休休。

蟋蟀

蟋蟀钻进房内,一年快结束了,
今天不再行乐,时光不复返啊,
欢乐且勿纵度,想到国难家患,
行乐不要太荒诞,记住贤士良言。

蟋蟀钻进房内,一年又近尾声了,
今天不再行乐,时光太匆匆啊,
欢乐且无纵度,勿忘家患国难,
人生不要太荒诞,记住贤士良言。

蟋蟀钻进房内,车马也休息了,
今天不再行乐,时光不停止啊,
欢乐且无纵度,工作要尽职守,
行乐不可太荒诞,记住贤士良言。

《唐风》蟋蟀

Cricket

When the cricket moves into the house,
Year's end is drawing near.
If you don't enjoy life today,
Time evaporates without a trace.
But don't live life to excess.
Think also of your responsibilities.
Enjoy, but don't be idle.
Remember the golden adages.

When the cricket moves into the house,
Year's end is drawing near.
If you don't enjoy life today,
Days, months will not return.
But don't live life to excess.
Think also of your patriotic duty.
Enjoy, but don't be idle.
Remember the golden rules.

When the cricket moves into the house,
Horses and wagons are at rest.
If you don't enjoy life today,
Days, months will fly by.
But don't live life to excess.
Think also of your duty to others.
Enjoy, but don't be idle.
A good person maintains a balance.

诗经·国风——英文白话新译

山有枢

山有枢,隰(xí)有榆。子有衣裳,弗曳弗娄(lǚ)。
子有车马,弗驰弗驱。宛其死矣,他人是愉。

山有栲,隰有杻(niǔ)。子有廷内,弗洒弗埽(sǎo)。
子有钟鼓,弗鼓弗考。宛其死矣,他人是保。

山有漆,隰有栗。子有酒食,何不日鼓瑟?
且以喜乐,且以永日。宛其死矣,他人入室。

山地上有刺榆

山地有刺榆,湿地有白榆。
你有美丽衣裳,却不穿装。
你有豪华车马,却不驾驰。
节省着等死吗? 等别人来享受吗?

山地有臭椿,湿地有椴树。
你有亭园楼阁,却不清理安居。
你有钟鼓,却不奏乐歌舞。
节省着等死吗? 等别人来享受吗?

山地有漆树,湿地有栗树。
你有酒有肉,却不设宴庆祝。
活着要享受呵,秉烛夜游。
节省着等死吗? 等别人来享受吗?

《唐风》山有枢

Mountain Elms

Thorn elms in the highlands, white elms in the lowlands.
You have such beautiful clothes, but do not wear them.
You have carriages and horses, but do not ride them.
Do you leave life's pleasures to others?

Heaven Tree in the highlands, lime tree in the lowlands.
You have a large garden and house, but do not
    clean and live in them.
You have bells and drums, but do not play them.
Do you leave life's pleasures to others?

Varnish trees in the highlands, chestnut trees in the lowlands.
You have good food and wine, but do not
    entertain with them.
Life should be lived, days continuing into nights.
When you die, other people will enjoy, those things
    that you ignored.

诗经·国风——英文白话新译

扬之水

扬之水，白石凿凿(zuò zuò)。
素衣朱襮(bó)，从子于沃。
既见君子，云何不乐？

扬之水，白石皓皓。
素衣朱绣，从子于鹄(gǔ)。
既见君子，云何其忧？

扬之水，白石粼粼(lín lín)。
我闻有命，不敢以告人。

清清流水

溪水浅浅清清，溪底白石洁净。
潘先生白衣红领，我要跟他去沃城。
在沃城可以见到桓叔，怎不快乐盈盈。

溪水浅浅清清，溪底白石晶莹。
潘先生白衣红领，我要跟他去沃城。
在沃城可以见到桓叔，当然心情高兴。

溪水清清浅浅，溪底白石闪闪。
我要传给桓叔密令，不敢说于外人听。

《唐风》扬之水

Stream Water Runs Clearly

Stream water runs clearly.
The stream bed glitters with white pebbles.
There is Mr. Pan with a red collared white shirt.
I will follow him to Wo, where I can see my Lord Heng-shu.
I am, of course, elated.

Stream water runs clearly.
The stream bed sparkles with white pebbles.
There is Mr. Pan with a red collared white shirt.
I will follow him to Wo, where I can see my Lord Heng-shu.
I am, of course, elated.

Stream water runs clearly.
The stream bed is jeweled with white pebbles.
I have a secret message for my Lord Heng-shu.
I can tell no one else.

诗经·国风——英文白话新译

椒聊

椒聊之实,蕃衍盈升。
彼其之子,硕大无朋。
椒聊且(jū),远条且。

椒聊之实,蕃衍盈匊(jū)。
彼其之子,硕大且笃。
椒聊且,远条且。

花椒树种子

花椒树果实重重,装满了一升升。
祝福你那些儿子呵,高大无朋。
像花椒树一样,茁长茂盛。

花椒树果实重重,装满了一捧捧。
祝福你那些儿子呵,高大允中。
像花椒树一样,枝叶葱葱。

《唐风》椒聊

Pepper Tree Seeds

Seeds of the pepper tree, filling pail after pail.
Bless all your sons, may they be strong,
Like the prosperity of the pepper tree.

Seeds of the pepper tree, filling hand after hand.
Bless all your sons, may they be handsome,
Like the prosperity of the pepper tree.

诗经·国风——英文白话新译

绸缪

绸缪(chóu móu)束薪,三星在天。今夕何夕?
见此良人。子兮子兮,如此良人何!

绸缪束刍(chú),三星在隅。今夕何夕?
见此邂逅。子兮子兮,如此邂逅何!

绸缪束楚,三星在户。今夕何夕?
见此粲者。子兮子兮,如此粲者何!

洞房之夜

柴楷紧紧的捆在一起,参星出现在东方了。
今夜,这样美丽的夜哟,我们单独一起了。
亲爱的,亲爱的,我们该怎样庆祝呢。

干草密密的捆在一起,参星移到南天了。
今夜,这样美丽的夜哟,我们绸缪了。
亲爱的,亲爱的,我们要怎样庆祝呢。

荆柴紧紧的捆在一起,参星降到窗外了。
今夜,这样美丽的夜哟,我们该怎样欢乐呢。
亲爱的,亲爱的,我们被无穷的祝福了。

《唐风》绸缪

Wedding Night

Tall straws, bound tightly.
The Three Stars appear in the eastern sky.
What night is this night?
My love, my love,
At last we are alone!
How shall we celebrate?

Tall straws, bound tightly.
The Three Stars have moved to the southern sky.
What night is this night?
My love, my love,
At last we are alone!
How shall we spend the rest of this night?

Thorn-wood, bound tightly.
The Three Stars have moved to the window's ledge.
What night is this night?
We are having such a magical time.
My love, my love,
Sweetly we are blessed by heaven.

诗经·国风——英文白话新译

杕杜

有杕(dì)之杜,其叶湑湑(xǔ xǔ)。
独行踽踽,岂无他人?不如我同父。
嗟行之人,胡不比(bì)焉?
人无兄弟,胡不佽(cì)焉?

有杕之杜,其叶菁菁。
独行睘睘(qióng),岂无他人?不如我同姓。
嗟行之人,胡不比焉?
人无兄弟,胡不佽焉?

棠梨树

孤零的棠梨树,叶子密密葱葱。
一人独行,冷冷清清,
虽然有路人为伴,终不如自己弟兄。
过路的君子先生,请分担些忧愁吧,
可怜我无兄无弟,请伸一伸援手吧。

孤零的棠梨树,叶子密密葱葱。
一人独行,冷冷清清,
虽然有路人为伴,终不如自己同宗。
过路的君子先生,请分担些忧愁吧,
可怜我无兄无弟,请伸一伸援手吧。

《唐风》杕杜

Pear Tree

A pear tree stands alone;
Its leaves grow thick and green.
Cold and miserable, I walk alone.
Travelers share the road —
No one is my sibling.
People over there — can you share my sorrow?
I have no brothers — can you lend me a hand?

A pear tree stands alone;
Its leaves grow thick and lush.
Cold and miserable, I walk alone.
Travelers share the road —
No one is my family.
People over there — can you share my sorrow?
I have no brothers — can you lend me a hand?

诗经·国风——英文白话新译

羔裘

羔裘豹袪(qū),自我人居居！岂无他人？ 维子之故。
羔裘豹褎(xiù),自我人究究！岂无他人？ 维子之好。

羊皮袍子

羊皮袍子豹皮袖,他的态度太跋扈,
我当然可以找别人,只是有些不忍心。

羊皮袍子豹皮袖,他的行为太骄横,
我当然可以找别人,只是有些舍不得。

《唐风》羔裘

Lamb Skin Coat

Lamb skin coat with leopard fur cuffs.
His aloofness plagues me.
Of course I can find others —
But I am not ready to forget him.

Lamb skin coat with leopard fur cuffs.
His condescension wounds me.
Of course I can find others —
But I am still in love with him.

诗经·国风——英文白话新译

鸨羽

肃肃鸨(bǎo)羽,集于苞栩(xǔ)。
王事靡盬(gǔ),不能蓺(yì)稷黍,父母何怙(hù)?
悠悠苍天,曷(hé)其有所?

肃肃鸨翼,集于苞棘。
王事靡盬,不能蓺黍稷,父母何食?
悠悠苍天,曷其有极?

肃肃鸨行,集于苞桑。
王事靡盬,不能蓺稻粱,父母何尝?
悠悠苍天,曷其有常?

秃鹫羽毛

秃鹫沙沙飞翔,跌落在橡树上,
整天为了官事忙,没有时间种米粮。谁会照顾我爹娘?
苍天啊苍天,何时生活才安康?

秃鹫沙沙飞翔,跌落在枣树上,
整天为了官事忙,没有时间种米粮,父母饿了无饭吃,
苍天啊苍天,这种日子何时了?

秃鹫沙沙飞翔,跌落在桑树上,
整天为了官事忙,没有时间种米粮,父母年老无人养,
苍天啊苍天,何日生活才正常?

《唐风》鸨羽

Vulture's Feather

Whoosh, whoosh — the vultures fly,
    to gather on the oaks.
Day and night busy with the King's affairs;
No time to plant millet; no time to care for my parents.
Oh heaven! Oh heaven!
When will this end?

Whoosh, whoosh — the carrion birds fly,
    to gather on the jujubes.
Day and night busy with the King's affairs;
No time to plant millet. My parents have nothing to eat.
Oh heaven! Oh heaven!
When will this end?

Whoosh, whoosh — the scavengers fly,
    to gather on the mulberry trees.
The King's affairs never cease.
No time to plant millet. How can my parents survive?
Oh heaven! Oh heaven!
When can we live normally?

诗经·国风——英文白话新译

无衣

岂曰无衣七兮,不如子之衣,安且吉兮!
岂曰无衣六兮,不如子之衣,安且燠(yù)兮!

无衣

谁说我没有衣裳穿？我有七件哟。
只是没有你做的那般舒适又温暖。

谁说我没有衣裳穿？我有六件哟。
只是没有你做的那般舒适又温暖。

《唐风》无衣

No Clothes

Who says I have no clothes?
I have seven sets — O.
But none are as comfortable
As the ones you made for me — O.

Who says I have no clothes?
I have six sets — O.
But none are as comfortable
As the ones you made for me — O.

诗经·国风——英文白话新译

有杕之杜

有杕(dì)之杜,生于道左。
彼君子兮,噬肯适我?
中心好(hào)之,曷饮(yìn)食(sì)之?

有杕之杜,生于道周。
彼君子兮,噬肯来游?
中心好之,曷饮食之?

棠梨树

一棵孤独的棠梨树,站在大道左边,
那位伟岸的男人,肯不肯来看我?
心中既然如此喜欢,何不请他共餐。

一棵孤独的棠梨树,站在大道转弯处,
那位风流自处的男人,会不会来看我?
心中既然如此喜欢,何不请他共餐。

《唐风》有杕之杜

A Lone Pear Tree

To the left of the path, a lone pear tree stands.
That princely, handsome man, will he come to see me?
Since I love him so, why not invite him to dine?

On the curve of the path, a lone pear tree stands.
That princely, handsome man, will he come to see me?
Since I love him so, why not invite him to dine?

诗经·国风——英文白话新译

葛生

葛生蒙楚,蔹(liǎn)蔓于野。予美亡此,谁与独处?
葛生蒙棘,蔹蔓于域。予美亡此,谁与独息?
角枕粲兮,锦衾(qīn)烂兮。予美亡此,谁与独旦?
夏之日,冬之夜。百岁之后,归于其居!
冬之夜,夏之日。百岁之后,归于其室!

葛藤

葛藤缠围了黄荆,茑萝覆盖了墓地,
吾爱埋葬于斯,谁与他为伴?只有他自己。

葛藤缠围了酸枣,茑萝覆盖了墓地,
吾爱埋葬于斯,谁与他为伴?只有他自己。

陪葬的角枕鲜丽,陪葬的丝被灿烂,
吾爱埋葬于斯,谁与他为伴?一人独眠。

夏日长长,冬夜漫漫,百年之后,与你为伴。

冬夜长长,夏日漫漫,等我死后,与你为伴。

《唐风》葛生

Climbing Vines

Climbing vines encircle the hawthorn tree.
Bindweed spreads over the cemetery.
My love is buried here.
Any companions?
No, he is alone.

Climbing vines entwine the jujube tree.
Bindweed spreads over the cemetery.
My love is buried here.
Any companions?
No, he is alone.

With him, a shiny ivory pillow.
With him, a colourful silk coverlet.
My love is buried here.
Any companions?
No, he is alone.

Long days,
Summertime.
Long nights,
Wintertime.
When I am dead, I shall be with him.

Long nights,
Winter time.
Long days,
Summer time.
When I die, I shall join him.

诗经·国风——英文白话新译

采苓

采苓采苓,首阳之颠。人之为(wèi)言,苟亦无信。
舍(shě)旃(zhān)舍旃,苟亦无然。人之为言,胡得焉?

采苦采苦,首阳之下。人之为言,苟亦无与。
舍旃舍旃,苟亦无然。人之为言,胡得焉?

采葑(fēng)采葑,首阳之东。人之为言,苟亦无从。
舍旃舍旃,苟亦无然。人之为言,胡得焉?

采甘草

我去采甘草,在首阳山顶。
别人讲的话,不要去听。
不理它,不理它,不要回应它。
无聊的谣言,永不得逞!

我去采苦菜,在首阳山下。
别人讲的话,不要去信它。
不理它,不理它,不要回应它。
无聊的谣言,不值一哂!

我去采芜菁,在首阳之东。
别人讲的话,不要去听。
不理它,不理它,不要回应它。
无聊的谣言,算是什么!

《唐风》采苓

Gathering Licorice

I was gathering licorice at the top of Shou-yang Mountain.
The stories people tell — do not trust them at all.
Ignore them, ignore them — do not respond.
The stories — just rumours — don't believe a word.

I was gathering dandelions at the foot of
    Shou-yang Mountain.
The stories people tell — do not trust them at all.
Ignore them, ignore them — do not respond.
The stories — just rumours — not worth worrying about.

I was gathering turnips to the east of Shou-yang Mountain.
The stories people tell — do not trust them at all.
Ignore them, ignore them — pay them no heed.
The stories — just senseless rumours —
    do not be concerned at all.

Zou-yu

Forest of luxurious reeds — one arrow hit five pigs!
Zou-yu, sir, you are great!
Meadow of opulent daisies — one arrow hit five pigs!
Zou-yu, sir, you are great!

《召南》贶箓

秦风
Airs of Qin
126—135

诗经·国风——英文白话新译

车邻

有车邻邻,有马白颠。
未见君子,寺人之令。

阪有漆,隰有栗。
既见君子,并坐鼓瑟。
今者不乐,逝者其耋(dié)。

阪有桑,隰有杨。
既见君子,并坐鼓簧。
今者不乐,逝者其亡。

马车邻邻

马车邻邻奔驰,拉车骏马四匹。
来到君王府,先请差役传信息。

高地上有漆树,低地里有栗树。
见到君王面,并坐鼓琴瑟。
今天快乐要及时,莫等老大徒叹息。

高地上有桑树,低地里有杨树。
见到我君王,并坐鼓笙簧。
今天行乐要及时,莫等老死无时机。

《秦风》车邻

Rushing Carriage

Clunk, clunk...a carriage comes.
White heads mark the four horses.
Before I can meet my lord,
Ask the eunuch to announce me.

Lacquer trees on the highland,
Chestnut trees on the lowland.
I have seen my lord. We sat, playing lutes.
Be merry today; don't wait till we are old.

Mulberry trees on the highland,
Poplar trees on the lowland.
I have seen my lord. We sat playing flutes.
Be merry today; don't wait till we are dead.

诗经·国风——英文白话新译

驷驖

驷驖(tiě)孔阜,六辔在手。公之媚子,从公于狩。
奉时辰牡,辰牡孔硕。公曰左之,舍(shě)拔则获。
游于北园,四马既闲。辀(yóu)车鸾镳,载猃(xiǎn)歇骄。

四匹青马

拉车四匹青马,六条缰绳在握。
秦公出外行猎,他的爱子跟着。

赶出公兽和母兽,都是肥大凶恶。
秦公喊:"向左转",一箭中的。

猎完行经北园,四马得得悠闲。
车慢行铃叮叮,两头猎犬车上行。

《秦风》驷驖

Four Black Horses

Four big black horses.
Holding six reins expertly,
Lord Qin is out hunting.
His beloved son in his wake.

The guards drive out the wild beasts,
All fat and furious.
Lord Qin: "Turn left!"
The first arrow hits its target.

Back from the hunt,
Touring through the North Park.
Bridle bells ring; horses trot.
Bearing two hounds, the wagon rolls slowly.

诗经·国风——英文白话新译

小戎①

小戎俴(jiàn)收,五楘(mù)梁辀(zhōu)。游环胁驱,阴靷鋈(wò)续。
文茵畅毂(gǔ),驾我骐馵(zhù)。言念君子,温其如玉。
在其板屋,乱我心曲。

四牡孔阜,六辔在手。骐骝(liú)是中,騧(guā)骊是骖(cān)。
龙盾之合,鋈以觼(jué)軜(nà)。言念君子,温其在邑。
方何为期?胡然我念之?

俴驷孔群,厹(qiú)矛鋈錞(dūn)。蒙伐有苑,虎韔(chàng)镂膺。
交韔二弓,竹闭绲(gǔn)縢(téng)。言念君子,载寝载兴。
厌厌良人,秩秩德音。

轻兵车

兵车轻小车厢浅,五束皮革缠车辕。
绳索环扣马相联,拉车主绳串铜环。
车座铺着虎皮垫,花马拉车他持鞭。
想念夫君在战场,温文如玉好人缘。
他住西戎小板屋,思念悠悠乱心曲。

四匹雄马都壮大,六条缰绳右手拿。
杂花大马在中间,黄马黑马列两边。
画龙盾牌排一起,缰绳贯穿白铜圈。
我的夫君在西戎,何时才能还家园。
他的为人脾气好,昼夜相思泪涟涟。

披甲战马齐步跑,三柄长矛镶银套。
盾牌画着五彩羽,虎皮弓袋饰铜花。
两弓交叉放袋中,再用竹架紧扣着。
思念夫君在西戎,睡去醒来不安宁。
他的为人品德高,言行彬彬有礼貌。

---

① 160篇风诗以此篇最难译,从2004年5月开始到2006年3月共校正过十几次,在台湾新竹交通大学图书馆曾仔细看过秦朝出土的小兵车(复制品),得益不少。

《秦风》小戎

Small War-Chariot

The small war-chariot with a shallow body —
Its poles bound with fine leather strips.
Leather reins and brass spurs direct the horses —
Tiger skin covers the cabin seat.
Brass rings connect the ropes.
My husband is in the war far away.
He lives in a wooden hut out in the west.
He is as gentle as jade, respected by all.
I miss him. I grieve....

Four horses, massive and mighty —
In his right hand, my husband holds the reins.
In the middle, the piebald and bay —
On the outside, the black and brown.
Dragon-painted shields sit by the driver.
My husband is in the war of the west.
When will he return?
He has a mild temper, loved by all.
I miss him. I grieve....

The armoured horses run as one —
Three long spears boast silver butts.
Peacock feathers are painted on the shields —
The quiver is made of tiger skin.
The bows cross diagonally in a bag, secured by bamboo frames.
My husband is in the war of the west.
He is an honest man, enjoying a good reputation.
Whether awake or sleeping,
I miss him. I grieve....

---

[1] Among the 160 poems in this book, I found this one the most difficult to translate. I started it in May, 2004 and by now (December, 2007), I have edited it a dozen times. I saw a replica of a war-chariot (from Qin Dynasty) in the library of National Chiao Tung University in Taiwan in March, 2005.

诗经·国风——英文白话新译

蒹葭

蒹葭(jiān jiā)苍苍,白露为霜。所谓伊人,在水一方。
溯(sù)洄从之,道阻且长。溯游从之,宛在水中央。

蒹葭萋萋,白露未晞。所谓伊人,在水之湄(méi)。
溯洄从之,道阻且跻(jī)。溯游从之,宛在水中坻(chí)。

蒹葭采采,白露未已。所谓伊人,在水之涘(sì)。
溯洄从之,道阻且右。溯游从之,宛在水中沚(zhǐ)。

芦苇

芦花一片白苍苍,露水变霜白茫茫。
我所思念的伊人,在河水的那一方。
逆着流水去找她,道路阻险又漫长。
顺着流水去找她,她又到了水中央。

芦花一片白凄凄,露水一片仍潮湿。
我所思念的伊人,在河边的青草地。
逆着流水去找她,道路阻险又崎岖。
顺着流水去找她,她又到了小岛地。

芦苇一片苍黄,朝露闪闪发亮。
我所思念的伊人,在河岸的那一旁。
逆着流水去找她,道路阻险又漫长。
顺着流水去找她,她又去了小岛上。

《秦风》蒹葭

Reeds

White infinity of reed plumes.
White frost forms
From evening dew.
At the water's edge, a lady whom I love —
Upstream I attempt to reach her,
The journey stretching long and hard.
Downstream I struggle to reach her,
Receding into a misty shroud.

White infinity of reed plumes.
White dew still, moist.
The lady whom I love —
Limns the shore, like ice.
Fading upstream she eludes me,
On a long, arduous journey.
I pursue her downstream,
Shimmering on a barren mound.

Brown infinity of wilted reeds,
Still, wet with white glittering dew.
My lady love is beyond the bank.
Upstream I search for her in vain,
On the steep endless journey.
Downstream I seek her,
Where she seems to stand
On a small isle of sand.

诗经·国风——英文白话新译

终南

终南何有？有条有梅。
君子至止，锦衣狐裘。
颜如渥丹，其君也哉！

终南何有？有纪有堂。
君子至止，黻(fú)衣绣裳。
佩玉将将(qiāng qiāng)，寿考不亡！

终南山

终南山有什么，有楸树有梅树。
襄公来到山上，穿了狐裘锦裳。
脸色红润如丹砂，领袖仪表堂堂。

终南山有什么，有杞树有棠梨。
襄公来到山上，青上衣红下裳。
袍上佩玉锵锵，祝他万寿无疆。

《秦风》终南

Zhong-nan Mountain

What grows on Zhong-nan Mountain?
Rowan trees and mei plum trees.
Lord Xiang ascends the mountain
In a fox fur coat and golden robe.
His face is darkly tanned,
The handsome leader of our land.

What grows on Zhong-nan Mountain?
Matrimony vines and pear trees.
Lord Xiang ascends the mountain
In blue coat and red robe.
His jade ornaments ring "Jiang, Jiang."
May he live ten thousand years.

诗经·国风——英文白话新译

黄鸟

交交黄鸟,止于棘。谁从穆公？子车奄息。
维此奄息,百夫之特。临其穴,惴惴(zhuì zhuì)其栗(lì)。
彼苍者天！歼我良人。如可赎兮,人百其身。

交交黄鸟,止于桑。谁从穆公？子车仲行(háng)。
维此仲行,百夫之防。临其穴,惴惴其栗。
彼苍者天！歼我良人。如可赎兮,人百其身。

交交黄鸟,止于楚。谁从穆公？子车𬭚(zhēn)虎。
维此𬭚虎,百夫之御。临其穴,惴惴其栗。
彼苍者天！歼我良人。如可赎兮,人百其身。

黄鸟

黄鸟唧唧叫,密集枣树上,谁陪穆公殉葬,子车奄息啊。
这位奄息,百夫莫敌,走近墓穴,浑身战栗。
苍天啊苍天,为甚么活埋好人,
如果可以赎身,宁可百人换一人。①

黄鸟唧唧叫,密集桑树上,谁陪穆公殉葬,子车仲行啊。
这位仲行,德行落落,走近墓穴,浑身哆嗦。
苍天啊苍天,为甚么活埋好人,
如果可以赎身,宁可百人换一人。

黄鸟唧唧叫,密集黄荆上,谁陪穆公殉葬,子车针虎啊。
这位针虎,强壮英武,走近墓穴,浑身哆嗦。
苍天啊苍天,为甚么活埋好人,
如果可以赎身,宁可百人换一人。

① 春秋秦国穆公去世,177位活人为他陪葬,其中包括子车家的奄息、仲行和𬭚虎三兄弟。

《秦风》黄鸟

Yellow Finches

The yellow finches cry
As they flock to the jujube tree.
Who is to be buried alive with Lord Mu? [1]
Mr. Zi-ju, Yan-xi.
This Yan-xi — brave and intelligent,
Trembles helplessly when approaching the tomb.
Oh heaven! Oh heaven!
Why does a good man have to die!
If only he could be replaced —
Hundreds of us are willing to take his place.

The yellow finches cry
As they flock to the mulberry tree.
Who is to be buried alive with Lord Mu?
Mr. Zi-ju, Zhong-hang.
This Zhong-hang — an extraordinary scholar,
Trembles helplessly when approaching the tomb.
Oh heaven! Oh heaven!
Why does such a man have to die!
If only he could be replaced —
Hundreds of us are willing to take his place.

The yellow finches cry
As they flock to the hawthurn tree.
Who is to be buried alive with Lord Mu?
Mr. Zi-ju, Zhen-hu.
This Zhen-hu, who has defeated hundreds of enemies,
Trembles helplessly when approaching the tomb.
Oh heaven! Oh heaven!
Why does such a man have to die!
If only he could be replaced —
Hundreds of us are willing to take his place.

---

[1] When Lord Mu of Qin died, 177 people, including the three brothers (Yan-xi, Zhong-hang and Zhen-hu) of the Zi-ju family were buried alive with him.

诗经·国风——英文白话新译

晨风

鴥(yù)彼晨风,郁彼北林。
未见君子,忧心钦钦。
如何如何?忘我实多。

山有苞栎(lì),隰有六驳(liù bó)。
未见君子,忧心靡乐。
如何如何?忘我实多。

山有苞棣(dì),隰有树檖(suì)。
未见君子,忧心如醉。
如何如何?忘我实多。

鹞子

一只鹞子飞去如风,消逝在苍郁的北林。
很久不见你,心中悲伤难忍。
为什么?为什么?你难道真的忘了我?

山坡上有橡树,低地里有梓榆。
很久不见你,心中忧虑。
为什么?为什么?你难道真的忘了我?

山坡上有唐棣,低地上有豆梨。
很久不见你,内心忧凄。
为什么?为什么?你竟忍心忘了我?

《秦风》晨风

Falcon

Falcon flies as wind, lost from view in the north woods.
I have not seen you for so long, grief pains my heart.
Why? Why so? Have you already forgotten me?

Oak trees in the highlands, elm trees in the lowlands.
I have not seen you for so long, grief gnaws my heart.
Why? Why so? Have you truly forgotten me?

Plum trees in the highlands, pear trees in the lowlands.
I've not seen you for so long, grief consumes my heart.
Why? Why so? Have you forgotten me completely?

诗经·国风——英文白话新译

无衣

岂曰无衣？与子同袍。
王于兴师，修(xiū)我戈矛，与子同仇！

岂曰无衣？与子同泽。
王于兴师，修我矛戟(jǐ)，与子偕作！

岂曰无衣？与子同裳。
王于兴师，修我甲兵，与子偕行！

无衣

谁说没有军衣？我们俩同穿一件袍子。
周天子动员了他的兵士，我们快点修理矛戟，
你和我，同仇敌忾。

谁说没有军服？我们俩同穿一件内衣。
周天子动员了他的兵士，我们快点修理武器，
你和我，共同出击。

谁说没有军装？我们俩同穿一件下裳。
周天子动员了他的士兵，我们快点准备武装，
你和我，同赴战场。

《秦风》无衣

No Clothes

No clothes? You and I can share the same uniform.
King Zhou is calling up his soldiers.
We had better sharpen our swords and axes.
We are facing the same enemies.

No clothes? You and I can share the same shirt.
King Zhou is calling up his soldiers.
We had better sharpen our spear and lances.
We are fighting the same enemies.

No clothes? You and I can share the same apron.
King Zhou is calling up his soldiers.
We must prepare to take our shield
As we are marching to the battlefield.

诗经·国风——英文白话新译

渭阳

我送舅氏,曰至渭阳。何以赠之? 路车乘(shèng)黄。
我送舅氏,悠悠我思。何以赠之? 琼瑰(guī)玉佩。

渭水之北

我送舅父到渭水之北。
赠他些什么呢?
大车一辆,黄马四四。

我送舅父到渭水之北。
临别依依,赠他些什么呢?
一件佩玉,几块宝石。

《秦风》渭阳

North Side of River Wei

On the north side of River Wei, "Goodbye, my uncle!" I say.
What should I present him with as a gift?
A wagon and four bay horses.

Already missing him deeply, "Goodbye, my uncle!" I say.
What should I present him with as a gift?
Some precious stones and a jade piece from my pocket.

诗经·国风——英文白话新译

权舆

於(wū),我乎!
夏屋渠渠,今也每食无余。
于嗟乎! 不承权舆。

於,我乎!
每食四簋(guǐ),今也每食不饱。
于嗟乎! 不承权舆。

思旧

唉,我这一生,
曾住过华厦大屋,今也食不饱腹。
可怜呵,时光流转,何须数。

唉,我这一生,
曾经是酒溢菜丰,今也剩饭残羹。
可怜呵,时光流转,何等不同。

《秦风》权舆

Good Old Time

Alas, what is this life of mine?
Once I lived in a grand mansion.
Today, not enough on my plate.
Why, why can I not continue as I began?

Alas, what is this life of mine?
Once I was served banquets.
Today, there are hardly leftovers.
Why does time pass with such changes?

陈风
Airs of Chen
136—145

诗经·国风——英文白话新译

宛丘

子之汤(dàng)兮,宛丘之上兮。洵有情兮,而无望兮。
坎其击鼓,宛丘之下。无冬无夏,值其鹭羽。
坎其击缶(fǒu),宛丘之道。无冬无夏,值其鹭翿(dào)。

宛丘

在宛丘之上,你的舞姿飞扬。
我爱上你了,就怕高攀不上。

鼓声咚咚敲打,在宛丘之下。
不管是冬是夏,你挥动鹭羽婆娑。

土盆敲得呛呛,在去宛丘的山路上。
夏天热,冬天凉,你举着鹭羽舞荡。

《陈风》宛丘

Wan Mound

You dance at the summit of Wan Mound, round and round.
I am in love, but fear it is an unrealistic dream.

Drums sound dong! dong!
    around the bottom of Wan Mound.
Be it winter, be it summer, you dance, with an egret feather.

Earth pots tap tsong! tsong! on the pathway to Wan Mound.
Be it winter, be it summer, you dance, with an egret feather.

诗经·国风——英文白话新译

东门之枌

东门之枌(fén)，宛丘之栩(xǔ)。子仲之子，婆娑其下。
榖旦于差(chā)，南方之原。不绩其麻，市也婆娑。
榖旦于逝，越以鬷迈(zōng mài)。视尔如荍(qiáo)，贻我握椒。

东门外的榆树

东门外有榆树，小山上有橡树。
子仲家的女儿，树下婆娑起舞了。

选一个好日子，南方的草原地，
不要忙着织麻了，快步跳舞吧。

快乐的时光太短暂，大家及时行乐呵。
你美的像一朵金花，还送我秦椒一大把。

《陈风》东门之枌

Elm Trees Outside the East Gate

Elm trees stand outside the East Gate.
Oak trees stand on the small hill top.
Under the trees, Zi Zhong's daughter dances,
Oh! So beautifully!

Please choose a good time on south plains
For us to dance,
Dance, with flying feet.
Stop the busy work of weaving.

Joyful days are so short —
Let's rejoice together.
You are lovely as a golden flower, and
You've given me a bouquet of Jio branches.

诗经·国风——英文白话新译

衡门

衡门之下,可以栖迟。泌(bì)之洋洋,可以乐(yào)饥。
岂其食鱼,必河之鲂(fáng)? 岂其取妻,必齐之姜?
岂其食鱼,必河之鲤? 岂其取妻,必宋之子?

陋室

柴门土屋,自可居住;
泌水自由的流,粗茶淡饭不须愁。

要吃鱼,不一定是黄河的鳊鱼;
要娶妻,不一定是齐国姜氏女。

要吃鱼,不一定是黄河的鲤鱼;
要娶妻,不一定是宋国侯门女。

《陈风》衡门

Humble Shack

'Though a humble shack,
    it houses me in comfort.
Freely flows the River Mi —
    I am content with peasant meals.

I like to eat fish —
    they don't have to be Yellow River flounders.
I'd like to have a wife —
    she needn't be the daughter of Jung from Chi.

I like to eat fish —
    it doesn't have to be Yellow River carp.
I'd like to have a wife —
    she needn't be a noble daughter of Sung.

诗经·国风——英文白话新译

东门之池

东门之池,可以沤(òu)麻。彼美淑姬,可与晤歌。
东门之池,可以沤纻(zhù)。彼美淑姬,可与晤语。
东门之池,可以沤菅(jiān),彼美淑姬,可与晤言。

东门护城河

东门外的护城河,泡大麻的好处所。
美好的姬家三姑娘,可以和她唱情歌。

东门外的护城河,泡纻麻的好处所。
美好的姬家三姑娘,可以和她话家常。

东门外的护城河,泡菅草的好处所。
美好的姬家三姑娘,可以和她谈情话。

《陈风》东门之池

The Moat Outside the Eastern Gate

The moat outside the Eastern Gate,
The perfect place for steeping hemp.
The lovely third daughter of Ji's family
Can answer back to songs of love.

The moat outside the Eastern Gate,
The finest spot for steeping hemp.
The lovely third daughter of Ji's family
Can respond with witty banter.

The moat outside the Eastern Gate,
The loveliest place for steeping pampas grass.
The lovely third daughter of Ji's family,
Can dazzle with her intelligence.

诗经·国风——英文白话新译

东门之杨

东门之杨,其叶牂牂(zāng zāng);昏以为期,明星煌煌。
东门之杨,其叶肺肺(pèi pèi);昏以为期,明星晢晢(zhé zhé)。

东门外的杨树

东门外的白杨,树叶沙沙作响。
讲好了,当太阳下山,在东门见面。
现在天已暗,金星闪闪。

东门外的白杨,树叶沙沙作响。
讲好了,当太阳下山,在东门见面。
现在天已暗,金星闪闪。

《陈风》东门之杨

Poplar Trees at the East Gate

Outside the East Gate the poplars sing.
You said we were to meet there at sunset.
It's late now; the golden star is shining.

Outside the East Gate the poplars quake.
You said we were to meet there at sunset.
It's late now; the golden star is twinkling.

诗经·国风——英文白话新译

墓门

墓门有棘,斧以斯之。
夫也不良,国人知之。
知而不已,谁昔然矣。

墓门有梅,有鸮(xiāo)萃(cuì)止。
夫也不良,歌以讯(suì)之。
讯予不顾,颠倒思予。

墓门

墓门外有枣树,用斧头去砍掉。
这个人不善良,全国人民都知道。
知道了他也不改,一直就是那么坏。

墓门外有梅树,树上有野猫子的窝。
这个人不善良,唱只歌劝劝他。
听了歌他也不改,失败了也许会想我。

《陈风》墓门

Tomb's Gate

Jujube trees stand outside the tomb's gate.
They should be felled by axes.
That man is not good.
Everyone knows it.
Fully aware,
He does not care.
His spirit's always been evil.

A mei plum tree stands outside the tomb's gate.
An owl nests in it.
That man is not good.
Sing a song to warn him.
Although he's warned, he does not care.
He will think of me after he falls —
Perhaps.

诗经·国风——英文白话新译

防有鹊巢

防有鹊巢,邛(qióng)有旨苕(tiáo)。
谁侜(zhōu)予美,心焉忉忉(dāo dāo)。
中唐有甓(pì),邛有旨鹝(nì)。
谁侜予美,心焉惕惕。

防备谣言

堤岸上怎么能筑鹊巢?
丘陵恶土怎么会生苕草?
担心离间我们的宵小,使我忧伤烦恼。

破瓦怎么会铺在中庭道?
丘陵恶土怎么会生绶草?
担心离间我们的宵小,使我忧伤烦恼。

《陈风》防有鹊巢

Avoid Gossip

How can a magpie build a nest on a river bank?
How can sweet grass grow in poor soil?
I am worried; the gossips may hurt us.
    Sorrow fills my heart.

How can broken tiles pave the court path?
How can sweet grass grow in poor soil?
I am worried; the gossips may hurt us.
    Sorrow fills my heart.

诗经·国风——英文白话新译

月出

月出皎兮,佼(jiǎo)人僚(liáo)兮;舒窈纠兮,劳心悄兮。
月出皓兮,佼人懰(liǔ)兮;舒忧(yǒu)受兮,劳心慅(cǎo)兮。
月出照兮,佼人燎(liǎo)兮;舒夭绍兮,劳心惨兮。

月出

白白月亮出来了,那位女郎好窈窕哟;
风致多姿又明亮,惹得我思念又忧伤哟。

皓皓月亮出来了,那位女郎好撩人哟;
轻愁颦眉的模样儿,惹得我思念又心急哟。

光光月亮出来了,那位女郎似仙子哟;
风情万种花自怜,惹得我思念又心酸哟。

《陈风》月出

Moonrise

Rising white moon — an enticing young maiden,
So charming, so lovely — longing for her, I wait.

Rising bright moon — an alluring young maiden,
So sensual — I suffer, in anticipation.

Shining, rising moon — an inviting young maiden,
So enchanting — my heart is breaking.

诗经·国风——英文白话新译

株林①

胡为乎株林,从夏南!
匪适株林,从夏南!

驾我乘(shèng)马,说(shuì)于株野!
乘(chéng)我乘驹,朝食于株!

株林

"灵公,为甚么去株林?""去拜访夏南呀!"

"我不是去株林,是去看夏南呀!"

驾了我的四匹骏马,去株林城外野餐呀!

驾了我的四匹骏马,去株林城内早点呀!

---

① 陈灵公与夏南寡母夏姬(住株林,有名美女)暗通款曲,时常去株林幽会,被问为何去株林时支吾其辞,最后两句可解读为陈灵公否认之后的内心独白。

《陈风》株林

Zhu-lin[①]

"Lord Chen, why did you go to Zhu-lin?"
"I went there to see Mr. Xia-nan!
I did not go to Zhu-lin,
But to see Mr. Xia-nan."

Driving my four beautiful horses,
I went to Zhu-lin for a picnic.
Driving my four beautiful horses,
I went to Zhu-lin for breakfast.

[①] Lord Chen had an affair with Xia-ji, the most beautiful woman in Chen, the widowed mother of Xia-nan who lived in Zhu-lin. Lord Chen went to Zhu-lin often to meet with Xia-ji, but denied it when asked. It may help to imagine the second, final stanza as interior monologue, following Lord Chen's denial.

诗经·国风——英文白话新译

泽陂

彼泽之陂(pō),有蒲与荷。
有美一人,伤如之何?
寤寐无为,涕泗滂沱(pāng tuó)。

彼泽之陂,有蒲与茼(jiān)。
有美一人,硕大且卷(quán)。
寤寐无为,中心悁悁(juān juān)。

彼泽之陂,有蒲菡萏(hàn dàn)。
有美一人,硕大且俨(yǎn)。
寤寐无为,辗转伏枕。

池塘岸上

池塘的岸上,长着菖蒲与荷花,
有位姣好的女子,很想结识她,
爱她,昼夜相思,什么也不能作,
想到深处,泪下如雨。

池塘的岸边,长着菖蒲与水莲,
有位姣好的女子,身体多姿丰满,
爱她,昼夜相思,什么也不想作,
心中闷闷不乐。

池塘的岸上,长着菖蒲与荷花,
有位姣好的女子,身体丰满活泼,
爱她,昼夜相思,什么也不能作,
伏在枕上左右翻播。

《陈风》泽陂

The Pond's Edge

At the pond's edge,
Cattails and lotus grow.
I have fallen in love with
A young maiden on the opposite shore.
Day and night I think of her,
Unable to do my chores.
My tears fall like rain drops.

At the pond's edge,
Cattails and lotus grow.
A young maiden,
Shapely and fair.
Missing her day and night.
My heart is filled
With grief.

At the pond's edge,
Cattails and lotus grow.
Over there a maiden fair —
Shapely, well mannered.
Missing her day and night,
I can do nothing more.
My face on the pillow turns left and right.

桧风
Airs of Kuai
146—149

诗经·国风——英文白话新译

羔裘

羔裘逍遥,狐裘以朝。岂不尔思?劳心忉忉(dāo dāo)。
羔裘翱翔,狐裘在堂。岂不尔思?我心忧伤。
羔裘如膏,日出有曜(yào)。岂不尔思?中心是悼。

羊皮袍子

穿了羊皮袍子去游乐,狐皮袍子上官廷,
我是如此想念你,内心忧伤又泣零。

穿了羊皮袍子去游赏,穿了狐皮袍子去公堂,
我是如此想念你,内心烦恼又悲伤。

羊皮袍子油光光,太阳照得闪闪亮,
我是如此想念你,内心疼痛又凄凉。

《桧风》羔裘

Lamb Skin Coat

In a lamb skin coat you attend festivities;
In a fox fur coat you see the Lord.
How can I not think of you —
My heart aches with sorrow.

In your lamb skin coat you go for a stroll;
In your fox fur coat, you hold court.
How can I avoid thinking of you?
My heart sighs, deeply grieving.

Your bright lamb skin coat
Shines brilliantly like the sun.
I cannot help but think of you.
My heart is broken into shards.

素冠

庶见素冠兮,棘人栾栾(luán luán)兮,劳心忉忉(tuán tuán)兮。
庶见素衣兮,我心伤悲兮,聊与子同归兮。
庶见素韠(bì)兮,我心蕴结兮,聊与子如一兮。

白冠

再看一看你的白冠,那样清瘦单寒,
我会永远想你,内心痛苦辛酸。

再看一看你的白衫,内心悲苦无限,
但愿与你同行,一起去黄泉。

再看一看你的膝垫,内心无限凄怜,
但愿与你同行,一块去黄泉。

White Cap

One last time let me look upon
Your white cap;
So thin, you lie so ashen.
My heart brims over with sorrow.

One last time let me gaze upon
Your white robe;
My heart over-flowing with grief.
I wish we could be together,
    holding hands in the next world.

One final time let me behold
Your white knee-pads;
I am feeling so abandoned.
How I wish we could be
    holding hands in eternity.

诗经·国风——英文白话新译

隰有苌楚

隰(xí)有苌楚(cháng,chǔ),猗傩(ē nuó)其枝。
天之沃沃,乐子之无知。
隰有苌楚,猗傩其华。
天之沃沃,乐子之无家。
隰有苌楚,猗傩其实。
天之沃沃,乐子之无室。

隰地里有狋桃藤

隰地上有棵狋桃藤,枝叶茂盛。
婀娜舒展,羡慕你天真自然。

隰地上有棵狋桃藤,花开如梦。
婀娜嫣嫣,羡慕你无家牵绊。

隰地上有棵狋桃藤,果实重重。
婀娜高贵,羡慕你无家之累。

《桧风》隰有苌楚

Kiwi Vine in the Wetland

A kiwi vine in the wetland, robust and splendidly boughed.
How beautiful! I envy so your innocence.

Wetland kiwi vine with such brilliant flowers,
Untamed ripeness by no family bound.

Wetland kiwi, proudly displaying your treasures,
Free, unfettered offering, my envy for you — profound.

诗经·国风——英文白话新译

匪风

匪风发兮,匪车偈(jié)兮。
顾瞻周道,中心怛(dá)兮。
匪风飘兮,匪车嘌(piāo)兮。
顾瞻周道,中心吊兮。
谁能亨(pēng)鱼?溉之釜鬵(xún)。
谁将西归?怀之好音。

大风

大风猛吹,马车狂奔。
回首西来路,心中苦闷。

大风旋转,马车快赶。
回首西来路,心中怆然。

谁会烹鱼鲜,我可洗碟碗。
谁要回去西方,问候我的同乡。

《桧风》匪风

Strong Wind

Mighty blows the whirling wind; swiftly runs my wagon.
Looking back to the west from whence I came,
Anguish overwhelms me.

A strong wind swirls; my wagon speeds along.
Looking back to the west from whence I came,
I am so heavy hearted.

Who will cook a fresh fish? I shall wash the dishes.
Is anyone returning to the west?
To my friend—please convey fond wishes.

曹风
Airs of Cao
150—153

诗经·国风——英文白话新译

蜉蝣

蜉蝣之羽,衣裳楚楚。心之忧矣,於(wū)我归处?
蜉蝣之翼,采采衣服。心之忧矣,於我归息?
蜉蝣掘阅,麻衣如雪。心之忧矣,於我归说(shuì)?

蜉蝣

蜉蝣的翅膀闪亮,穿起漂亮新衣裳。
内心一直在思量,不知走向何方?

蜉蝣的翅膀闪亮,穿起漂亮新衣裳。
心中一直在忧戚,不知何处去休息?

蜉蝣爬出洞穴,白衣如雪。
心中一直在忧虑,不知何处是归宿?

《曹风》蜉蝣

Mayfly

Bright winged mayfly, wears exquisite clothes.
How sad, my heart — where should I go?

Bright winged mayfly, wears such pretty clothes.
How sad, my heart — where should I repose?

Mayfly crawling from your hole, wings so white, like snow.
Sad, my heart — where, my destiny?

诗经·国风——英文白话新译

候人

彼候人兮,何(hè)戈与祋(duó)。彼其之子,三百赤芾(fú)。
维鹈(tí)在梁,不濡其翼。彼其之子,不称(chèn)其服。
维鹈在梁,不濡其咮(zhòu)。彼其之子,不遂(suì)其媾。
荟兮蔚兮,南山朝隮(jī)。婉兮娈(luán)兮,季女斯饥。

小军官

那位迎宾的小官人,肩着矛戈和长棍。
穿了红盖膝的新贵们,一群竟有三百人。

鹈鹕栖在水边的栏杆上,没有沾湿翅膀。
那三百个新贵们,不配穿了好衣裳。

鹈鹕栖在码头的栏杆上,没有把喙弄湿。
那三百个新贵们,官阶奢侈。

冉冉升起的雾哟;南山头挂着彩虹哟!
如此美丽婉约哟,小官人的幼女挨饿哟!

《曹风》候人

Man of Arms

The man of arms, a low ranked officer, nothing but a stick.
The high ranked ministers, three hundred strong,
   wear noble uniforms.

The pelicans perched on the bridge rail,
   do not wet their wings.
Those ministers — unworthy of their attire.

The pelicans, perched on the bridge rail,
   do not wet their beaks.
Those useless ministers — an embarrassment to their ranks.

Fog is rising; a rainbow hangs over the south hill.
The man of arms' young daughter — so gentle, so tender —
   starves.

诗经·国风——英文白话新译

鸤鸠

鸤鸠(shī jiū)在桑,其子七兮。
淑人君子,其仪一兮。
其仪一兮,心如结兮。

鸤鸠在桑,其子在梅。
淑人君子,其带伊丝。
其带伊丝,其弁(biàn)伊骐。

鸤鸠在桑,其子在棘。
淑人君子,其仪不忒(tè)。
其仪不忒,正是四国。

鸤鸠在桑,其子在榛(zhēn)。
淑人君子,正是国人。
正是国人,胡不万年!

布谷鸟

布谷鸟在桑树上,养育七只幼鸟哟。
做一个好人,要公平不偏心哟。
公平不偏心,要心地正直哟。

布谷鸟在桑树上,她的幼鸟在梅树上。
做一个好人,衣带是丝制哟。
衣带丝制,皮帽上有玉饰哟。

布谷鸟在桑树上,她的幼鸟在枣树上。
做一个好人,要仪态端正哟。
仪态端正,可为邻人的风范哟。

布谷鸟在桑树上,她的幼鸟在榛树上。
做一个好人,是人民的榜样哟。
人民的榜样,祝他健康长寿哟。

《曹风》鸤鸠

Cuckoo

The cuckoo perches on the mulberry tree —
Caring for her seven chicks equally.
To be a good person and trustworthy,
One must observe the rules of fair-play,
The rules of fair-play
Are the roots of justice.

The cuckoo perches on the mulberry tree —
Her young sit among the mei plums.
To be a good person,
One should wear silk clothes,
Wear silk clothes,
And one's cap be adorned with jade.

The cuckoo perches on the mulberry tree —
Her young sit on a jujube.
To be a good person,
One must behave civilly,
Behave civilly,
Being a mentor for the neighbors.

The cuckoo perches on the mulberry tree —
Her young sit on a hazelnut tree.
To be a good person,
One should be a model for the citizenry,
A model for the citizenry,
May he be healthy and live for ten thousand years.

下泉

冽(liè)彼下泉,浸彼苞稂(láng)。
忾(kài)我寤叹,念彼周京。
冽彼下泉,浸彼苞萧。
忾我寤叹,念彼京周。
冽彼下泉,浸彼苞蓍(shī)。
忾我寤叹,念彼京师。
芃芃(péng péng)黍苗,阴雨膏之。
四国有王,郇(xún)伯劳之。

下泉

冰冽的下泉水,淹死了簇簇的狼尾草。
夜里醒来长叹息,思念周朝的京畿。

冰冽的下泉水,淹烂了簇簇的牛尾蒿。
夜里醒来长叹息,怀念周朝的京师。

冰冽的下泉水,淹灭了簇簇的蓍草。
夜里醒来长叹息,怀念周朝的京师。

谷苗蓬勃欣欣,田原风调雨顺。
邻国诸候来朝,赞扬郇伯的功劳。

《曹风》下泉

Deep Spring

Freezing water from the Deep Spring,
Floods and kills the fox-tail grass.
Waking in the night, I sigh, thinking of Zhou's capital.

Freezing water from the Deep Spring,
Floods and drowns the ox-tail grass.
Waking in the night, I sigh, thinking of Zhou's capital.

Freezing water from the Deep Spring,
Floods and slays the Shi grass.
Waking in the night, I sigh, thinking of Zhou's capital.

Millet shoots grow splendidly,
Nurtured by the rain and soil.
People now have a great leader, thanks to Xun-bo's efforts.

豳风
Airs of Bin
154—160

诗经·国风——英文白话新译

七月

七月流火,九月授衣。
一之日觱发(bì fā),二之日栗烈。
无衣无褐,何以卒岁?
三之日于耜(sì),四之日举趾。
同我妇子,馌(yè)彼南亩,田畯(jùn)至喜。

七月流火,九月授衣。
春日载阳,有鸣仓庚。
女执懿筐,遵彼微行(háng),爰求柔桑。
春日迟迟,采蘩祁祁(qí qí)。
女心伤悲,殆及公子同归。

七月流火,八月萑苇(huán wěi)。
蚕月条桑,取彼斧斨(qiāng),
以伐远扬,猗(yī)彼女桑。
七月鸣鵙(jué),八月载绩。
载玄载黄,我朱孔阳,为公子裳。

四月秀葽(yāo),五月鸣蜩(tiáo)。
八月其获,十月陨萚(tuò)。
一之日于貉(hé),取彼狐狸,为公子裘。
二之日其同,载缵(zuǎn)武功。
言私其豵(zōng),献豜(jiān)于公。

五月斯螽动股,六月莎鸡(suō jī)振羽。
七月在野,八月在宇,
九月在户,十月蟋蟀入我床下。
穹窒(qióng zhì)熏鼠,塞向墐(jìn)户。
嗟我妇子,曰为改岁,入此室处。

The Seventh Month

The "fire star" moves to the west in the seventh month.
In the ninth month, we hand out winter clothing.
North wind in November —
Bitter cold in December.
Without padded garments,
How can we survive until the new year?
In January we repair farm tools.
We work in the field in February.
Here come my wife and children,
Bringing food to the south acres.
The inspector is satisfied.

The "fire star" moves to the west in the seventh month.
In the ninth month we hand out winter clothing.
In March the sun begins to warm.
On the treetops the yellow finch begins to sing.
Young girls carrying their deep baskets,
Walk on the country path,
Collecting mulberry leaves.
In the slow, lazy spring sun,
Young girls fill their baskets with asters.
Their hearts are sad and heavy.
Is our young lord going to return?

The "fire star" moves to the west in the seventh month.
In the eighth month we harvest reed grass.
In March we work in the mulberry patches.
Bringing our cutters and hatchets,
Pruning the long branches,
Pulling down the tall boughs for tender leaves.
In July the butcherbird cries;

六月食郁及薁(yù),七月亨(pēng)葵及菽。
八月剥枣,十月获稻,
为此春酒,以介眉寿。
七月食瓜,八月断壶,
九月叔苴(jū),采荼(tú)薪樗(shū),食(sì)我农夫。

九月筑场圃,十月纳禾稼,
黍稷重(chóng)穋(lù),禾麻菽麦。
嗟我农夫,我稼既同,上入执宫功。
昼尔于茅,宵尔索绹(táo),
亟其乘屋,其始播百谷。

二之日凿冰冲冲,三之日纳于凌阴。
四之日其蚤,献羔祭韭。
九月肃霜,十月涤场。
朋酒斯飨,曰杀羔羊。
跻(jī)彼公堂,称彼兕觥(sì gōng),万寿无疆。

七月

七月火星移向西,九月忙着授寒衣。
十一月北风呼呼叫,十二月大雪纷纷飞。
没有冬袍和棉袄,如何挨到年尾梢。
正月修农具,二月下田去。
老婆和孩子,送饭南田吃。
田官见了心满意。

七月火星移向西,九月忙着授寒衣。
三月太阳暖洋洋,黄莺飞舞又歌唱。
姑娘外出提筥筐,走在田埂小路上。
小心翼翼采蚕桑,春日迟迟任徜徉。
采了菁蒿满筥筐,姑娘发愁心慌慌,
就怕公子不还乡。

《豳风》七月

The silk must soak in dyes.
Some black, some yellow.
But red is the most pleasing.
It will be kept for our young lord.

Foxtails flower in April.
Cicada calls in May.
Autumn is our harvest time.
Yellow leaves fall in October.
In November we hunt
Fox fur for our young lord's coat.
In December grain is stored.
We have some leisure time.
We practice martial arts.
Young boars are for ourselves;
Large ones are for our lord.

In the fifth month locusts kick their legs;
In the sixth month katydids rub their wings.
In July, crickets are singing in the wild;
In August, they move near the eaves.
They crawl inside my door in September;
They hide under my bed in October.
We must seal all the holes in the house,
Smoking out the rats from their nests,
Repairing the north window and plastering the door.
Oh, come my wife and children, come into the house;
The new year is near.

In the sixth month we eat plums and grapes.
In July we boil sunflower seeds and soybeans.
We heap jujubes in August.
We cook rice in October,

诗经·国风——英文白话新译

七月火星移向西,八月割苇好日子。
三月去桑园,拿了斧和剪,修理桑树颠。
拉下高枝采嫩叶,七月伯劳唱。
八月染丝忙,染成黑色和黄色。
唯有红色最漂亮,留为公子作衣裳。

四月狗尾草结子,五月知了唧唧啼。
八月庄稼收成时,十月黄叶飘飘离。
十一月出外去打猎,捉到狐狸剥了皮,
好为公子作皮衣。十二月冬藏有空闲,
大家一齐武功练,猎得小兽留自己。
猎得大兽给官吃。

五月蝗虫弹腿唱,六月振翅纺织娘。
七月蟋蟀在郊野,八月屋檐下,
九月入我房,十月床下藏。
堵死房洞熏老鼠,泥了门户塞北窗。
我的老婆和孩子,年关就到,快快进房。

六月吃李子和葡萄,七月煮葵和豆苗。
八月打枣,十月割稻。
发酵制春酒,喝了可以长寿。
七月吃甜瓜,八月摘葫芦,
九月收麻种,采苦菜,积火柴。
农夫肚子饱起来。

九月整理打谷场,十月晒粮纳入仓。
春谷,秋谷,小麦,芝麻,
黄豆,黍子和高粱,一起都储藏。
庄稼收获刚结束,又要进城为公忙。
白天割茅草,夜晚搓绳子。
爬上屋顶修房子,马上下田播种子。

十二月锯冰呛呛响,正月放入储冰房。
二月开冰窖,祭祖宗,献上酒菜和羊肉。
九月霜降,十月天凉。
家酒尽兴喝,杀猪又宰羊。
家人全聚公堂上。
举杯庆贺:"万寿无疆!"

344

《豳风》七月

Fermenting spring wine.
Drink to the blessing of our long life.
In the seventh month we eat melons.
In the eighth month the gourds mature.
In the ninth month we gather hemp seeds.
We collect sow thistles and store firewood.
This is how we feed ourselves.

We prepare the cereal stockyard in September;
In October we dry our grain.
Spring millet, autumn millet, sorghum, soybeans,
Hemp, sesame and wheat —
All of them are stored.
When we have finished our farm chores,
It is time to work for our lord.
Cutting sage and rushes during the day,
Twisting rope at night.
Climbing up to repair the roof.
It's springtime and we have to work the farm.

"Chung, Chung, Chung" — we cut ice in December,
Placing it in the cellar in January.
In February we worship our ancestors,
Offering them ice cubes, lamb and scallions.
It is frosty cold in September.
After cleaning our stockyard in October,
We kill a hog and take two bottles of our spring wine,
Walking together to the central hall,
Where we raise our wine cups overhead
To toast our lord:
"May you have a long life!"

诗经·国风——英文白话新译

鸱鸮

鸱鸮(chī xiāo)鸱鸮,既取我子,无毁我室。
恩斯勤斯,鬻(yù)子之闵斯!

迨天之未阴雨,彻彼桑土,绸缪牖(yǒu)户。
今女(rǔ)下民,或敢侮予?

予手拮据(jié jū),予所捋荼(tú),予所蓄租,
予口卒瘏(tú),曰予未有室家!

予羽谯谯(qiáo qiáo),予尾翛翛(xiāo xiāo),
予室翘翘(qiáo qiáo),
风雨所漂摇,予维音哓哓(xiāo xiāo)!

夜猫子

夜猫子,夜猫子,既已抓走了我的孩子,
不要再毁掉我的家室。我一辈子辛勤终日,护养子嗣。

趁着天还未雨,剥些桑皮修补门户。
"树下那些匪徒,不要再把我欺负。"

我用手撕抓,采些芦花,积些材料建窝,
我的嘴已磨破,房屋仍未建妥。

我的翅羽已失色,我的尾羽已脱落,
我的房室在风雨中飘摇,
怕极了,怕极了,只有大声惊叫。

《豳风》鸱鸮

Owl

Oh, Owl, Owl, you have taken my children;
Do not destroy my house.
So long and hard I laboured, to raise a family.

Before it is dark and raining,
I must gather mulberry bark to repair the window and doors.
"People down there, don't you dare bully me!"

My hands are worn to the bone,
Collecting rush flowers for the building.
My mouth is bloody and sore. Yet my house is unfinished.

My wing feathers have lost their hue:
    my tail is unplumed.
My house shakes in the wind and rain.
Terrified, scared, am I crying in vain?

诗经·国风——英文白话新译

东山

我徂(cú)东山,慆慆(tāo tāo)不归。我来自东,零雨其濛。
我东曰归,我心西悲。制彼裳衣,勿士行枚。
蜎蜎(juān juān)者蠋(shǔ),烝在桑野。
敦彼独宿,亦在车下。

我徂东山,慆慆不归。我来自东,零雨其濛。
果臝(guǒ luǒ)之实,亦施(yì)于宇。
伊威在室,蟏蛸(xiāo shāo)在户。
町畽(tīng tuǎn)鹿场,熠耀(yì yào)宵行。
不可畏也?伊可怀也。

我徂东山,慆慆不归。我来自东,零雨其濛。
鹳(guàn)鸣于垤(dié),妇叹于室。
洒埽(sǎo)穹窒,我征聿至。
有敦瓜苦,烝在栗薪。自我不见,于今三年。

我徂东山,慆慆不归,我来自东,零雨其濛。
仓庚于飞,熠耀其羽。之子于归,皇驳其马。
亲结其缡(lí),九十其仪。其新孔嘉,其旧如之何。

《豳风》东山

Eastern Hills

I went to war in the Eastern Hills, unable to come home
 for years.
I return now — misty rain follows me.
I am about to leave the East; my heart has already gone West.
I've put on my plain clothes,
Replacing my military uniform.
Silk worm crawls on the mulberry leaf.
I curl to sleep beneath the chariot.

I went to war in the Eastern Hills, unable to come home
 for years.
I return now — misty rain follows me.
Gourd vine covers the wall; gourds hang under the eaves.
Sawbugs invade my house; fire flies blink in the night.
Above the windows, spiders weave webs; deer dash
 before our door.
Are these to be feared?
No, I miss them enormously.

I went to war in the Eastern Hills, unable to come home
 for years.
I return now — misty rain follows me.
Storks cry on the dirt mound.
In our bedroom, my wife weeps, preparing to clean the yard.
Husband will be home soon.

诗经·国风——英文白话新译

东山

我去东山作战,久久不得回家,
如今东方归来,一路细雨绵绵。
刚要离开东方,心已回到故乡,
脱去军衣,换上民装。
野蚕在桑叶上弓身爬,
我独个儿睡在车底下。

我去东山作战,久久不得回家,
如今东方归来,一路细雨绵绵。
蔓藤贴在墙上,瓜儿吊在檐下,
土龟侵入正房,蜘蛛门窗结网。
野鹿门前奔跑,萤火虫入夜闪亮,
荒凉光景不可怕,怀乡之情更增加。

我去东山作战,久久不得回家,
如今东方回来,一路细雨绵绵。
鹳鸟土墩上叫,妻子卧房里哭,
快快收拾庭院,丈夫就要回家。
圆圆的葫瓢,躺在柴堆上,
离家去东山,整整已三年。

我去东山作战,久久不得归家,
如今东方回来,一路细雨绵绵。
黄雀飞翔,翅羽闪亮,
当年妻子出嫁,嫁队白马红马。
母亲为她结佩巾,仪式庄严欢欣,
三年之后再相逢,比起初婚更钟情。

《豳风》东山

Gourd ladles on the firewood pile.
I have not seen them for three years.

I went to war in the Eastern Hills, unable to come home
    for years.
I return now — misty rain follows me.
Goldfinches fly, displaying their bright plumes.
Remembering my wedding day — white and red horses
    at the party.
My mother tied her silk scarf; the ceremony proceeded
    with dignity.
I shall see my wife again — after three years.
I am more excited than on my wedding day.

诗经·国风——英文白话新译

破斧

既破我斧,又缺我斨(qiāng)。
周公东征,四国是皇。
哀我人斯,亦孔之将!

既破我斧,又缺我锜(qí)。
周公东征,四国是吪(é)。
哀我人斯,亦孔之嘉!

既破我斧,又缺我銶(qiú)。
周公东征,四国是遒(qiú)。
哀我人斯,亦孔之休!

破斧

我的战斧已破,我的战斨已缺。
周天子大军东征,四国惶惶。
我们这些小民呀,也可平安还乡。

我的战斧已破,我的战锜已缺。
周天子大军东征,四国得到感化。
我们这些小民呀,也有了自己的家。

我的战斧已破,我的战銶已缺。
周天子大军东征,四国得到安宁。
我们这些小民呀,也可享受太平。

《豳风》破斧

Broken Axe

My axe is broken, my lance is dulled.
King Zhou's army marches east, the four states are blessed.
We can now return to our land.

My axe is broken, my lance is dulled.
King Zhou's army marches east, the four states are grateful.
We can now have a home of our own.

My axe is broken, my lance is dulled.
King Zhou's army marches east, the four states have peace.
Now we can rest.

诗经·国风——英文白话新译

伐柯

伐柯如何？匪斧不克。取妻如何？匪媒不得。
伐柯伐柯，其则不远。我觏(gòu)之子，笾(biān)豆有践。

作斧柄

如何作斧柄？非用斧头不行。
如何找妻子？要靠媒人才行。

作斧柄，作斧柄，方法就在手中。
看到一位女子，花篮一样美丽。

《豳风》伐柯

Making an Axe Handle

How to make an axe handle?
One needs an axe.
How to find a wife?
One needs a matchmaker.

To make an axe handle,
The skill is in your hand.
I saw a young woman, as beautiful —
As a woven flower basket.

诗经·国风——英文白话新译

九罭

九罭(jiǔ yù)之鱼,鳟(cǔn)鲂(fáng)。
我觏之子,衮(gǔn)衣绣裳。
鸿飞遵渚(zhǔ),公归无所,于女(rǔ)信处(chǔ)。
鸿飞遵陆,公归不复,于女信宿。
是以有衮衣兮,无以我公归兮,无使我心悲兮。

鱼网

放下捕小鱼的网,却网住了大鱼鳟和鲂。
我见到的那位公子,锦袍华裳。

大雁沿着沙洲飞,飞向何方?
请你不要急着走,多住两天何妨。

大雁沿着陆地飞,何时还乡?
请你不要急着走,多住两天何妨。

那位华袍锦裳的公子,我要和你在一起。
不要忘记回来啊,不要使我心碎。

《豳风》九罭

Fish Net

The fish net set for small minnows,
　　catches large rudd and bream.
The young lord I met wears
　　a colourful embroidered robe.

A wild goose flies over the island —
　　where is he going?
Don't be in a hurry; please stay with me
　　for two more days.

A wild goose flies over the countryside —
　　when will he return?
Don't be in a hurry; please stay with me
　　for two more days.

My young lord with the colourful embroidered robe —
　　I want to go with him.
Do not forget to come back;
　　do not break my heart.

诗经·国风——英文白话新译

狼跋

狼跋(bá)其胡,载疐(zhì)其尾。公孙硕肤,赤舄(xì)几几(jǐ jǐ)。
狼疐其尾,载跋其胡。公孙硕肤,德音不瑕(xiá)。

狼走路

老狼前进踩下巴,老狼后退绊尾巴,
公孙先生大肚子,一双红鞋好神气。

老狼后退绊尾巴,老狼前进踩下巴,
公孙先生大肚子,做人耿耿有廉耻。

《豳风》狼跋

Wolf Walking

A wolf steps forward, snags his dewlap;
Steps backward, trips on his tail.
The fat Mr. Kun-sun, a good man;
His red curved shoes, elegant.

A wolf steps backward, trips on his tail;
Steps forward, snags his dewlap.
The fat Mr. Kun-sun, a good man;
His conduct, admired.

诗经·国风——英文白话新译

【附录】夜读蒹葭

秋深了,书房外的凉台被月光染成苍白,一棵道格拉斯杉木的影子投射在凉台上,安静地踱步——因为风的缘故,孤影独往来!

视线再回到书桌上,再回到正敞开着的一本诗经《蒹葭》篇,过去一周我都在试着译这篇诗,迟迟不动笔,因为不能捕捉作者写诗时的心情。快三千年了,作者是男是女?是殿阁的大学士,还是乡间的种田人?

假如他是一个中年的失意书生,感情和事业都在低潮,辛苦的追寻着失去的爱,追寻着人生的意思,又假如他姓姜,于是,我们有了这样一段对话:

贾:"姜先生,我是贾福相,种田出身,专业海洋生物,教了一辈子书,退休十年,读了一些中国古典,过去三年全心翻译国风,对这篇《蒹葭》有些偏爱,能否告诉我一些您的生平?"

姜:"我不会像你一样提名道姓的无聊,何况我的生平与《蒹葭》无关。"

贾:"是否有关,见仁见智,每人有不同的想法。好,不谈生平,你能不能告诉我你写这篇诗的动机?或者你心中的听众是谁?"

姜:"这又是个胡涂的问话,动机是有所为,是要达到一种目的,诗没有动机,小说和戏剧要听众、要鼓掌的人,诗没有,诗是为自己而写,为诗而写,了不起是两人的对话,诗也不一定发表。"

贾:"寂寞的时候才能写诗吗?"

(附录)夜读蒹葭

姜:"孤独的时候写诗,寂寞是苦恼的事,写诗时不苦恼,而是充满了生的思念和希望,在熙熙攘攘的人群中没有诗。"

贾:"我预备把《蒹葭》译成白话和英文,读来读去有很多不懂的地方。"

姜:"诗不要懂,诗是要感觉,是心灵的交通,要找言外之意,象外之象,景外之景,懂了的部分已不是诗了。译诗是一种错误,诗是不能译的。"

贾:"很多人同意你的看法,但我只赞成一部分,文字是一种符号,是一种密码,好的符号和密码是可以交通的,是可以翻译的,不然像我这样一个乡下人20岁前怎么会知道莎士比亚?怎么会知道歌德?怎么会知道大小仲马?"

姜:"那是故事不是诗。"

贾:"我所译的白话和英文《蒹葭》当然与你的《蒹葭》不完全相同,翻译是一种再创造,是一种脱胎换骨的过程。严复先生用'食桑吐丝'来形容,丝自然不是桑叶,但没有桑叶就没有丝,译者是蚕,把桑叶吃下,在丝囊中经过不少发酵变化而吐出了丝,说不定我翻成的白话和英文《蒹葭》有些章句比原来更耐读。"

姜:"承教,承教,你当然知道诗经中的每一篇都已经过不少乐官的编选,几百年下来,与原作不一样了。"

贾:"好,再回到《蒹葭》篇,你的风景部分我有经验,小时候住在山东平原,入秋,芦花似雪,沿着河岸一望无际,早起时草地上一片露水,在阳光下白闪闪的,如果温度降到冰点下,白露变成霜了,走在霜地上,沙沙作响,一步一脚印,那是种难忘的感觉,若干年前我访问澳洲叩克大学,有一位从苏格兰来的教授曾说他愿意花一个月的薪水买一分钟走在霜地上的感觉。"

姜:"好啦!很多人都有些芦花和霜露的经验。"

他的声音有些不耐烦,我知道自己又犯了多话的毛病,应该找机会结束这段谈话了。

贾:"对于你的'伊人'两千多年来有不同的看法,诗序说是讽刺秦襄公,因为他身处周地而不懂周礼;有人说'伊人'是情人,可能是男也可能是女,还有人说'伊人'是一种理想,或一位贤者。"

姜:"只有这四种说法吗?你的看法呢?"

贾:"我喜欢简单的故事,我以为这是一位中年男人对一个姣好女子的爱慕,大做白日梦么,可望不可及,用诗来寄情。"

姜:"你预备这样翻译吗?"

贾:"还没有决定,所以问你,至少你可以给一个暗示吧!"

姜:"不要再旧话重提,反正怎么翻译都是错的。"

贾:"错就是对,是不是?"

我们谈话到此为止,月亮又西移了几度,杉树的影子又走远了些,我突然觉得空空洞洞,心中一无所有,振笔疾书,是在帮姜先生写白话蒹葭吗?

芦花一片白苍苍,露水变霜白茫茫。
我所思念的伊人,在河水的那一方。
逆着流水去找她,道路阻险又漫长。
顺着流水去找她,她又到了水中央。

（附录）夜读蒹葭

芦花一片白凄凄,露水一片仍潮湿。
我所思念的伊人,在河边的青草地。
逆着流水去找她,道路阻险又崎岖。
顺着流水去找她,她又到了小岛地。

芦苇一片苍黄,朝露闪闪发亮。
我所思念的伊人,在河岸的那一旁。
逆着流水去找她,道路阻险又漫长。
顺着流水去找她,她又去了小岛上。

　　走出书房,月在中天,我如何来庆祝这时的心情呢?想高歌庆祝。世上有谁会知道一个译者替古人说话的快乐?

　　一只满足的蚕!

[Appendix]
Evening Reading of "Reeds"

Edmonton, Alberta, Canada
May 2005

Late night. The deck outside my study's window was bleached white by the moon. The shadow of a Douglas fir projected onto the deck moved slowly in the wind as if an old man was pacing back and forth alone.

My eyes returned to my desk to focus on the *Shi Jing*, opened to the poem "Reeds." For the past week I had tried to translate this ancient treasure of a poem. I had had difficulty starting because I could not capture the mood of the poet when he wrote it. Some 3,000 years had passed between us. Was the poet a man or a woman? Was the poem's voice even that of the poet? Was the poet a court scholar? Or a peasant in the village?

My assumption for working is that "he" was a middle-aged scholar, suffering the ebb of a career and of romance, in pursuit of a lost love, in search of the meaning of life. I assumed again that his surname is Ching. He and I then have the following dialogue:

Chia: Mr. Ching, my name is Fu-Shiang Chia. I grew up on a farm. My profession is that of a marine biologist. I have devoted my life to teaching and research. It has been ten years since I retired. During this time I have re-read the Chinese classics. For the past three years I have focused myself entirely on translating the *Shi Jing*. The poem "Reeds" is my favourite. Would you mind telling me about your life?

Ching: I would not be a nuisance like you. Besides, my life had nothing to do with the poem "Reeds."

Chia: Whether or not your life is related to "Reeds" depends on how you look at things. Each person makes his own observations. So, let's not talk about your life. Can you tell me your motive for writing the poem, and who was your audience?

Ching: Once again this is a nonsensical question! Motive is a purpose. You want to reach a certain target. Poetry has no motive. Novels and plays need audiences, people to applaud. Poetry needs none. Poems are written for oneself; a poem is written for the sake of the poem itself. Sometimes it's a dialogue between two people, and not necessarily to be published.

Chia: Do you write a poem when you are lonely?

Ching: No. You write a poem when you are alone. Loneliness is a miserable feeling. You are not miserable when you are writing a poem. A poem can be filled with longing and hope for life. One could not write a poem in a noisy crowd.

Chia: I intend to translate your "Reeds" poem into modern Chinese and into English, but even after reading it many times, I cannot understand some parts.

Ching: A poem is not to be understood. It is to be felt. It is a communication between souls, expressed between the lines, beyond the expressed phenomena, beyond the setting or scenery which are expressed. The part you understand is no longer a poem. It is a mistake to translate a poem. Poems cannot be translated.

Chia: I am sure there are people who agree with you, but I agree only partially. Language is a code. Good code can be communicated and also translated. Otherwise how can a person like me, from the village, have read Shakespeare before I was twenty? How could I have read Goethe and Dumas Sr. and Jr.?

Ching: Those are stories, not poetry.

Chia: My translations of "Reeds" into modern Chinese and into English are of course not identical with your original. Translation is a recreation. The translated version is different from the original. Mr. Yang, Fu, the great Chinese translator, described the translation process as the transformation of mulberry leaves into silk. Silk, of course, is not mulberry leaves, but there would be no silk if there were no mulberry leaves. The translator is the silkworm, swallowing the mulberry leaves and storing them in a silk gland, where numerous enzymatic activities take place. Then it spits out the silk. It is possible that my translations of your poem into modern Chinese and English may be better than your original poem.

Ching: Thank you for the lecture. But you should know that the *Shi Jing* was compiled over a period of six hundred years. What

	you have on hand may not be the same as the original.
Chia:	Let's return to the poem again. I've had some experience of the scenery of your poem's setting. When I was a little boy I lived on the prairie of Shandong province. In late autumn, reed plumes — white as snow — appeared. They paved the entire banks of rivers. In the morning dew they shone like pearls under the sunshine. If the temperature dropped below zero, the dew became frost. If you walked on it you could hear the sound "sha sha." You could examine your own footprints. The feeling was unforgettable. Some years ago, while I was visiting Cook University in Australia, I met a professor from Scotland who told me that he would not mind paying a month's income to experience a single minute of walking on the frosty grass.
Ching:	Alright. Many people have experienced reed blooms and morning frost.

Ching's voice became impatient. Once more I thought I was talking too much and needed to find an excuse to end the conversation.

Chia:	With regard to the person in your poem, there have been different interpretations. In the "Great Preface" it is said you were making fun of Lord Chin, because his kingdom was in Zhou district and he didn't understand the customs of his own district. Others have said the person is a lover, maybe a woman, maybe a man. Still others said the person is an ideal, a sage.
Ching:	Are those the only four possible interpretations? What do you think?
Chia:	I like simple stories. I believe the poem is spoken by a middleaged man, expressing his love for a woman. He was daydreaming and could not reach her. So he expressed his love in a poem.
Ching:	Do you want to translate it that way?
Chia:	I haven't yet decided. That's why I questioned you.
Ching:	Let's change the subject. Whatever you express will be wrong. Whatever way you translate it will be wrong.
Chia:	Wrong is right? Isn't it so?

We stopped our conversation at this point. The moon had moved west a few degrees. The Douglas fir's shadow had followed. I felt suddenly empty. Nothing left in my mind. Quickly I put the translation on paper. Am I writing the "Reeds" poem for Mr. Ching?

REEDS

White infinity of reed plumes.
White frost forms
From evening dew.
At the water's edge, a lady whom I love —
Upstream I attempt to reach her,
The journey stretching long and hard.
Downstream I struggle to reach her,
Receding into a misty shroud.

White infinity of reed plumes.
White dew still, moist.
The lady whom I love —
Limns the shore, like ice.
Fading upstream she eludes me,
On a long, arduous journey.
I pursue her downstream,
Shimmering on a barren mound.

Brown infinity of wilted reeds,
Still, wet with white glittering dew.
My lady love is beyond the bank.
Upstream I search for her in vain,
On the steep endless journey.
Downstream I seek her,
Where she seems to stand
On a small isle of sand.

I walked out of my study. The moon was in the middle of the sky. How should I celebrate this moment? I want to sing a song. How many people in the world can comprehend the happiness of speaking for such an ancient poet?

A content silkworm.

诗经·国风——英文白话新译

关于封面的艺术

封面的鱼翠与荷花是喻仲林的遗作,是1976年我与妻子由郭钟祥介绍在台北喻的画室购得。我用此画作为封面第一纪念我与仲林的长年友谊,第二诗经首篇《关雎》的雎鸠,在若干译书中译为鱼鹰、水鸟、鸭子等。我选了鱼翠,因为此鸟:一、体小艳丽,二、雌比雄好看,三、贴着水面曲线飞行,像女人走路时的摆动,四、定居岸边可能与《关雎》作者比邻,五、潜水捕鱼姿态优美,因此用来比喻"窈窕淑女",我觉得比雄壮体大,高空飞翔,筑巢树颠的鱼鹰更为合适。

2007年时1月,我与旅居美国加州的仲林大嫂通信,谈及封面的事,12月初又与她电话长谈,我们相信,仲林如果地下有知,也一定会含笑同意。

封底是我妻子Sharon的一幅油画(梅花),我特别钟情。三年前她在艾德门顿市开画展时,我建议她这一幅画是"非卖品",不然我会出资购买,于是她就送给了我,过去三年一直挂在书房,与我日日为伴。

国风160篇有许多用赋、比、兴的体裁以花来表示爱慕、向往和风情,如唐棣、荷、桃、红蓼、木槿、芍药,而这幅梅花清新自然,如一支民歌,美在其中,美在其外,与国风中各花可以互通款曲。

以上两件艺术品美化了我的译书,志此以作纪念。

贾福相
2007年12月9日
Salt Spring Island

关于封面的艺术

A Note About The Book Cover Art

The painting of a lotus and kingfisher on the front cover of this book is by the late Mr. Zheng-Lin Yu. In 1976, through the introduction of Professor Tom Kuo, my wife and I bought this painting from Mr. Yu during a visit to his studio. I used it on the front cover to remember my long years of friendship with him. Also, I translated the bird Jiu-Jio in the first poem of the Shi-Jing as Kingfisher. It is translated in most books as osprey, sea hawk, water bird, duck or not translated at all. I chose kingfisher because this is a small and beautiful fish-eating bird; the female has more colorful plumage than the male, and when flying it curves just above the water like the movement of a young maiden. Living in caves by the waterfront, possibly next door to the poet, it looks graceful when diving to capture fish. Using this bird to conjure the idea of a lovely young woman seems more appropriate to me than using the large powerful osprey which soars at high altitude, and builds nests on the treetops.

In November of 2007 I wrote to Mrs. Yu, who is now living in Southern California, about using this painting as a book cover. I talked with her in December; we both agreed that Mr. Yu would be happy with that.

The back cover of the book is an oil painting of mei plum flowers by my wife, Sharon. I told her that it was one of my favorites among her works; she decided not to sell it in her exhibition in Edmonton three years ago and gave it to me. It has been hanging in my study since, keeping me company every day. Many of the one hundred sixty poems in the *Airs of the States* have use flowers to express longing, happiness, love and beauty — as lotus, peach, hibiscus, peony and others. Sharon's painting of mei plum flowers is simple and clean, like a short and classic folk song, beauty inside, beauty outside; it can represent all the flowers used in the one hundred sixty poems.

These two paintings have beautified my book. This note is to express my appreciation.

Fu-Shiang Chia
Salt Spring Island
December 9. 2007